THE RELUCTANT VAMPIRE

THE AFTER DARK SERIES
BOOK THREE

DEAN ALAN CONRAD

Acknowledgments

For my parents, LaMar and Louise Major Conrad. Although sadly they did not live to see this trilogy published, they might have had an inkling they would arrive, after I turned our basement into a mad scientist's laboratory one summer and collected entrance fees from relatives and neighbors. Did I raise some eyebrows? That was the plan.

CHAPTER ONE

A GREAT EXPLOSION SNAPPED BO BENTWOOD INTO consciousness.

It was followed by an avalanche of rushing dirt that buried him deeper inside the hill above the old cemetery. The revived vampire that had been Bo Bentwood moved inside the wood-lined vault, placed there after he was fatally shot and fed—against his dying pleas—the blood of the ancient vampiress Eva. The chrysalis that contained his body during his metamorphosis shattered with the explosion. The amniotic-like fluid that had cradled him for four days, and had let the vampire disease infiltrate his body's every cell, bled into the ground.

Bo stretched his limbs. The bullets that had shattered his femur and penetrated a lung were gone. The twisted spent rounds lay beside him. The bones were mended, and the wounds healed. During his change, Bo's blood was replaced with a syrupy black liquid infused with the vampire disease. His heart no longer beat. The blood remained stationary in his veins until the vampire disease it carried was needed to heal his corpse.

Bo felt no discomfort in his dark tomb underground. His

heightened senses smelled the grave and the retched fluid that had encased his body during the transformation. He heard tiny creatures move through the earth. Breathing was unnecessary, although he could still inflate his lungs to smell his surroundings. He found the darkness and the smell of moist earth pleasant.

His mind raced, calculated, and replayed the hours leading to his death. The trip to the movies with the vampiress with a stop at a restaurant, where he consumed his and Eva's cheeseburgers. The thief who accosted them outside, brandishing a gun. The vampiress's feigned concern. He escaped on foot to the mall while Eva killed the thief. A race to get among people and what he thought was safety and freedom from the vampiress.

Then two cars of gangbangers slid to a stop. They sprayed bullets at one another and into the crowd. Bo took two shots, one to the leg, and one to the chest. He crumpled to the ground. The vampiress was at his side in a flash. Lifted him like a baby and blurred with him back to her crypt in the vampire colony above the cemetery.

The vampiress had become attached to Bo, a rare sign of devotion among the undead. She displayed the only affection he had ever seen in a vampire. Bo wanted to die. His friends Lisa and Jimmy pleaded with the vampire to let him go. The vampire Shadows Kazmer and Patty wanted the vampiress to turn Bo. As Bo took his last few breaths, the vampiress bit her own wrist and drizzled her cold, syrupy blood between Bo's lips. The disease-infused blood congealed and ran down his throat. The blood hastened Bo's demise and started the metamorphosis.

Bo immediately sensed his increased abilities when he regained consciousness. He tensed his muscles and felt the strength in them. He believed the blood of the ancient vampiress had given him powers greater than those of an ordinary newbie vamp. He no longer seemed to have a connection with the vampiress. Perhaps she could no longer control him as she had done when he was mortal. The mental connection Bo had felt with the vampiress was no longer there. Perhaps she was dead. Perhaps the Brethren had killed her during their attack on the vampire colony. Bo was dead and sealed inside his wooden vault before any attack occurred.

As he lay entombed underground, Bo thought of the vampiress. *If that bitch is still alive, I'll stake her for feeding on my blood, for turning me into a monster. I hope the Brethren got her. And now, the Brethren will hunt me.*

The vampire disease had preserved Bo's body. Made it strong. Increased his senses tenfold. However, there was a price. The disease that gave him eternal youth demanded blood to sustain itself and him. An unquenchable thirst raged in Bo's throat. He extended his claws and started to dig his way to the surface.

KAZMER WAS the first to emerge from the vampire colony's collapsed crypt. He had flung himself into a crypt off the main vault just before Del Hatch and the Brethren detonated the structure. His hand landed on his grave-digging tools, a pick and a long-handled shovel. The blast knocked Kazmer senseless.

He awoke at the back of the crypt, which amazingly had remained intact, even though the main vault imploded and the vampire house on the hill collapsed and slid down the hillside in a great conflagration. Kazmer used his cigarette lighter to check his surroundings after sniffing the dank air for natural gas that might have escaped underground from the home.

He grunted several times as his head cleared. He gathered his tools and started to dig. This wasn't the first cave-in Kazmer was swallowed by. Digging up might collapse what was left of the vault and bury him again. He decided to dig through the dirt in front of him, where the ground was soft, unlike the hardened material at the back of the crypt. He swung his pick in slow, measured strokes, stopping to shovel the fallen dirt back and occasionally rest a minute. Kazmer wanted a cigarette but knew oxygen in the void grew scarce. He would pass out if he couldn't reach the exterior and fresh air. As miners in Europe, Kazmer and his brother Lazlo had dug their way out of several cave-ins. Not this time. Lazlo was dead, shot by the Brethren with their crossbows.

Kazmer thought *If I was…*He stopped a moment and continued. *If I were a vampire, I would not need to breathe. Would not get tired. Would dig until I find Master Bo. Bo would be proud at my English.*

Kazmer continued to dig. His progress was hindered by several small cave-ins, which required him to retreat and shovel more dirt away from the small tunnel he dug. The ground got softer. *Part of the cave-in*, Kazmer thought. *Getting closer. Need fresh air.* He returned up the shaft to the small crypt. Found the air there no better. He snapped off the shovel handle. To conserve his strength and oxygen, Kazmer returned to his newly dug shaft and kneeled, using the shovel handle to loosen the earth in front of him, and the shortened shovel blade to push dirt behind him. His progress got slower. His head heart. His muscles burned. His heart pounded.

My mind is making tricks. I hear people talking. Maybe it is my ancestors. Maybe it is those I have killed who wait for me now. No, can't be. There is only one voice, and it speaks in English.

With the last of his strength, Kazmer dug a cone-shaped space in front of his face. Finally, dirt fell away and he felt cool air enter his little tunnel. He sucked on the air. Heard the voice again. It was night. Now Kazmer smelled burnt wood. *Must be from the house on the hill.*

After he rested to regain strength, Kazmer enlarged the hole to the exterior. He managed to stick out his head and saw a man walking slowly across the bank toward him. He carried a cell phone and talked. That was the voice he heard. Kazmer withdrew into the hole and patted the side of his hoodie. His stiletto knife was still safely tucked away. He and it survived the blast. Kazmer decided to remain in his tunnel until the man left. He had no idea how much time elapsed since the Brethren's attack on the vampire colony or how long he was unconscious underground. He hoped Bo had not emerged and fled. He must find Bo. As a new vampire, Bo would need training only he could provide. Otherwise, Bo would never survive. He would make an easy target for the Brethren. Perhaps he would get caught in the sun's rays and burn to ashes. Kazmer concentrated on the voice as it grew closer. If necessary, he would kill the man with the annoying voice and bury his body in the hole where Kazmer lay.

"If it weren't for the moonlight, we'd be up shit creek. I kid you not. You know John Bargain does not falsify and Bargain Videos are the real deal." Bargain stopped a moment and panned his cell phone around. "You can see the aftermath of the great explosion earlier today. Police think it was a gas leak inside the old house; a house that was not supposed to have any utilities. Wink. Wink. So, this gas leak exploded and collapsed this hillside into the cemetery below. Covered three mausoleums. The middle one is of interest. It's not exactly King Tut-worthy, but something maybe just as incredible. I kid you not. I was there. I was inside that place. Saw the whole shebang blow. I know what happened but hesitate to incriminate myself in any way. More about that later. You know I don't incriminate unless there is a good reason. Check it out. I did a video last summer. I'll leave the link below. While we're at it, please subscribe, give me a like, and hit the little bell so you get notifications on future videos.

"Ahead, you can see the remains of the house, all twisted and charred, almost beyond recognition. Looks like some fabulous pirate ship that ran aground in a storm, and washed up high on the beach. There were plenty of fire trucks here, but there wasn't enough water pressure to put out the blaze. Therefore, the men in the red trucks sat around to make sure the sparks didn't catch anything else ablaze until the house burned out. Not enough water pressure? Maybe it was—you heard it here on Bargain Videos—the destruction of *vampire* evidence. Yes. Vampires exist. I have seen them. I have even incinerated two of the goblins by exposing them to sunlight. So there! I have the burns to prove it. See my wrapped hand? I have video, too...that is still being ...edited...with help from my new friend, who I will call Persimmon—not her real name. Who would name a child after a fruit? That video will explain everything. It will show a lot of what went down today. I kid you not.

"You might be asking yourself, 'How come you're here at night on a hillside where surviving vampires might be digging out?' I'll tell you. Persimmon gave me a crucifix to wear around my neck. I'll show it to you. What makes this cross special is that it has been blessed by a priest in Rome, the Vatican even. So you know it's legit. The so-called vampire priest, a cardinal even. That's the difference. A vamp can stroll through the cemetery below, among all those crosses on graves, and never feel a twinge, because they are not blessed. The little jewel around my neck was blessed.

"So, I am here at Persimmon's request to shoot video and watch for any stinkers crawling out that might have survived. I hope she's right. I hope this blessing works, or I'll have my throat ripped out. I'll be drained of blood in the time it takes someone to down a pony bottle of Miller Lite. But if you saw Persimmon you'd do anything she asked. Yes. She is that hot.

"I'm going to take five. Sit down and watch for vamps digging out. You'll be the first to see one. Right here on Bargain Videos. And remember, as always. Hit the subscribe button below and the little bell that will alert you when I post a new video. With stuff like this, you don't want to miss a single episode."

Kazmer could take no more. He put his shovel back to work. As he dug to enlarge an escape route, dirt trickled from the hole, and rolled down the embankment next to Bargain.

"How now! A rat!" Bargain stood suddenly. Backed away from the ever-widening hole. "Here comes one now. A big rat at that. I remember a little Hamlet. I wish I had his sword. Oh boy! Moment of truth. Let's see if this blessing works. I hope to God it does."

Kazmer's head and shoulders emerged from the hole. He spit

dirt. His head was covered with soil. Bargain raised the cross in front of his face. Pointed it at Kazmer. Kazmer wiggled free to his waist. Bargained continued to video with his free hand. Kazmer pulled himself from the hole and slid down the bank a few feet before standing to face Bargain.

"Take this, bloodsucker," Bargained shouted, keeping the cross pointed in Kazmer's direction.

"I'm not vampire...yet." Kazmer brushed off his clothes and adjusted his pants.

"It looks like a homeless guy was caught in the explosion, and got swallowed up in the avalanche. False alarm. No vamp this time. The cross had no effect on him. Plus, he didn't attack my neck."

Kazmer stared at Bargain, narrowed his eyes to two slits. "Kazmer is not homeless. Have nice apartment with nice things to look at."

"I hit a nerve." Bargain dropped the cross on a chain around his neck.

Kazmer walked away, stopped, and turned back to Bargain. "You talk too much, Mr. Video. All vampires gone. Dead." He walked away across the bank in the moonlight, sliding several feet downhill after every few steps.

Bargain swiveled the cell phone back to his face and smiled. "You heard it from the source. A man who should know, who's spent time underground. All the vamps are gone. Dead!"

CHAPTER TWO

It was daylight and Kazmer sat about fifteen yards up the bank on the collapsed vampire vault. He waited patiently, smoking his rank-smelling hand-rolled cigarettes. Kazmer had waited through the night hidden in the cemetery until John Bargain and his annoying monologue finally left the area. He returned to the bank in the hope Bo would emerge. Kazmer had just crushed out a smoke when a policeman below, patrolling the edge of the great debris field from the avalanche, called to him.

"Hey, get out of there. That ground isn't stable. It might slide again. Nobody wants to dig your ass out of this mess." The cop took a few steps on the bank and skirted some rocks that had rolled to the bottom.

Kazmer looked up. "I wait for my dog. He got buried in the explosion. I think he will dig his way out and come to me."

"How the fuck did that happen?"

"We always walk in the cemetery. I am respectful of dead. Don't let my dog...Fritz...do his business on graves. We were walking where you are now. There was a boom. I look up and the whole mountain is coming down. I ran. Fritz went the wrong way. Was covered with dirt."

"That's tough, buddy. I lost a German shepherd a few years back to a shark. He went right off my kayak off the point. I know how you feel."

"Sorry to hear that. My dog is all that I have. He is strong. Maybe not too smart because he got confused and ran the wrong way, but I think he will dig himself out. The dirt is soft." Kazmer raised a paper bag at his side. "I brought food and water. He will need it after digging all night."

"All right. But be careful. If you hear or feel anything, any tremor, get off that bank and don't stop running. The city's engineer said this whole hillside is unstable."

"Yes, sir," Kazmer said and smiled.

After the cop was gone, Kazmer rolled another cigarette and sighed deeply before lighting it. Normally, he would roll two, one for his brother Lazlo. Lazlo always joked that Kazmer rolled a better cigarette because his fingers were strong from handling the knife he used to kill. Kazmer regretted not taking Bart's nice smoking jacket with the paisley design. Even though it wouldn't fit him, had a hole in the side where he plunged his stiletto knife blade, and was stained with Bart's blood, the jacket would look nice in his apartment closet, among the other things he and his brother had collected over the years. Occasionally, they would walk about the rooms, inspecting the closets. Now all the things they shared belonged to him.

"Here is your warm winter coat, my brudder," Lazlo would say and run the coat sleeve material between his thick fingers.

"It is nice," Kazmer would reply. "Too bad it is too small to wear."

"True, my brudder. Still, it looks nice in the closet. When we are richer, all our clothes will be nice and fit. You will see. Someday."

They would move to the bedroom, where there were two single

beds, rummage through a jewelry box, try on rings that slid no farther than their first knuckles, and wiggle their gnarled fingers at the mirror on the wall. The brothers smiled in amusement and the pleasure they felt having such wonderful things. Then they would sit in the living room and watch television. Chambered Glocks rested on the coffee table between bowls of pretzels and potato chips. They sipped Coca-Cola. It was good to feel rich. It had been a long time since the brothers visited their apartment and enjoyed its contents. An automatic payment was made every month to the landlord, who had never seen the brothers Lazlo and Kazmer In fact, he hadn't talked to them over the telephone in years. Still, their rent and utilities were paid on time. They were the perfect tenants.

Now that life was gone. Lazlo was dead. Killed by the Brethren with their crossbows. They would never sit on their sofa, drink Coca-Cola, watch *The Three Stooges*, trade glances, and laugh at the trio throwing pies.

"Who would waste a good pie by throwing it away?" Kazmer said one day, his thick shoulders heaving with mirth.

"I would hit myself in the face with the pie, my brudder, to eat more if it, but that, too, would be a waste. It is a sin to waste food."

"You could shave."

The brothers roared.

"You are too funny, my brudder."

Kazmer knew he must forget his brother and focus his attention on serving Bo, in the hope that Bo would transform him into a vampire someday. That was the goal. There was no way to tell whether the vampiress had survived the explosion. He did not know whether the vampire disease would be strong enough to pull her separated body parts back together.

The sun climbed higher in the sky. Kazmer raised his hood to keep the rays off his head. He craved another cigarette and pulled out his pouch of loose tobacco. To his left, there was an exclamation of surprise and pain. Kazmer saw a pale hand withdraw into the dirt. Kazmer scrambled toward the hole, shoving the tobacco pouch inside his hoodie.

"Master Bo, is it you? Are you there?"

"Kaz? The fucking sunlight burned the shit out of my hand."

Kazmer pressed his head toward the hole Bo had opened, looked inside, and surveyed the blistered hand. "I see you, Master. I am here to serve you. I will block the sun." Bo had retreated inside the cavity he had dug, away from the direct sunlight. His face was pale, dirt-smudged. His fangs were extended. "You must wait until tonight to come out," Kazmer added.

"No shit, Einstein. I gotta eat. This isn't going to cut it." Bo tossed to the hole's edge a desiccated rat he had drained.

"Find your dog?" The cop was back, climbing slowly up the bank. It seemed for every two steps he advanced he slipped back one.

Kazmer's eyes narrowed to two slits. He turned to the cop. "False alarm. It was only a rat." Kazmer raised the rat over his head and dropped it.

"Tough break, man. Good luck with your dog." The cop turned around and slid down the bank into the cemetery. In a moment, he was out of sight among the foliage and graves.

"Kaz, I can't wait till dark to eat," Bo implored from his hole. "This thirst is killing me."

Kazmer grunted. He reached inside his hoodie and pulled out a bag of blood. He shoved it inside the hole. "I had it next to my body to keep it warm," Kazmer said. "I hope you like it."

"What the fuck! Where—"

"I have my ways. I worked in a hospital when I first come to this country. In the morgue, where no one else would work."

Bo grabbed the bag, tore off the top, and downed the contents. He pressed the pouch to get out every drop possible. Then he lay back. "I never thought anything could taste so good."

CHAPTER THREE

An early morning breeze swept across the beach. The sun was still low in the sky, partly obscured by haze. A crowd had gathered near the surf. Those in long trousers had their pant legs rolled up to keep them dry. Here and there the shore was sprinkled with runners, walkers, and Frisbee throwers with dogs. At the center of the crowd stood a tall black man and a diminutive white woman with flowers in her hair, and flowers in her hands. Both wore shorts and T-shirts. The assembly joked and tittered. The bride hopped up and down in the surf. She sniffed her bouquet and threw out her arms, screaming into the waves. The groom threw back his head and laughed. The crowd stamped their feet in the shallow water. Those with bandaged injuries remained away from the roiling surf. Some sat on blankets in the sand. Moving around the group was a young man videoing the occasion with a cell phone on a gimble.

Finally, a tall dark-haired woman walked between the couple, stood with her back to the ocean, and addressed everyone. It was Persimmon.

"We are here this morning to witness the marriage of our

friends Overboard George and Mad Maggie. They have come a long way, both separately and now together, to this place on this beach, this moment in time." Persimmon was quiet for a moment while she surveyed the faces in the crowd.

Mad Maggie dropped her head for a moment and cried. Then looked up at Overboard George.

"It's the nicest wedding I've ever been to," Old Harriet bawled. "I'll never forget it." Old Harriet's beehive hairdo was gone, mostly incinerated in the attack against the vampire lair. Her hair was now short and shaped against her head. She wore a flowered dress and carried a bag of rice she intended to throw at the couple.

Persimmon looked at the couple while a flock of gulls circled overhead and eventually drifted off. "Do you have your vows?"

"We do. We've been working on them in our free time, deciding what we wanted to say," Mad Maggie said.

"And the rings?"

Dressed in a powder-blue jumpsuit zipped up the front, with his pantlegs rolled up to the knees, and a straw hat to ward off the sun, Del Hatch took a step forward and patted a pocket on his chest.

Persimmon smiled and said, "Let's begin." She invited Overboard George to start.

George cleared his throat. "This wasn't easy for me to make a set of vows. Not that I couldn't keep a vow. It's kind of like giving a speech. There are so many words in the English language. Every time I made a vow in my head, I thought there must be a better way to express it if you know what I mean. Finally, I realized the important thing was expressing myself. It didn't matter exactly how I said it."

"That's okay, OG," Mad Maggie said, looking up at Overboard George with tears in her eyes.

"Just as this ocean here is eternal, that's how my love for you is, Mags. It won't fluctuate like the tides, but it will be constant. I swear. I promise to take care of you to the best of my ability, no matter what happens. I promise to listen more than I lecture. I will not do any dope or stimulant for the rest of my life. I will strive to improve our condition in life until we reach the point where people who see us will say, 'There goes a respectable couple.' We didn't start real young in life and maybe that's a good thing, but I hope in the future—in many distant years—you, Mad Maggie, will be able to say, 'I married a good man.'"

A murmur swept through the crowd. Persimmon nodded to Mad Maggie to continue. Mad Maggie opened her mouth and jumped with a start. She looked down to see a plastic milk jug had come in on the surf and struck her leg. George picked it up before it was swept back out and threw it up to the sand. The gulls were back, apparently thinking so many people must have food.

Mad Maggie cleared her throat. "OG and me have come a long way. He's clean and he helped me not be so crazy like I used to be. The only thing I think of killing now is vampires."

The crowd tittered. "That's a good thing," someone interjected.

"It wasn't a love at first sight thing between me and OG. It came slowly, developed out of trust and respect and helping each other. After a while, I realized it would be impossible to continue without OG, because he had my best interest at heart, and I had his. It was a natural progression. Now, we want to look forward and not backward to the dark places we came from. I don't know where this life will take us, but I hope we can follow the Brethren, who have been so kind and accepted us despite all the baggage and flaws we carried in it. We didn't get involved young, as I said, but we are still young enough that maybe someday there'll be a little OG running around on a beach, chasing birds, and having fun. One thing I know *now* and don't have to wait years to tell you, OG, I already found a good man."

The group applauded. Persimmon looked toward Del Hatch and waved her fingers. Del unzipped his breast pocket, strode forward, and handed the rings, two simple gold bands, to the couple. Then he backed away. Overboard George slipped Mad

Maggie's ring on her finger, and she slid the larger ring on OG's finger.

Persimmon wiped a tear from her eye. "Okay. Overboard George and Mad Maggie, I declare you are married. You may kiss the bride."

The couple kissed and the crowd applauded and surged forward to congratulate them. Almost just as quickly, the group dispersed. Overboard George looked at Mad Maggie. "We could take a dip if the water wasn't so cold."

"Not today. I just had my hair done. Looks nice for the first time in years," Mad Maggie said. She thought for a moment and called to Persimmon. "What about our memberships? Is there an initiation into the Brethren? Can we do it now, or is it a secret ceremony? One we do where nobody will see?"

Persimmon put two fingers to her mouth and gave a sharp whistle. "That's right," Persimmon said, moving back between the couple. She called to the group. "There's one more thing we have to do."

The group returned to their original places. Looked on expectantly as they had for the wedding vows. Persimmon took a deep breath. OG and Mad Maggie joined hands again. They looked nervous and grinned at each other.

"Okay. So, you guys want to join us?" Persimmon said, loud enough for all to hear.

The couple nodded.

"All right. You're in. You are now Brethren. Any other East Coaster vampire hunters want in?"

Old Harriet raised her hand.

Del Hatch said, "You can't have too many affiliations, especially a first-class outfit like the Brethren." He raised his hand.

"You're all in," Persimmon said with a wave of her arms.

CHAPTER FOUR

As soon as the sun was down, Bo dug his way out of the dirt bank and brushed off the soil that had accumulated on his body. Kazmer sat nearby smoking his rolled cigarettes, watched Bo emerge from the ground. Kazmer greeted Bo with a deep bow and handed him a stack of new clothes. Bo pulled on the clothes.

"I can't explain how I feel, Kaz. Like I could take on the world."

"Not so fast, Master," Kaz warned. "You must take it slow. Learn the ways of the vampire. Your new powers are...how do you say it?"

"Intoxicating!"

"Dangerous."

"There are things the mistress would have taught you, but she is not here, so I must show you as best I can. But I don't know everything."

"I'm thirsty, Kaz. I need blood. That's all I can think about. A few days ago, the thought of drinking blood would have made me puke."

Kazmer grunted and pulled a second bag of blood from inside his hoodie.

Bo grabbed the bag, tore off the top, and sucked greedily at its contents. "How did you get these?" Bo said when he squeezed out the last few drops.

"I make friend at the hospital. At one time you could get old blood, but now there is a shortage. Blood never gets thrown out. It is used for patients. So, it costs more. The hospitals keep track of such things. But, when the price is right you find a way."

"I'm still thirsty, Kaz. What do we do?"

You will always be thirsty, Master. It is the vampire disease that controls your brain. You must learn to fight back. Be cautious. The disease wants only to be fed. Sometimes it will put you in danger. That is why you must learn the ways of the vampire before you get in trouble. Be wise."

"Right now, Kaz, I don't think that's possible. No one can stop me."

"You can't be seen. Humans cannot find out about you."

"Then I'll blur."

"No, Master. Another vampire should show you how to blur. Or you will..."

Bo was gone. He screamed in delight. He raced up and down the hillside, throwing up a rooster tail of dirt. Then disappeared into the street. Kazmer heard Bo's voice recede in the distance.

Kazmer grunted. "This will not end good. No. This will not end well."

Kazmer walked across the hillside and stood in the street where Bo had disappeared. In a moment, Bo blurred through the intersection below. Kazmer caught a momentary view of the flash in the streetlight at the corner. A blue blur, jeans on the bottom, light blue shirt on the top. Just as fast, Bo was gone again. His laughter echoed in the distance. A car drove through the intersection. There was a crash, the sound of crumpled metal. Then all was quiet. Kazmer took a few steps downhill toward the corner. He stopped. Below, Bo turned the corner and walked toward him. In the distance, Kazmer saw Bo was covered with gore. It was not the dark, syrupy blood of a vampire. It was the bright red arterial blood of a human.

Kazmer approached Bo until they stood a few steps apart. Kazmer grunted. Bo's head was caved in, lopsided. The left eye was gone. The right eye dangled outside its socket by the optic nerve and a few veins that looked like a single, thick frayed thread. Bo took the eyeball in his fingers, and lifted it carefully to point at Kazmer. Bo opened his mouth and blood poured out and ran down his chin.

Kazmer grunted. "Good thing I bought more than one set of clothes. I had a feeling..."

"Kaz, I was just in my first car accident."

"I heard the noise."

"I killed somebody. I drank the blood."

"It won't be the last killing, Master. It was only the first. You will always remember it."

Bo's eyeball slipped through his fingers and snapped back into his skull's orbit with a pop. The vampire disease worked to reassemble his damaged skull and had reattached the nerves to the brain and the muscles that held the orb in place. While he talked with a slur, his jaw reattached. The skull reformed into its previous shape, and new skin and hair grew. An ear took shape on the side of his head.

Kazmer watched nonplused while the healing continued. "I was blurring. I wanted to turn the corner. I saw the car. I wanted to go around it, but in that instant, I ran into it. Couldn't help it. I don't know whether I was too fast or too slow. I dented the hood and went through the windshield. I had to lift my head to see her. One eye was gone, the other hung by whatever."

Kazmer grunted and nodded his head in agreement as if he had witnessed the crash.

"I drank all the blood. Every drop I could suck. It was difficult at first because my jaw was broken. I couldn't stop feeding. She was bleeding. After I smelled the blood I couldn't control myself. I crawled through the hole in the windshield. The glass splintered and fell inside the car. The look of amazement on her face! She knew it was coming. She knew I was unnatural. She knew she was going to die. Kaz, there was so much blood in her. The taste was better than that bagged blood. Her heart was still pumping when I bit her neck. Her blood flowed into my mouth and down my throat. I hardly swallowed. It was wonderful."

"Are you in pain, Master?"

Bo looked at Kazmer. His face was still healing. "No pain. Just thirst. It's as if I never drank."

"That's how it is, so I have heard. We must go, Master. Get the woman out of the car. We can't leave a drained body for police to find. Bring her purse. I will get my van. I have a hiding place for you in the daylight hours.

KAZMER DROVE through the city's outskirts. The night was cool. In the distance, there were gunshots and sirens. The woman's exsanguinated body rolled back and forth in the back of the van. Bo was quiet, looking out the passenger side window.

"Can't you go faster?" Bo said.

"Never go over the speed limit unless you are chased. It is a rule. Never get caught, especially with a body in the back. There are hours left before sun comes up. We are in good shape."

"Says you."

"Yes. I say it. Just now I say it. Even though you are the master, Mr. Bo, you must listen to me to learn the vampire ways. You should learn as a disciple to another vampire. I do not know all the rules for survival, but I, Kazmer, will teach you what I know. It is better than nothin'."

"Okay, Kaz. I get the point."

"No, that is what you do not want—the point of a stake. The Brethren will know you survived if they find bodies without blood."

"They might think Eva survived. That's more plausible," Bo said. His reconstruction was complete.

"The mistress would not be so sloppy," Kazmer said. "The Brethren know she can control the disease."

"Is she dead, Kaz? I don't feel a connection anymore."

"I don't know. It would be up to her to keep the connection open, I think. You would not know how to open the connection with her. That is something you will learn in time, I think. It is not something I can teach you."

"I'd stake that bitch myself if she were here," Bo said, "for turning me. I begged her to let me die. I don't want to be a vampire. To stink like she did. To kill people like the one in the back. That was an accident." Bo looked into the back of the van as the body rolled side to side on a curve in the roadway. Then he snapped his head back to Kazmer.

"Killing for a vampire is never an accident," Kazmer said.

They had reached a desolate stretch of highway. Kazmer pulled off the road and drove up a barely discernable lane that ended in the overgrown, pock-marked parking lot of an abandoned motel. Kazmer pulled the van behind the building and shut off the engine.

"What a dump," Bo said.

Kazmer turned to Bo. "I find this place yesterday. I seal off windows to keep out light. This is a good place for you to rest until we find a better one. There is always a better place to hide. There is always a worse place to hide. What matters is not being found."

They climbed out of the van. Kazmer opened the back and pulled out the body. Then he unfolded a large tarp and covered the vehicle with it. He motioned with his head for Bo to follow and led the way into the motel through a back door. It appeared that the Bella Vista was abandoned suddenly. The office contained a board on the wall with room keys. There were broken lamps and paper scattered over the counter and floor. Litter lay across the lobby, where chairs were overturned, and the cushions slashed. Kazmer snapped on a cigarette lighter to see, but Bo could see clearly in the near dark and led the way down a hall to the rooms. There were broken doors and holes in the walls and ceilings. Wires dangled. More junk lay in the hall.

"Drug users stayed here, I think," Kazmer said. "There are needles in the rooms. Old cans of food. Empty beer cans. Booze bottles. The drug users have gone. Rats ate the food they left. Then the rats moved out. Just us now. I think nobody come here for a long time. This place is *dead*. Now, the room at the end. This is the place I fix up. No light will enter the windows. You will be safe, Master. The door has a good lock. We can put a chair under the doorknob, too."

"Thanks, Kaz. It looks like you even straightened up."

"I try. You can lay..."

"Lie."

"My mistake, Master. I am sorry. You can lie in the closet or on the bed. The mattress has stains. We can flip it, or maybe there is a better mattress in another room."

"After being underground and trapped in the vampire's casket with her stinking corpse on top of me, this mattress will do, Kaz."

Kazmer grunted in apparent agreement. "I will take the closet, then. First I will bury the body in the old garden outside." He switched off his lighter and left Bo alone. Eventually, Kazmer returned, crawled into the closet with a groan, and sat with his back against the wall.

Bo settled on the bed, sighed, and held his head in his hands. "You know, Kaz, when I woke up and was underground and it was still daylight, I had time to think."

Kazmer grunted. "Lots of time," he said, as he tried to roll a cigarette in the dark.

"I knew I was a vampire. I knew it immediately. The bullet wounds didn't hurt. I felt the power in my body. I heard worms and bugs crawl through the dirt. I even ate some. Then I caught a rat and drained it. None of them were appetizing. All I wanted was human blood. I imagined drinking it, gulping it, feeling my body fill with it. I imagined the strength that blood would give me. I wanted it more than anything. That blood. That strength."

Kazmer had managed to roll a cigarette and flicked on a lighter flame. He inhaled deeply and slowly released the smoke in his lungs. His sweaty face glistened in the point of the cigarette's orange light. "I am listening, Master," he said calmly.

"Even though I had that craving, it was really a lust I couldn't control, I decided underground that I would never take a human life. I would feed on worms and bugs, rats, anything to sustain me, even blood in a bag, but I wouldn't kill anyone because I knew if I killed one person I'd never control that vampire disease."

CHAPTER FIVE

It was nearly dawn when Bo lay on the mattress in the abandoned motel. Kazmer closed the door to the hall, locked it, and pressed the back of a chair he scrounged from another room under the doorknob. It was a sturdy chair that, along with the lock, should keep out intruders.

"We will be safe now, Master."

"You don't have to call me Master. It's Bo. Just Bo. No formality, the way it was with Eva. Understand?

"Understand. Tomorrow, I will get you nice casket to rest." Kazmer smiled in the darkness.

"No casket. I don't want a casket. I spent enough time alive in a casket with *her*. Besides, a casket would be too awkward. Too difficult to move. To hide. We need something easy."

"Easy peasy?" Kazmer said.

"Exactly, Kaz." Bo thought for a while. "Do you know what you could get? One of those mummy sleeping bags. They cover you completely. No light will get in. You could get one, too, Kaz. Roll it up every morning—night, whatever—and go. They'd be a lot easier to move, especially if we have to bug out of a place. Plus, a sleeping bag won't raise suspicion the way a casket would."

"Good idea, Mr. Bo. I understand why you were a college student. You are smart. I will look at sleeping bags tomorrow."

<hr>

DURING THAT DAY, Kazmer uncovered the van, drove to a sporting goods store, and bought two large mummy bags. He combed the streets for a better place to hide and stopped to eat before he returned to the motel for the night. There was still an hour before sunset when Kazmer returned to the motel room and unlocked the door. Bo was still in the same position on the mattress. Kazmer unrolled the sleeping bag next to Bo to ensure it was large enough for him to fit inside. There was room to spare. He unrolled his identical bag and spread it over Bo's bag. This was a good idea. If Bo should have to go underground to hide during daylight hours, the hole he dug would be smaller than the one needed to conceal a casket. Kazmer and his brother Lazlo had done a lot of unnecessary digging serving vampires who demanded caskets. Bo would be a good boss. Better than Eva, the ancient vampiress. Bo would not be so demanding. There was a lot he still did not know, and did not understand. Bo's big problem would be staying out of trouble and keeping his identity a secret from humans, especially the Brethren. If humans found Bo, they would find Kazmer. Bo had to learn how to control the vampire disease.

Kazmer spread his sleeping bag in the closet and climbed in. Zipped it up partially. He was asleep in a moment. It was dark when he woke and rolled over. He flicked his cigarette lighter on and saw Bo seated on the bed's edge, hands holding his head.

"How is it, Mr. Bo?"

"I must feed tonight. The thirst—I can't rake it."

"We can find a derelict. Two derelicts. Leave some blood in both. Otherwise, I will have to bury the bodies."

"No humans, Kaz. Never again. Let's stop at the blood bank and talk to your friend. He might help us."

Kazmer shook his shaggy head. "He was not my friend. He needed money. Last time I saw him he said no more blood. That is all. He said the hospital might think he is in a cult, Satan worshippers who use blood in ceremonies. He must be careful."

"What about old blood? The stuff they would throw out." Bo sounded hopeful.

Kazmer had begun to roll a cigarette in the dark. He had become somewhat adroit at the process. "There is no blood thrown out. Not like years ago. He said so many people are shot and stabbed the blood supply is always low. Nothing extra."

"I need blood, Kaz. Tonight!"

Kazmer thought a moment and finished making the cigarette. He held it near his lips and spoke. "If you won't attack humans, we will have to get animal blood. We'll go inland where there are farms. You can drink a cow or pig, even a goat, until you are full."

"I don't know," Bo said, slowly, drawing out the words while he thought about the idea.

Kazmer inhaled deeply and held the smoke in his lungs a long time before releasing the rank smoke slowly. "There is another... alternative. I could kill a human and let you drink the blood. It would kill two stones with one bird, I think they say."

Bo stared for a moment, looking at Kaz through the dark. Kaz held up the flame on his lighter. "Kaz, they do not say that. Nobody does. You don't kill stones. It would still be murder. I won't drink the blood of people you kill for me. There'd be no difference. Let's try animal blood. I could kill a steer. I ate enough steak and hamburger as a human."

Kazmer unlocked the room door and moved down to the hall and outside. He pulled the tarp off the van and climbed in. Bo was in the passenger side before Kazmer closed his door. Kazmer started the engine and pulled out, cautiously, ensuring no one saw them leave the motel. He hit the highway and drove east, inland to farmland. Eventually, he exited the highway and entered two-lane roads that rose and fell, twisted with the land's terrain. They passed orchards and vineyards. Eventually, they drove past farms.

"Watch for barns, places a farmer would keep animals at night," Kazmer said. "I will pull over and let you hunt. I will stay with the van just in case."

"Sounds like a plan, Kaz."

"This is a good plan," Kazmer said, inhaling on his cigarette. He steered with one hand to wipe loose tobacco flakes from his mouth. "Farmers find dead animals in their fields all the time. They say it is Satanic cults, even aliens from other plants, experimenting, even eating. If we had the time, we could make crop circles in the fields. My brother Lazlo, God rest his soul, and I liked to make crop circles and watch the news to see if they were reported."

"Not tonight, Kaz. I'm not in the mood."

"Not tonight," Kazmer repeated. "Someday, maybe."

Kazmer drove on, slower now. "Watch for the buildings, Mr. Bo. I might not see them in the dark unless they are next to the road."

"Over there, Kaz. Across the field. There's a building. I smell the animals."

Kazmer pulled the van off the road. "I don't smell anything, but I will wait here, Mr. Bo. If the farmer chases me, I will be up the road," Kazmer pointed his hand holding the cigarette at the windshield. "Good luck." Kazmer turned off the engine.

Bo slipped from the van and pressed the door closed silently. He sniffed the air again. Kazmer smiled at Bo in the dark as if he were a parent watching a child leave for school. The orange end of his lit cigarette illuminated his face. Then Bo was gone. He blurred across the field and stopped at the building's metal wall. To the south, the farmhouse had a light upstairs. Bo watched. The light blinked out and another light turned on downstairs. Someone inside the farmer's house stirred.

Bo knew the night was closer to dawn than sunset. *In and out. I hope I like this stuff. I hope this animal blood satisfies me for a while. If not, I don't know what I'll do. I could try deer or animals in the forest. Deers destroy crops. Farmers would love to see the deer population shrink. They'd love it. Wouldn't think twice about dead deer in the trees. If there's a way, I'll beat this vampire disease. I'll tame it. I can go anywhere and hunt deer. Anywhere.*

With one eye on the farmhouse, Bo edged around the building's exterior. He heard animals inside. Pigs. *Some pigs are big. Hold a lot of blood. A big pig—maybe two small ones— should last me. Kazmer likes pork. He can slice off a roast for himself. We'll live like kings.* Bo reached the building's closed door. It wasn't locked. He pulled it open. Stepped inside. Closed the door again. The swine stirred. Moved around, almost expectantly, crowded around a trough. *They think they're getting fed. Too bad. I'm the one feeding.*

Bo vaulted over the enclosure that confined the pigs. The animals scattered. Grunted. Squealed Then quieted again. Bo held out his arms. The pigs tried to return to the trough. Bo singled out a large sow. The teats on its belly were visible. Bo walked silently, waving his arms up and down. The pig moved away from the other animals. Across the buildings, chickens clucked in cages. *I'll grab some eggs for Kaz while I'm here. Maybe a chicken, too. Won't he be surprised!*

Bo backed the sow into a corner. It stared at Bo with its almond-shaped eyes. "That's a nice girl," Bo cooed. He knelt by the animal. He felt his fangs and claws extend. He scratched his claws across the pig's back. It seemed to enjoy the touch. "Hold still, little one." Bo leaned toward the pig. He smelled barnyard dirt and manure in its sparse hair. The pig grunted lowly. Bo opened his mouth and raked his fangs across the back. He sensed a large vein in the neck. He dropped his head toward it. He felt unimaginable pleasure in his mouth. The thirst at the back of his throat demanded blood.

The building lit up. A pale dropped and spilled the pigs' slop on the ground and rolled away. A teenage girl stood frozen inside the door. Her hand was still on the light switch. In the instant she inhaled the air to scream, Bo vaulted over the enclosure and attacked the girl's throat. His fangs made a popping noise as they penetrated her flesh. He hit a vein and drank greedily. Gulped the hot blood while the girl's heart hammered in terror. Soon the heart slowed and fell silent. Bo gorged himself. He could not stop. He was sloppy and blood splattered over the girl and Bo. Eventually, she was drained. Bo threw back his head and relished the last few gulps. For a moment he savored the taste. Then the gnawing thirst in his throat returned.

Bo stared at the body. The lifeless, blue eyes stared back. The throat was ripped open. Bo grabbed a leg and pulled the body from the building. The head drug along the dirt floor, moved side to side as if the teenager was in some animated conversation with friends. After he was outside, Bo hoisted the girl over his shoulder and crossed the field toward the van. Her oversized rubber boots fell off. First the left. Then the right. Her bare feet dangled.

***

Kazmer made out Bo's outline come toward him. He soon realized that Bo carried a body over his shoulder. Kazmer dropped to the ground from the van. The door remained open. Kazmer palmed his .9 mm pistol. Kazmer watched. Wondered what happened in the building. It was too dark for him to see the girl approach the building from the farmhouse. Bo dropped the corpse over the fence, leaped over himself, and picked up the girl again. He stopped in front of Kazmer.

"I wanted to surprise you, Kaz."

"I am surprised. You took a human life."

"I didn't plan on it." Bo unslung the body, held it briefly across his chest, and handed it to Kazmer, who took the corpse and walked to the van's rear.

Bo said, "I had planned to bring you a pork roast and eggs to make, but..."

"That would be nice. So, instead you brought me a drained girl who will be missed, and I will have to bury. No matter. You should stick to derelicts who nobody misses."

Kazmer opened the van's back door and lay the body inside. He picked up a foot and examined it. "Did you put the ring on the toe?"

"No. It's popular with some girls. It's what they do."

Kazmer grunted. "Seems strange, but good to know for when I have girlfriend." He slid off the ring, dropped the foot inside, pocketed the ring, and closed the van's rear door. "She will think ring for toe make good present."

"She surprised me, Kaz. I was ready to sink into a pig, a big sow, when she came through the door and turned on the lights. I was on her in a second. I couldn't help myself."

"Not a problem, Mr. Bo. We will get through this. You will learn the vampire ways. This is the first step."

———

THEY RETURNED to the motel and covered the van. Kazmer carried in the body. Rigor mortis was setting in. "Don't put her in our room, Kaz. I can't take it."

"I will bury her tomorrow," Kazmer said. "Now I need to rest. I am falling asleep."

"Rest, Kazmer. I will sit up with you. Just remember. She will be the last human I kill. No more. I don't care about the thirst. I plan to go into the woods. To hunt deer. Drink their blood. No more cities. No more farms. I'm staying away from people. I won't kill people if I'm not around them. Do you understand?"

"I understand. Before you drink deer blood, we should move. I want to show you something." Kazmer led the way down the hall and into the lobby. "I didn't see this until today in the light."

Lengths of copper wire and a pile of copper pipes were stacked. "Somebody will be back for this stuff," Kazmer said. "They will sell the copper, have money for drugs."

Bo said. "We could turn it in for cash before they come back."

"Not a good idea. We don't want to be recognized. Police will be looking for this girl. I have found a new place to go. The girl disappear. We disappear from here."

"What about her parents, Kaz? What will they think?"

"Maybe they think she go off with a boy. Girls do that sometimes."

"She might not have a boyfriend."

Kazmer scratched his chin. He looked at the body and brushed her hair off her face. "Pretty girl like this will have boyfriend."

CHAPTER SIX

AFTER THE GIRL'S BODY WAS BURIED, KAZMER RETURNED TO the motel room. Bo rested inside his mummy sleeping bag on the bed. He had climbed into it for the first time at dawn. Before he disappeared inside for the day, Kazmer said, "With your permission, we will move tonight after dark. There is not much to carry. I don't like this place anymore."

With just his nose and eyes showing outside the bag, Bo asked, "Kaz, do I stink?"

"Smell like the dead. It is natural for vampires."

"That's what I thought. What do we do about the stink?"

Kazmer pursed his lips. He was midway through rolling a cigarette. He paused with the smoke raised to his lips to lick the paper's edge. "Tonight, we check in at a real motel. Get showers—me, too. Then we check out and go to the new place."

"Sounds like a plan. See you at sundown."

Inside the Brethren's hideout, Persimmon spread a city map on the kitchen island. She sighed. "It looks like we're back to visiting cemeteries and abandos for the vamps," she told Goldenrod, using the Brethren's slang for abandoned buildings.

"I'll take cemetery watch any day, even night," said Goldenrod, who preferred to be called Gold. She also used the moniker Kelly Gold. She fixed a length of blond hair into a ponytail. "Abandoned buildings are not my forte. Too many steps."

Cemetery watch amounted to finding vampire Shadows, the humans who acted as undead servants in the hope of being turned someday. The Shadows weren't always too smart and exposed themselves by coming and going from the vampire lairs. Because most of the Shadows were killed in the Brethren attack on the vampire lair, cemeteries, for now, would get minimum coverage. The focus would be on abandos as potential vampire lodgings but more likely to contain the homeless and drug addicts.

Persimmon stared at Gold.

"All right, if I have to do abandos let me take John Bargain," Gold said. "He is one of us, isn't he?"

"I suppose. He has his own apartment, but he's been hanging around here trying to interview everyone," Persimmon said. "You can take him. Let him interview you. He'll need to be trained starting with Brethren 101."

"Is he still pissed? Are you giving him his video of the assault?"

"Can't." Persimmon threw up her hands. "I don't think the world is ready to be told vampires exist or watch them burn to ashes. I don't think the world is ready to find out about *us*. It was a good vid. Maybe we can use it for training. Give him credit. At the very least we can pay him. That will make him happy."

Overboard George and Mad Maggie enjoyed the honeymoon the Brethren treated them to. They couldn't remember staying in a motel where they were not looked down upon because a governmental agency picked up the tab for a few nights. They had just returned from the pool and sauna, showered, dressed, and got ready to go out for dinner to a restaurant down the block.

"This is our last night," Overboard George said. "Then it's back to work chasing vampires. I wonder if there's any news on Eva. I think she died in that avalanche after Del Hatch blew up the vampires' big vault. I think a beam or big rock crushed her. Smashed her heart and she burned up underground."

"I don't know," Mad Maggie said, brushing her hair in the room's mirror. "I'd like to think so. She was quite the enemy. Just think. Vampire hunters could go their whole lives and never see an ancient vampire, and we got involved with two from the start. We staked Gerrard in our first fight. Then tracked her across the country. That's something."

"It is. I think that's why the Brethren are happy to accept us. Make us one of their own." George paused a moment. Checked out his own appearance in the mirror. "I wonder if Del Hatch caught a Bigfoot yet. He should be in Washington State by now."

"I wouldn't put anything passed that man," Mad Maggie said. She set down her brush and smiled at Overboard George in the mirror. He smiled back. "What do you say we hit the restaurant before it gets crowded."

Overboard George laughed.

"What's funny, Babe?"

"This money on the dresser."

"Tip for the maid?"

"Yeah. There was a time when I'd steal that money if I could. Now I can tip the maid."

"You have arrived, OG."

They walked to the door to the hall. George paused. Put his eye to the peephole in the door.

"Another reason to be tall," Mad Maggie said, rising on her toes beside George. "I can't see shit through that thing."

"These little fisheye windows always amazed me. When I was using and could get a motel room, I'd stand for hours at the door, waiting for something to happen in the hall. Kind of like when we sat on the sidewalks watching traffic. Always waiting for something to happen."

"Did anything ever happen?" Maggie smiled.

"No. But you never know." He trained an eye at the peephole. Grinned at the empty hall.

Overboard George spun around. His eyes were wide. His mouth quivered.

Maggie cupped a hand over her mouth. Laughed.

"Mother fucker!" George hissed. He backed up a step and pointed toward the hall. "I just saw Bo and his Shadow. The big guy. Walked right by the door."

"Come on." Mad Maggie smirked. She reached for the door handle but realized George was serious.

"It was Bo. Only now he looks like Mr. White Bread. He's very pale."

They returned to the door. George pressed an eye to the peephole.

"What do ya see, OG," Mad Maggie whispered.

"Nothin'." He moved his head around the peephole to get a view down the hall.

They heard the noise of a card key swipe and a door lock.

Overboard George looked down at Mad Maggie.

"They're next door," George whispered.

"No."

"Yes."

A door opened and then closed. Locks engaged.

"We have no weapons," Mad Maggie said. "I didn't bring my machete."

"Me, too. I didn't expect to need weapons on our honeymoon. Call Persimmon. Tell her what happened." George pulled back from the door. "Wait. I'm going over to check the room number, so we give her the right one."

"No. What if they're looking out their peephole and see us? We'll be sitting ducks without weapons."

Overboard George scanned their room. "Maybe there's something we can break up to make a couple of stakes."

"They'll hear us, OG. I'm calling Persimmon."

With the call made, Overboard George kept his eye to the peephole. Mad Maggie sat on the bed wringing her hands. George whispered, "It don't make sense that they'd come here, around all these people, and maid service, too, going in and out." Overboard George opened the door and stuck out his head. He returned inside in an instant and turned to Mad Maggie. "Smells like something dead out there."

Mad Maggie, who now had her ear at the common wall between the rooms, ran to George. He placed a hand on the doorknob.

"Want to get a whiff? It's fading."

"I smelled enough death this last year." She locked the door and pointed a finger at George. "I'll bet they came here to get cleaned up. Shower the stink off themselves. Remember how we used to get washed in the bus station's restroom? Go between buses, when it was mostly empty. Wash our clothes, too, when money was tight. I loved that hand soap in the dispensers. How many times did you get chased out of that bathroom at the bus station?"

"Can't count it was so many," Overboard George said.

Persimmon texted back. She was on her way. She told OG and Maggie to stay safe.

George heard the lock open next door. He pressed his eye to the peephole and traded places with Maggie, but neither could see any movement in the hall. He unlocked the door and pulled it open a few inches to listen. The hall was unnaturally quiet. After a few seconds of hearing only his own breathing, feeling his heart thumping, a door closed at the end of the hall. He looked back at Maggie.

"I think they're gone."

Mad Maggie ran to the common wall between the rooms. She listened for movement next door. She looked back at George, frustrated. Overboard George turned from the peephole and shrugged his shoulders. Maggie flew to the window. Parted the shades. A white van cruised slowly through the nearly empty parking lot below. Mad Maggie motioned for George to join her. Pointed at the van's slow progress.

"There they go," Overboard George said. "Fresh as daisies. By the time we got downstairs, they'd be long gone. We won't know what direction they're going. Our only hope is Persimmon spots them by chance and follows."

Overboard George and Mad Maggie stood at the window. In a moment Persimmon's black SUV roared into the parking lot, and stopped at the main door.

"Let's go, meet them downstairs," Maggie said.

"Let's wait. Bo's gone. We might miss them downstairs. We'll be in the lobby and they'll be up here. Damn!"

"There'll be other chances, OG."

"But we were so close. We could have spit on them."

There was a knock on the door. George opened it. It was a breathless, Persimmon, Goldenrod, and a new Brethren arrival, the female Cacti.

"Where?" Persimmon said.

"They're gone," Mad Maggie said. "They pulled out right after you texted us. We watched them leave the parking lot in a white van. Exited that away." Mad Maggie pointed with her thumb."

"That makes sense," Persimmon said. "You'd need something like a van to carry a casket."

"Sorry, Persimmon," OG said.

"Don't worry. At least we know they're still in the area. A new vampire like Bo is bound to make mistakes. We'll get him. First, we need to get in next door."

Gold rummaged through her wallet. She marched down the

hall to the next room. "This the vamp spa?" she said in front of the door.

"That's the place," OG said.

Gold slipped a card in the lock, jiggled it and the lock opened. She smiled at the group.

"How?" Persimmon said.

"I call it a skeleton card. Opens everything but a can of tuna."

They pushed open the door with a bang. Maggie hit the lights. The room was empty. The shower still dripped and was steamy. The exhaust fan hummed. Towels lay on the wet floor.

"I wonder whether they showered together," Gold said.

"That's a gruesome thought," OG said.

"It does appear Bo's Shadow has some experience. Knows how to move through the world," Persimmon said. "How to rent a room and drive. That's good to know. He probably had to do all kinds of things for Eva."

The group examined the room closer. Overboard George used a coat hanger to turn over towels on the bathroom floor. The complimentary soaps, shampoos, and lotions were gone. The beds appeared to be untouched, not even sat on.

The only new evidence was Bo seemed to like to clean the smell off his corpse. "Don't know of too many vamps who bathe unless they plan to go out in public," Gold said. "That's interesting. I know they don't like perfumes or colognes. They mask their ability to smell at long range. Lisa told me colony Shadows were punished severely for using any body fragrances."

Cacti approached OG and Maggie to introduce herself and shake hands. "It's a pleasure to meet part of the East Coasters who killed the powerful Gerrard, Eva's brother. He's been on the Brethren's most wanted list for a century. Well done. And you are newlyweds."

"Thanks. Where you from?" Mad Maggie asked.

"I just got in from Flagstaff," Cacti said.

"Desert country," Maggie said.

"That too,' Cacti said. "I got my name because of this." She ran her hand over her short, spiked hair. "Plus, I can be quite prickly with people I don't like."

Everyone laughed. The Brethren returned to their stronghold. Overboard George and Mad Maggie had one more night at the motel.

After they got back to their room, George told Maggie, "You know, we never made it to dinner. Let's get going before the restaurant closes. I don't plan to eat out of a dumpster. Those days are over."

When they reached the lobby, Gold said, "I have an idea." She went to the desk and asked the young man, "Do you have surveillance cameras in the parking lot?" She smiled broadly and rested her hand near the young man's.

He looked up. Swallowed. "Why do you ask?"

"Somebody hit my car and took off. I think it was a white van."

"I can call the police for you. To open a claim."

"I'd rather do this myself. It might have been my ex. Know what I mean?"

"Not exactly." The young man swallowed hard again. Looked skeptical, wary of Gold.

She brushed back her long blond hair. "If I could look at the footage from just a few minutes ago I could tell for sure. If it was an ex. If he wasn't the one, you can call the police."

There was a pause. The young man stared.

"I won't get you in trouble," Gold said. "And I don't plan any action against the motel. It's not your fault people don't know how to drive." Gold smiled again.

The man looked around nervously. "Let me see what I can do." He typed furiously at the keyboard. "Okay, I see a white van in the parking lot. It's on the move. Exiting."

"Can I come around and look," Gold said.

"Nobody's supposed to be back here. It's off limits unless you're an employee."

"I'm not telling," Gold said. She raised an index finger to her lips and whispered "Shhh."

"Okay. Just for a minute."

Gold vaulted over the counter. Landed next to the man. He stepped back, amazed.

"You said I have only a minute. I wanted to make the most of it."

Persimmon and Cacti stood outside the lobby door facing away from the motel.

He set to work. Their heads were close in front of the monitor. He pointed. Gold pointed. He backed up the video. "Can you take it back to where they checked in? I see there's a camera on this desk."

The clerk sighed and complied. Looked nervously at the clock on the wall. "There. Stop it, where they're under the carport. Can you zoom in on the license plate?"

Gold squealed. "I can see it." She grabbed the man's arm and squeezed the bicep. "You are a computer genius."

The man smiled. Blushed.

"I have a friend in the DMV. Need a ticket fixed?"

The man's mouth dropped open. Shook his head no. He raised a pen and paper for Gold, but she vaulted over the counter and hurried away.

"You're welcome," he added as she disappeared outside.

CHAPTER SEVEN

They had been through a dozen abandos looking for vampires without success. They passed on the abandoned buildings where access was too easy. A vampire wanted protection from the sun's rays and the curious who might wander in. The homeless were always in search of a place that was safe and dry. Drug users sometimes wanted privacy to shoot up and sleep off the concoctions of fentanyl and animal tranquilizers that passed now as heroin. Although police didn't often interrupt the street corner sale of drugs, which was brisk, sometimes an address was better for making transactions than in the open.

The Brethren had fanned out across the city in search of the vampires that had escaped the assault on the cemetery lair. They knew Bo Bentwood escaped and traveled with his Shadow Kazmer. There had been no sign of the ancient vampiress Eva. The Brethren had combed the hillside that collapsed on the vampire vault. Other than Bo's trail to the exterior where he had dug himself out, and a pile of rolled cigarette remnants where Kazmer waited patiently for his master, there was no evidence another of the undead had survived. Still, there was always the chance that some loner vamp missed the Brethren assault and still roamed the city. These lone vampires were difficult to find. Their seemingly haphazard movements were almost impossible to trace. More often it came down to luck when capturing a loner. Then there was the sudden vacuum a collapsed undead colony might bring as, one by one, other vampires moved in. formed a new colony, selected a leader, and found a stronghold.

The city provided a smorgasbord of hapless victims. There were the homeless, the drug users who spent part of the day or night incapacitated after shooting up, and criminals, solitary rogues, or gang members. All had one thing in common: if they disappeared, they would be forgotten. Most were known by aliases, and if bodies were found, it was almost impossible to identify them.

Persimmon, Overboard George, and Mad Maggie made it quickly through the first several buildings. They split up to search various floors and found only an assortment of broken furniture and appliances. Some rooms had old mattresses where people had slept before eventually moving out. Homelessness in its various forms meant people traveled with all their meager possessions. No moving vans. A shopping cart or an assortment of bags was sufficient.

As the Brethren went from building to building, the homeless, looking for some reward, often helped the Brethren. "You looking for someone special? Give me a name. Maybe I can help. This ain't a good place to look for someone. This is Overdose Alley. We had a lot of deaths on this street. Anyway, there's nobody in that building."

Overboard George nodded and continued on his way. He knew who told the truth. Others asked for money or flipped open a coat to reveal packets of drugs fastened to the lining. The group walked around the people passed out on the sidewalk, moving down the street. Some junkies sat unconscious on steps, leaning against old handrails. Finally, they found a promising building. The door was wedged shut. Overboard George put his shoulder against it several times before it opened enough to admit the trio.

"The upper floors look dark," Mad Maggie said, standing in the foyer, pointing up the stairwell. "The windows must be covered."

"Looks really creepy," George added.

"We'll have to be careful," Persimmon whispered. "Don't talk. Hand signals only. Not that we didn't make noise forcing the door."

Persimmon took the lead. She slowly climbed the steps, cautiously, until they reached the second floor. Persimmon and Overboard George pulled out their pistols. Mad Maggie drew her machete. All three had wooden stakes as they moved down the hall. Each took a room. The windows were covered, Some with heavy drapes. Others spray painted black. The second-floor rooms were empty. They returned to the stairs. Persimmon nodded to climb.

Just as she stepped, a mournful wail rose above. Persimmon stopped. Looked at her friends. Raised an eyebrow.

"I think it's the wind," Mad Maggie said. "There must be a window open or broken out."

Overboard George nodded. "Could be," he whispered.

Something flapped, a slapping noise. The group traded glances.

"More wind," Mad Maggie murmured.

Persimmon winked. "Just so we're all on the same page."

"We are," George said. He holstered his pistol and picked up a discarded chair by a leg. "I see a vamp, this chair is going through the window. That will brighten up the place. Vamps won't like that."

Mad Maggie smiled. "My George is always thinking."

He waved his stake toward the steps. They climbed in near-complete darkness. When they reached the next landing the third floor had long shadows in the hall that crossed the floor and climbed the walls. Like the hall downstairs, this one had holes punched in the plaster, broken shards of wood laths, and peeling stained wallpaper. The floorboards squeaked. They explored each room together, stakes raised, moving into the dark corners, the closets that were like black holes. The rooms were empty.

It was clear the wail and the flapping, came from the fourth floor. They approached the staircase with caution, and paused a moment before they ascended. The steps creaked. The wail continued. The flapping was steady, rhythmic, like a heartbeat.

Overboard George whispered, "The first thing I'm gonna do—after I kill any vamps—is fix that noise."

"It is unsettling. I got only one nerve left," Mad Maggie said. "You better do your fixing fast."

Persimmon nodded. They climbed on. The first three rooms on the fourth floor were almost pitch black inside. The window glass had been spray-painted black. All were empty. So was the fourth. One room to go, through which a sliver of light shined, undulated into the hall. It was from that room the noises came—the wail, the flapping. They paused outside the room. The door was partially closed. The odor of death caught their noses.

"This is the door our prize is behind," George said lowly.

Persimmon counted on her gloved fingers: one, two, three. The trio burst into the room. One window was open at the top. The wind roared through the open space. An old shade covering the window raised in the noisy breeze, letting in light momentarily, and struck the wooden trim with a rhythmic beat. Overboard George charged the window, seized the shade, and ripped it down. All three breathed a sigh of relief.

Mad Maggie twisted her expression and raised two fingers, pinched her nose. The smell remained. They scanned the room. Persimmon spun and pointed. Legs protruded from the dark closet. They approached. Persimmon opened the door. Overboard George grabbed a sneakered foot and pulled out the body. The corpse remained seated in the same position it had been in, leaning against the closet's interior wall. Rigor mortis. A needle remained in the tied-off arm below the elbow. No vampire. An overdose.

"Must have been quick," Overboard George said. "Not even enough time to pull out the needle."

"Anybody get the address before we came in?" Mad Maggie said. Her friends were silent. "We'll have to go outside and call 911. Let the authorities know he's here. After all, he's someone's son."

Overboard George snorted. "Fool."

Persimmon said, "His pockets are inside out. Looks like we weren't the first to find him. Just a kid, too."

"They all just foolish kids," Overboard George said.

CHAPTER EIGHT

KAZMER ROOTED THROUGH ACCUMULATED JUNK ON, UNDER, and around the abandoned motel's front desk. Bo sat across the lobby on the end of a sofa, its faded leather cracked, a leg dangling over the end. Bo watched Kazmer intent on his search. The sun was rising, and Bo would have to move soon to the darkened room for the day, crawl inside his mummy sleeping bag, and pull the cover over his face. Enough light already filtered in to help Kazmer in his search.

"What are you doing, Kaz?"

"Looking for useful things we might need some time."

"If it weren't junk, somebody would have taken it. I thought vampires traveled with few possessions."

"True. Useful is important, too. We must leave this place soon. People will come back."

"Who?"

"The people who pulled the electric wires from the walls. Wrapped them up. Piled them near the door. That is a lot of work. They will return for the wire. Sell the copper inside for drug money. That is how it is."

"Do you think there might be drugs here?"

"I don't know. Drug users, gangs, they don't—what is the word —stockpile drugs. They use them or sell them."

"Do we have another place?"

Kazmer stopped his search to roll a cigarette. He looked directly at Bo. "I found a place not far from here while you rest. I believe you will like it."

"What about you, Kaz? Will you like it? Creature comforts don't mean much to me, but you have to stay warm and dry. Be able to get food."

Kazmer lit his cigarette and inhaled deeply. He examined the lopsided smoke for a second. "I have stayed in worse places. Worked long hours in worse places. This is my comfort, Mr. Bo. Tobacco."

"If that shit is as strong as it smells, you'll have lung cancer before the summer is over."

"Kazmer does not get lung cancer. Kazmer is strong."

"I hope you're right, Kaz. I'm going to the room. The sun's coming up and its light is getting uncomfortable here. My skin is crawling"

Kazmer grunted. "Lock yourself inside, Mr. Bo. I have another key to get in later."

AFTER BO LOCKED himself in the darkened room, Kazmer listened outside the door in the hall, his ear an inch from the exterior, for the sleeping bag zipper to close. The sun was almost up. Kazmer uncovered the van and drove for breakfast, fast food at a drive-thru. He proceeded to the city's edge, where an old factory lay in ruins. He sat at the entrance a minute, then snipped the lock with a bolt cutter he found inside the motel with the coiled wire the gang-bangers had collected. He let the gate swing open, drove inside the fence, and closed the gate, keeping it in place by wrapping the chain through it.

Kazmer moved the van inside the factory, driving through a hole at the end of the main building. Once inside, Kazmer covered the van with the tarp he brought from the motel and settled down to eat his breakfast. An old machine provided the perfect seat and table for his meal. Kazmer relaxed.

After he ate, he smoked a rank cigarette, blowing the smoke into the air above his head. It was such times he and his brother Lazlo had enjoyed. Smoking. Talking quietly. They always made plans. Now, however, with Lazlo gone, entombed inside the hillside avalanche set off by Del Hatch, those plans would never be realized. All the things they had collected in their apartment, which they enjoyed going from room to room to identify and admire, collected dust. There were clothing and jewelry that did not fit, gaudy bric-a-brac that had caught their eye during robberies and murders they committed over the years. There was no thought of the people whose lives they had ended. No notion of the grieving relatives left to mourn missing loved ones. The brothers had been as callous as the vampires they served.

At some point, Kazmer thought he would like to show Bo his apartment. Perhaps they would stay there. It would require quite a trip. Bo would have to overcome his squeamishness for killing humans, of course. That would come eventually, Kazmer believed. It did with other vampires. Kazmer hoped sooner than later as he stirred, crushed the remainder of his cigarette between a thumb and index finger, and felt the momentary burn as the lit tobacco was extinguished.

Kazmer stood and stretched. This old building would be a good place to hide. The floor was littered with rubble, bricks, and chunks of concrete. The old walls were festooned with graffiti, some painted in areas seemingly impossible to reach. Machines and parts too large to move lay about. It appeared anything that could be stolen was already gone. Through broken skylights, pigeons flew in and out, roosted on the iron beams overhead. Kazmer walked to an iron staircase, stopped a moment to scan the area above, and started a slow climb up. The stairs seemed sturdy and switched direction midway up. They reminded Kazmer of the switch-backed path that led to Eva's tomb high in the vampire's main vault. At the top of the steps, there was a large platform. Nearby was a room, an old office, Kazmer thought, that had a working door that could be barricaded from the inside with a heavy, old wooden desk that was part of the interior clutter. Kazmer looked down at the factory floor. It was a long drop. His eyes followed another set of steps upward from the platform and office to a door to the roof. Kazmer twisted his face and started climbing upward again. At the top, he pushed the door open and smiled. The flat roof was bathed in sunlight. Someone had gone to the trouble of hauling up chairs and a grill. Kazmer walked to the end of the building where a large water tank stood. A rusted door with a missing seal hung open. Kazmer walked inside. The place was dry. Someone had used the tank to reside. Wooden pallets and an old mattress lay at the center. Kazmer inspected the mattress, flipped it over, and kicked the pallets. he pursed his lips and nodded with approval. He returned to the door. Pulled it closed. A thin sliver of light spread around the hatch across the tank wall. Kazmer locked the door with difficulty. Opened it again. Eventually, the rusty lock broke free and worked smoothly.

This will be a good place for Bo to rest. No light. No people. Secure. I will take the office inside. Not so many steps.

Kazmer returned to one of the chairs on the roof, sat, and rolled a cigarette. The breeze on the roof carried away tobacco from his rolling paper and made the cigarette difficult to light. He settled back and relaxed, enjoyed the sunlight on his face, and dozed off.

Kazmer returned to the motel near sundown, after another stop for fast food and coffee. He ate in the lobby while there was still light, seated on the cracked leather sofa. After eating, he checked to ensure the coiled wire still lay on the floor near the door and returned down the hall to the darkened room. After slipping inside the room, Kazmer relocked the door, and pressed the chair back under the doorknob. There was no need to be quiet. After all, vampires slept like the dead. Bo would wake on his own accord. Kazmer slipped into his sleeping bag in the closet and felt the sunburn on his face before he fell asleep again.

It was pitch black in the room when Bo shook Kazmer's shoulder. Kazmer woke slowly.

"We have company, Kaz."

"So soon? I hoped we could move before the gangbangers returned for their wire. I hope they don't damage the van."

Kazmer strained his ears to hear the voices up the hall in the lobby. "How many?" he whispered. Kazmer flicked on his lighter for a moment to check the surroundings, the door, and the chair wedged under its doorknob. He crawled from the sleeping bag and felt his way to the locked door.

"Three. Two men. One woman. They might have guns."

"Don't drain them, Mr. Bo. No blood will look suspicious. I don't want to bury three bodies tonight if I don't have to."

"No humans, Kaz. No more murder," Bo whispered, inches away from Kazmer's face.

"But you must feed."

"Not on these three."

Although Kazmer could not discern the three voices, Bo could, even with the closed door. Their voices came in short, staccato blasts.

"Let's get the wire and go," one man said.

"I think somebody's here," the other said.

"What about the van," the woman said. "It has to be a hideout."

"We could use that van," the first man said, who had the deepest voice.

"It could be boosted. Hot. The cops might be looking for it."

"Fuck the van. We have a car," the woman said. "Check inside it. What if there's drugs."

"Could be drugs anywhere in here," the man with the fluty voice said. "It's been a week since we were here."

"I say we grab the copper and get out," the man with the deep voice said.

As the gangbangers talked back and forth, not careful about how loud their voices were, Bo repeated the conversation in a whisper for Kazmer. Occasionally, Kazmer grunted with the hint of a growl in his throat.

"What if there's a stash?" the woman said. "Let's go through the place. Quickly."

"You'll never find anything in this dump," the deep-voiced man hissed.

"I wanna look," the woman said. "We might get lucky."

She stepped down the hall and tramped on something that broke under her foot. "Fuck! Check out these rooms. Look for anything out in the open. Then we'll go."

"Hey, look for my bolt cutter. It's not with the wire. I want that cutter."

"Right."

Kazmer flicked on his lighter for a second and looked at Bo.

The trio moved down the hall. Kicked in closed doors. Turned over mattresses, rummaged through closets, inspected anything that might conceal drugs or valuables.

As they approached the last room where Bo and Kazmer were barricaded, Kazmer pulled out the chair from under the doorknob. "I don't want them shooting through the door. I could be hit."

Bo and Kazmer waited and listened. Bo had inherited some of the vampiress's strengths. He could detect their separate smells. They were not clean. The woman was menstruating. The smell of blood gnawed at the back of his throat. His fangs descended. His jaw trembled. His claws extended. The room seemed filled with the smell of blood.

The gangbangers continued down the hall.

Kazmer flicked on his lighter again. Looked at Bo for a moment before letting the flame die. "Remember, don't drain them. Take some from each. Three people will have enough blood for tonight."

Bo moaned. "No murder," he managed to hiss.

"You hear that?" the woman said. "Sounded like it came from the last room. A voice. Let's go."

Outside the locked door the trio hesitated. Inside, Bo smelled their breath. Their sweat. Gun oil. Their fear. It was intoxicating. The vampire disease's thirst made the back of Bo's throat raw. He imagined tearing them open, ripping the flesh, draining their blood. He imagined the taste of the hot liquid coursing down his throat, as it had when he exsanguinated the farm girl, soothing the demand only temporarily. There would be no sipping, no tasting. He would gorge himself on the hot tonic. His own body would be covered in blood. His teeth chattered. He could hear their three hearts pounding. It was almost musical. A heavy metal riff no human could play. Bo looked at Kazmer, whom he could see in the darkness. Kazmer had his stiletto knife ready, clenched in his fist. His heart was calm, beating slowly. There was a hint of a smile on his lips. Kazmer was ready.

The doorknob jiggled. "The fucker's locked."

"Get a key," the fluty-voiced man hissed, his voice rising in falsetto. "The keys are in the office.

"It wasn't locked before. Kick it in!"

The man with the deep voice took a step backward and raised a long leg to deliver a kick. His leg fired. The door opened. He missed the door and fell into the room. Kazmer stepped to the side. The fluty-voiced man screamed. Fired his gun wildly. Bo was hit with two bullets. The woman saw the shots had no effect. Black, syrupy blood spread across Bo's chest. She ran. The big man scrambled across the floor, tried to stand and aim his own pistol. Kazmer grabbed his hair, pulled back his head, and put his blade through the man's heart. Let him sink to the floor. Bo tackled the fluty-voiced man. Tore open his neck. Attached his mouth to a fountain of blood. Gulped mouthful after mouthful.

Kazmer tapped Bo on the back as if he were a wrestling referee. "One is getting away."

Bo's attention shot down the hall. He heard footsteps receding. He knew immediately it was the woman. The vampire disease demanded blood. He blurred down the hall, passed the woman, and waited for her at the office entrance. He caught her by the throat. Lifted her off the ground with one arm. Pinned her against the wall. She choked. Beat her fists against his arm. Bo looked at her curiously. Let her slide down the wall. Released his grip while she passed out. He bent his head toward her neck. Sniffed. Looked at her again. He grabbed an arm and dragged her down the hall to the first room. Threw her on the mattress. Kazmer appeared at the door. Flicked on his lighter. Raised an eyebrow and twisted his lips.

This is not a good time to lose your virginity, Master Bo.

CHAPTER NINE

Bo climbed on the unconscious woman. "She is mine," Bo hissed, baring his fangs when Kazmer's cigarette lighter flicked on. "I want her now."

"They fired their guns. Made too much noise. We must leave."

"I can't take it. I want her now." Bo picked her off the bed like a doll.

"I will take care of her, Mr. Bo." Kazmer raised his knife to strike.

"No!" Bo spun the woman away from Kazmer.

"There are homes close," Kazmer said. "They will call the police. Let me kill her or you kill her. We must go fast!"

Bo was transfixed by the limp woman hanging in his arms in the darkness.

"Now, Mr. Bo, or we will get caught. I cannot blur away to safety."

Bo turned his head. Stared at Kazmer. "Kaz," he said slowly, "you just kill me. You kill me."

"Good. We go fast," Kazmer said. His voice showed anxiety for the first time.

"All right. Get our sleeping bags. I'll meet you at the van."

Bo walked toward the motel office with the woman dangling under one arm.

"Drop her, Mr. Bo. If you won't kill her, drop her."

"No, Kaz!"

"You plan to save her?" Kazmer said. He was half down the hall to retrieve their sleeping bags.

"For a while. Now I need more blood."

"Bite her," Kazmer said.

"Not yet."

"You can take blood from the big man. I stabbed him to stop his heart. He did not bleed much."

Bo blurred down the hall to his darkened room. Hoisted the body into the air with one hand and slammed it down on the mattress. Kazmer followed. "A suggestion, Mr. Bo."

Bo turned to Kazmer, his mouth open, fangs extended. His eyes were two slits. "What?"

"Instead of biting the body, tearing the meat, you can suck the blood through my knife hole in the chest."

Bo raised a quizzical eyebrow. "You think of everything, Kaz."

"It will be like using a straw. Leave some blood to avoid suspicion. That is what my brother Lazlo always said—*avoid suspicion*."

Bo returned to the corpse, ripped open the shirt, planted his mouth over the wound, and sucked, slurping up the blood. After a while, Kazmer placed a hand on Bo's shoulder.

"Enough," Kazmer said. "Avoid suspicion."

Bo took two more long sucks and stopped, turning his head toward Kazmer. Blood ran from his mouth and down his chin. Bo slid out his long, vampire tongue and cleaned up the blood. He released the body and let it fall on the floor.

"We should go to the new place, Mr. Bo. It will be safer. More might look for these people. We can leave the bodies."

"I'm taking the girl. That's an order. I'm not done with her," Bo said.

Kazmer showed no emotion. "I have a good place to keep her, but she will need food, drink, as you did when you were the mistress's pet."

"How strange, Kaz. The kept has become the keeper."

"Not strange," Kazmer said, picking up several blankets and folding them quickly. "It is the way life changes. We will see many changes over the years. You will come to understand."

"Don't let me be cruel. I don't want her abused the way I was abused."

"I understand."

"I'll let her go before I treat her like I was treated."

Bo returned up the hall, threw the still-unconscious woman over his shoulder, and waited for Kazmer to uncover the van. It was still dark, the middle of the night, when Kazmer pulled out and drove toward the abandoned factory. There was little traffic, and Kazmer stayed below the speed limit. He stopped at a twenty-four-hour convenience store to fill the van with gasoline and buy sandwiches and coffee. Inside, the clerk eyed Kazmer suspiciously and checked out the van at the gas pumps. The plump, balding man seemed to breathe a sigh of relief when Kazmer pulled out cash to pay the bill. Kazmer turned to leave. Suddenly, he stopped. Tracked down an aisle and returned with a half dozen frosted cupcakes in a plastic container.

"Sweet tooth," Kazmer said, smiling. He peeled off more money to pay the clerk, collected his change, and walked out of the store.

"You buy a banquet, Kaz?" Bo wanted to know.

"She must eat if you plan to feed on her, Mr. Bo."

"Do you think we need to chain her?" Bo asked.

"If you want, I can buy chains and locks tomorrow, but she will not get away. Look at this new place first. Then decide."

They drove on in silence. Kazmer approached the factory's property gate, stopped, and turned off the headlights. He slid from the van, examined the chain he had cut earlier, saw the chain as he had replaced it remained undisturbed, unfastened the gate and let it swing open. After the van was through the gate, Kazmer fastened the chain to keep the gate closed, making it appear locked. He pulled the van inside the factory. Birds in the rafters stirred in the dark, squawked, flew, and settled again.

Outside the van, Kazmer pointed into the darkness. "There is an office up there."

"I see it," Bo said.

"Yes, the eyes of the vampire see many things. I will take the office. It has many windows to watch. There is an empty water tank on the roof for you and the girl, if you still want her."

"I do." Bo blurred up the steps. A split second later the roof door opened. Before it could swing closed Bo returned to the van. "I like the tank, Kaz. Well done."

Kazmer bowed.

"What did I tell you about that royal treatment, Kaz. I'm not liking it."

"I apologize."

"Don't."

Bo opened the back of the van, pulled out the woman feet first, threw her body over his shoulder, and was gone. The door to the roof banged shut. Kazmer pulled out the food he bought and a blanket for himself. He set everything on the steps. He locked the van and covered it with the tarp. Returning to the steps, Kazmer gathered everything and trudged up the steps. The first glint of morning appeared in the east. Kazmer settled inside the office, draped the blanket over his shoulders, and rolled a cigarette. It had been a long day, and he was tired. Still, he thought Bo was learning the vampire ways. He lit the misshapen cigarette rolled in the dark and sighed. Who knew what tomorrow would bring.

CHAPTER TEN

Del Hatch bloused his jumpsuit pant legs inside his boots, laced them up, and finished the job with double knots. He crawled from his tent into the clearing with other similar tents. He stood, stretched and smiled at the aroma of coffee. Other members of the Sasquatch Research Foundation—or SRF—were already at work. A fire was made, wood gathered, coffee made. A folding table had been set up with the fixings for breakfast. The camp cook, Jerry, whipped flapjack batter in a mixing bowl. Three men and two women greeted Del. One called him sleepy head.

"Looks like the sandman gave you an extra dose," Perry Byrd said, patting his expansive stomach. He grinned at Del with a gap-toothed smile and sauntered to the table to watch Jerry test the batter's consistency. Jerry nodded in approval and gave Perry a taste.

"I suppose so," Del said shyly "There's nothing like sleeping in the great outdoors."

"Leave him alone, Perry," Jim Nelson called from the fire, where he added a log to bring up the flame. "Del was out most of the night reconnoitering."

"I know," Perry said. "I heard him. Between the wood knocks, howls, and distressed animal howls he let fly, I didn't sleep either."

"That's good you heard me," Del said. He moved to the fire and accepted a cup of coffee. Smelled the aroma, blew over the dark surface, and took a sip. "I was up on the ridge. That means my shenanigans traveled a long way."

"Any response?" Jerry wanted to know. The others all paused for a moment to look toward Del.

"Nothing. Not a peep—at least not in a human's hearing range." Del sipped more coffee. "Who made the java? It's good this morning."

Jerry raised a free hand. He gave the batter one final stir, held up a full ladle, and let it spill back into the bowl. He spooned the creamy batter onto a griddle near the fire. The concoction sputtered and bubbled, instantly filling the air with a wonderful aroma of cinnamon, Jerry's secret ingredient.

"It doesn't get any better than this," Del Hatch said, smiling, looking at the blue sky visible between the treetops. With the flapjacks sputtering, Del returned to his tent with his coffee and checked his supplies for the day. Full canteen. Energy bars. Bear spray. Sasquatch sex lure. Smith & Wesson .9 mm with extra clips. Bowie knife. Backpack with a wood-knock bat. Tarp. Ghillie suit. Infra-red camera with extra batteries. Flashlight with extra batteries. His regular camera could take photos or videos. GPS. Plaster of Paris for making Sasquatch footprint casts. And, of course, a good old-fashioned compass. He planned to be back before dark, but he might find a cave or hole that needed exploring. Even an interesting game trail. Del arranged his equipment inside the backpack. His camera would hang on his neck on a strap. Del hefted the backpack and found the weight agreeable.

Jerry called Del back to the fire and moved his fingers back and forth across his closed lips, the sign for mealtime. The others were already in line with their plates. Jerry called, "There's butter and real maple syrup, thanks to Del!" The Sasquatch hunters hooted.

Del fell into line. Jerry passed out flapjacks, dropped a slab of butter on the griddle, let it melt, and poured more batter.

"Got the syrup at the trading post down in the valley," Del said, raising a fork. "I got a gallon, so don't be afraid to eat it."

"Is that the spot with the cigar store Sasquatch on the porch?" Doris Two Feathers asked.

"That's the place," Del said. "Nice folks run it. It's a little touristy but, hey, they got to make a living somehow."

With everyone served, including Jerry, the group found seats and focused on the flapjacks swimming in maple syrup. After breakfast, Perry and Doris washed the dishes. It was their turn. The others surrounded a topographical map of the area, which included a valley lake and high wooded ridges. All were experienced hikers and Sasquatch researchers. They would split into teams and go in separate directions. Communicate any findings via walkie-talkie. In addition, some members, including Del, had satellite phones. Del explored alone by choice. He liked the silence. He didn't want to deal with trail prattle. There was something to hear even in the silence of the deep woods—birds chirping, animals moving about, wind in the treetops. Most of all, Del hated when Sasquatch evidence was stepped on.

Del was always on the look for prints, snapped-off trees, game trails, the availability of prey in any given location, and hair and scat samples he stowed away in glass vials for laboratory analysis. He used latex gloves and tweezers to collect his samples and ensure he did not contaminate them. Del slipped into his backpack and told the other members still studying the map where he would be and approximately when he'd return. "Don't get frantic if I'm not back before sundown," Del said with a toothsome smile. "If I'm going to be late, I'll give you a yodel on the walkie-talkie."

Del gave the group a little salute to his baseball cap, the one with the Sasquatch on the front, and hustled off into the brush.

THE GOING WAS TOUGH, all uphill with thick underbrush. Periodically, Del Hatch rested a hand on his pistol or his Bowie knife, his spray cans of bear spray and Sasquatch sex lure—all arranged on his belt—when one of them got snagged. He stood a minute and listened. He wanted to return to the area he camped in last night, taking a different route to the ridge top, to look for evidence. Although he heard no response to his throaty howls, wood knocks, and recorded animal distress cries he played at full volume through his cell phone and a speaker, and he felt a presence in the woods. A feeling he did not normally experience. He would have expected rocks to be thrown in his direction—a Sasquatch warning —but there was nothing. Del knew he was being watched by someone or something that was close. It didn't scare him. It intrigued him. While he took a breather, he panned his surroundings with an infrared camera. No heat signatures. Not a coyote, not a deer, not a squirrel, not an owl. Even the mosquitos didn't bother him. It was as if he were off-limits to *everything*. It was like he was not even there.

Finally, Del reached the spot where he had spent most of the night. Sweat soaked his jumpsuit. As soon as he sat down on the bed of pine needles he had scraped together last night, and rested his pack at his side, the satellite phone rang. Del was ready for a swig from his canteen and a protein bar. A few minutes to enjoy nature.

He answered, expecting a breakthrough from one of the other researchers. It was John Bargain. The Brethren's very own John from Bargain Videos, news hound, vlogger, who had wanted to interview him since Del blew up the vampire lair with C-4, caused the vampire house on the hill to explode and slide down the hill with the rest of the avalanche.

"Is this a good time, Del. It's John Bargain"

"I know who it is," Del said, immediately disappointed one of the crew didn't get a Sasquatch on video.

"Where are you anyway?"

"Do you know where Martin is?" Del asked. Del liked John Bargain. After all, he had killed a couple of fangers himself and recorded the general assault on the lair with only a stake in his free hand. The kid had guts. Perhaps he was a little foolhardy in his constant search for a good story.

"Don't have a clue, Del. Should I know where it is?

"Probably not. It's a little town near the state forest up here in Washington State. I'm a couple of thousand feet up on a ridge north of Martin. It's Sasquatch country, as you might expect. That's about the best I can do without a map."

"Hey, can you link your satellite phone to your cell? That way I can see you."

"Hold on," Del said, as he dug through his pack. He pulled out his cell and a cord to connect the two devices. After a minute of starting the apps, the connection was made. "How's that? Can you see me now? I see you."

"That's great, Del."

"Where the hell are you."

"My apartment."

"Looks like you had a tussle with a bobcat. You need a haircut, son. High and tight. Don't tell me you just got out of bed."

Bargain smiled and panned his camera over. Kelly Gold, aka, Goldenrod, aka Gold, sat nearby cross-legged wearing only a bra and panties. She squealed and ran out of range, cursed Bargain.

"Come on, Gold. It's only Del Hatch."

"I hope you're not recording," Del said with a smirk.

"I'm always recording. That's my job."

Gold returned to bed in one of Bargain's shirts, which covered her midway down her shapely thighs.

"Hi, Del," Gold waved. "Miss you. Wish you were here."

Del Hatch raised an eyebrow. "I don't know. You know what they say, 'Two's company, three's a crowd.'"

"You see any Bigfoot yet?" Gold ran her fingers through

Bargain's hair, seized and shook his head, which made the video Del received squirrelly for a moment.

"I'm working on it," Del said. "Nothing yet, but I'm feeling lucky. Of course, not as lucky as you two."

The couple howled.

Del Hatch's head snapped to the left. "Now that's an interesting sound." He pursed his lips and turned back to his phone. "Check back with me later." The call went dead.

CHAPTER ELEVEN

The sun had slipped below the horizon, although some light remained in the abandoned factory, angling in through skylights and the hole in the wall at one end. Kazmer snoozed in the office. The kidnapped woman sat as far away from Bo Bentwood as possible inside the empty rooftop water tank, wrapped in a blanket, her back pressed against the curved wall. Bo lay on the pallets inside his mummy sleeping bag. The woman didn't realize it, but she could have escaped, worked the door latch open, stepped outside, crossed the roof, reentered the factory, and made her way down the steps, passed the office, down another flight of steps to the ground. She didn't know Kazmer slept soundly in the office. All she had to do was remain as quiet as possible. How far could she get? Where was she? What was this fiend that had killed her friends? Been shot without effect? Slept like a corpse inside the old water tank?

What did she have to lose at this point? She raised herself and stood. Paused. All was quiet. In the low light that filtered in around the door, she examined the floor. Her eyes had become accustomed to the dark. She planned a path that would make the least amount of noise to the door. She scanned the interior for a weapon—a length of pipe, a chain, a 2X4. She knew where the head was inside the sleeping bag. She would send him to hell; but if bullets hadn't hurt him, what would a pipe do? However, no potential weapons were visible in the low light. She walked quickly across the tank and stopped again, standing over him. Paused for a moment. Listened. No breathing came from within the sleeping bag. Perhaps he had died from the gunshot wounds. Still, there was no blood. She expected to see blood stain the sleeping bag.

She retreated to the door, grabbed the door handle with her right hand, and gave it a tug. It didn't move. Could it be locked? She used two hands. Still, the handle did not move. It had to open inward, judging from the wan light trickling inside. She pulled on the handle, turning it at the same time. Her blanket fell off her shoulders to the floor. She tugged on the door and used all her strength on the handle. Slowly, it moved a little at a time.

She stopped to look at the sleeping bag. There was no movement. No sound from within. He must be dead. She planted her feet and gave one more yank on the handle. The handle lock slipped from under the welded plate that held it in place. There was a clank, and the door swung open. She froze. Looked down at the sleeping bag. Still no movement. No sound from inside. She stepped over the door sill and into the twilight, immediately saw a trail of footprints across the dusty roof to a door in the distance. She reached inside, grabbed the blanket, and sprinted toward the door. She tried to wrap herself in the blanket as she ran, but the light blue fabric trailed behind her like a large pennant at a football game.

The air was cool and breezy on the roof. She reached the door to the building's interior and stopped to adjust the blanket on her shoulders. She looked back at the water tank. The tank's door was open. *I should have closed it. No time to go back now.* She used both thumbs to depress the rusty release on the inside lock. She strained mightily. The latch moved begrudgingly. Finally, it released. She pulled the door open and stepped inside. The birds in the rafters flew. They circled a few times—some exited through broken skylights—and returned to roost.

The girl held a blanketed hand to her mouth to suppress a scream. The farther she got away from the dead guy, the closer to freedom, the more difficult she found it to breathe. She turned back to the door, and let it close slowly. The latch clicked shut. The twilight waned. She looked back through the door's safety glass and its greasy patina. There was no movement inside the tank. The door still hung open. Just a black hole. She looked down at the office and its roof splattered with bird droppings. Was there safety there, or did the other man wait inside? *I must get as far away as possible.* She hiked up the blanket, and like a debutante attending her first cotillion, her presentation to local society, she moved slowly down the steps. Instead of a smile, she wore a grimace on her face. The blanket was caught in the door to the roof. She tugged several times until a corner of the blanket tore off.

She reached the office and cupped her hands around her eyes to peek through a dirty window. Kazmer slept, snoring, leaning back in an old wooden chair. His feet rested on a wooden desk; his arms hung at his sides. She crouched below the window ledge, duck-walked across the platform to the steps, and passed the office door and other windows. She heard Kazmer stir inside. His feet dropped to the floor. He snorted several times, bassoon-like, seemed to choke, and returned to snoring. She hiked up the blanket around her knees and took off toward the factory floor. A vehicle—probably a van—was parked near the steps, covered with a tarp. She ran over the jagged stones, crying as freedom loomed ever closer. She passed through the hole in the wall and followed fresh-looking tire tracks through softer dirt. She quickened her pace. Stopped. Turned around. Saw her footprints in the soil. She decided not to follow the tire tracks because her trail was too evident. She took a final look at the factory and veered away into high grass she hoped would conceal her.

It was not easy going. She tripped on rocks obscured by grass.

Cried out in pain. Saplings, briars, and burs scratched her arms. One whipped across her face and cut her cheek. The wound burned. Tree limbs, like unseen hands, caught the blanket and tried to rip it off. She clutched the blanket tighter. Forged ahead. It was difficult scrambling over the uneven ground while holding the blanket tight. Still, the blanket provided comfort. Ahead, she heard a car speeding along a road. She climbed a bank, holding the blanket between her teeth. Clutched at the grass with both hands. Near the top she lost her hold and slipped to the bottom, scraping both knees. She was breathless and cried. She looked up the steep bank and started to climb again. This time she made it. Across the top was a high chain-link fence with barbed wire on top. She groaned. *I'll never climb it. Have to look for a way through.* She followed the fence. Traveled some twenty yards before she realized she returned toward the factory. She stopped in terror. Another car passed. She wanted to scream but knew they wouldn't hear her. Wouldn't see her. Probably wouldn't stop anyway. But she had to try. Ahead a fence pole leaned toward the ground. The fence was down. Some drunk probably drove through it. Thank God.

She could step over the toppled fence and right onto the road. She could see the asphalt. It was almost dark. She hiked up the bur-encrusted blanket and stepped on barbed wire. It grabbed her ankle like the teeth in a trap. She screamed. Stepped again. Landed on more barbed wire with her other foot. Screamed again.

THE GIRL'S SCREAM, even at a distance, jolted Bo Bentwood awake. He clawed out of his sleeping bag. In an instant, he surveyed the water tank's interior. The girl was gone. The sun was down. No light around the hatch's edges. He jumped outside. Saw her footprints trailing across the rubber roof. Wide strides. She ran. He blurred to the rooftop door. Pulled it open. A corner of blanket fabric fluttered like a leaf to the factory floor. Bo watched it float downward. He vaulted over the railing, landing with a deafening crash outside the office. Kazmer woke with a start, flailing his arms and legs like an inexperienced swimmer thrown into deep water. Bo shoved open the office door. Kazmer stood, breathless.

"She's gone, Kaz! I want her back!" Bo roared. "I'll suck the blood from every ounce of her flesh."

"How?" Kazmer said, waving his huge hands in circles. "You were there. I was here."

"She's outside. I heard her scream. She's heading for the highway."

"There's a fence around the factory," Kazmer said. "She'll be trapped. You blur. I will follow."

Bo was gone before Kazmer finished his sentence.

John Bargain steered the car with his left hand. He held Kelly Gold's hand with his right. It had been quite a day. They were giddy as night hastened. They had woken up at his apartment, checked out abandos assigned to them in the morning, and taken a picnic lunch to a state park. It was so deserted they made love on a blanket in the afternoon. Now they were headed back to his place. A recently purchased bottle of wine lay in the picnic basket.

"Are you sure you know where you're going?" Gold said, straining to see out the windshield in front of them. "I never saw this road. It's the kind of place you might want to avoid in the dark. Too many dips and curves. Never know what you're going to run into."

"I know this road. I was hoping to pass this way while it was still light," Bargain said. "There's an old factory to your right somewhere. You can see it in daylight. I was hoping to do a vlog inside. There's a ton of graffiti on the walls. Some of it's almost art. Some of it is way out of reach. So high you'd wonder how they did it. I thought maybe you'd come along. And while we're there we could look for the undead."

"Sounds interesting," Gold said. "But during the day."

"Naturally."

She concentrated on the road ahead and gave his hand a squeeze."

"Do you know Party Pooper?" he asked.

"Should I?"

"He's a vlogger. Has a lot more subscribers than I do. He made a video inside the factory. On all the graffiti. It was really good. He does nice editing."

"Are you thinking of duplicating..."

"That's the thing," Bargain interrupted. "I don't like doing things other vloggers did unless I get a lot of requests—which I rarely get—or unless I come up with a new angle. That's where I am, working on a new angle."

"Well, good luck. I'll be happy to help, as long as your video doesn't have vampires," Gold said.

"Would it be out of line to ask the Brethren, maybe worldwide, to subscribe to my channel? It would put me over the top."

"I'd be happy to, but that's the kind of thing you should ask Persimmon. You know the Brethren. We stay anonymous."

"Of course. Completely anonymous. Nobody'd have to comment on the videos unless they really wanted to."

"Brake!" Gold screamed.

A form limped onto the road covered by a filthy blanket. Bargain hit the brake and steered around the form. A bloodied female stepped toward the car and hammered on Gold's window. Gold palmed her .9 mm pistol. Rolled down the window.

"Let me in. Get me out of here," the girl screamed. "I was kidnapped. They killed my friends."

Bargain unlocked the car doors. Gold relocked them.

"Please!" the girl screamed.

"Open the blanket," Gold said. "I want to see you don't have a weapon. Then you can get in."

She opened the blanket. Spread out the ends like wings.

"Get in." Gold unlocked the car doors.

The girl slid into the back seat. Secured the blanket around her again.

Bargain punched the gas and sped away. The girl turned, kneeled on the seat, and peered out the rear windshield. As they rounded a curve, she saw her kidnapper step on the roadway, crouching like he was ready to propel himself after the vehicle. She shivered. Somehow, she knew he could overtake Bargain's car if he wanted to. The car whizzed around a curve and he was lost from sight. The girl took a deep breath, turned around in the seat, and cried.

Bo was ready to blur away to catch the car when Kazmer put a hand on his shoulder.

"Let her go, Mr. Bo. There will be others. Many more."

"What if she tells about us?"

"Who would believe her?" Kazmer said. "She will be trouble. I know the type. We will need a new place, Mr. Bo. I have one in mind."

"So do I, Kaz."

CHAPTER TWELVE

"You better step on it," the girl told Bargain. "If he wants to, that guy can catch us, even without a car."

"What's your name, dear?" Bargain asked.

"Jane," the girl said.

"As in Jane Doe?"

"As in Jane Whatever. Does it matter?"

"It does if we're going to help," Gold said, turning to look at her in the backseat.

She turned around and looked out the back window. "You have to hurry."

Bargain blew a stream of air through his mouth, as if he had to explain something to a child he knew would not understand. "The first mistake people make when they're trying to get away is they drive too fast. They end up off the road, in a ditch, or wrapped around a tree. They're either dead or recaptured. Got it? I'm going plenty fast enough. Faster than the speed limit."

The girl sobbed. "Please, faster."

Gold raised her pistol over the seat, where Jane could see it.

"We're ready for anything. He has one, too." Gold inclined her head toward Bargain.

"It doesn't matter," Jane said. "I saw him shot twice. It had no effect. He didn't even bleed."

Bargain slammed on the brakes. The car stopped in the middle of its lane. Bargain and Gold stared at each other for a moment, then turned to Jane. A car driving in the opposite direction slowed and then sped off.

"Go! Go! Go! PLEASE!" Jane implored.

Bargain stepped on the gas and resumed driving. Jane settled back into the seat.

"What did he look like?" Gold said. "This guy who kidnapped you."

"I don't know." Jane waved her hands in front. Her blanket slipped down. She pulled it back up. "He was young. Blond. Good looking. He wouldn't have trouble finding a girl. He wouldn't have to kidnap one."

"Did you get a good look at him?" Gold said.

"Not really. It was dark in the motel where he took me."

"His skin?"

"Very pale," Jane said. She thought for a moment. "Very pale. Like an albino."

"Like he was dead?"

"Exactly. But he was very strong. No way was he dead."

Bargain and Gold traded a glance quickly. "Bo," they said in unison.

"So, we know he's still in the area," Gold said. "Was he alone?"

Bargain drove through the night. The road twisted, rose, and fell. He concentrated on the roadway. Only a few houses showed lights inside. There were no streetlights.

"I wish you'd go faster," Jane said."

Gold spoke slowly, to ensure Jane understood the message. "The thing that you escaped from is undead—a vampire."

"Just my luck," Jane said. "I'm rescued by two loonies who probably are on the run from an insane asylum."

Gold turned to face the back. "Jane, you must tell us everything that happened. Then we'll tell you what we know about vampires. We'll take you somewhere safe. We'll get you cleaned up and give you new clothes. Even have a doctor look at you."

"No police," Jane said. "I'd be arrested. There are warrants on me. And I never showed up on court dates. Went off the grid."

"That's all right," Gold said. "No police. *We* work off the grid."

"How do you know she's not a Shadow setting us up," Bargain said.

"I don't think so. She's been through a lot."

"What's a Shadow?" Jane asked. She leaned forward in the seat. "Can you turn up the heat? It's cold back here."

Bargain dialed up the heat.

"Was there anybody with the albino?" Gold said.

"A big guy. Hairy. He didn't seem to like guns. The *albino*—he wasn't afraid of nothing. He was shot twice, maybe more. It didn't slow him down."

"We know who they are," Gold said. "The albino is named Bo. His goon is human. His name is Kazmer."

"You're in with them?" Jane seemed more terrified than she had been since she first got in the car.

"We plan to kill them," Gold said, matter-of-factly. "You can help us by telling everything you know."

"I was with two guys—James and Craig," Jane said. "They had been working in this abandoned motel on Route 54, pulling out the copper. They had it stacked in coils in the lobby, hidden under some junk. They were waiting to make a deal. Had a buyer for the wire and pipe. We waited to set up a vmeeting for the swap. They promised me some meth if I helped. I was Craig's...friend. We lived on the street together. He was off the grid, too, and had a jail sentence waiting if he got caught. He was heavy into tranq and didn't want to go through withdrawal in jail. Anyway, when we got inside the motel, Craig's bolt cutter was missing. He was pissed. We knew someone was in the motel. The guys searched room by room checking everything out. They were packing, so I hung back. They thought whoever was inside had money or drugs we could boost. There was a nice van outside covered with a tarp. The guys wanted to take the van, too, but I said what if the cops were looking for it. When we got to the last room the door was locked."

Jane stopped suddenly. Through the car's rearview mirror, Bargain saw Jane's eyes fill with tears. She paused another moment and took several breaths before continuing. "It was dark, but the guys had flashlights. Craig went to kick the last door open, but it flew open itself. Craig fell into the room. He was shooting. James was shooting. The albino attacked. Craig didn't get up. I saw the big, hairy man in the room. He had a bloody knife. I knew Craig was dead. I took off down the hall. Didn't know where I was going. Didn't have a real plan. Just wanted to escape. I didn't get far when the albino was in front of me, waiting at the end of the hall. How is that possible? He was behind me one second and in front of me the next. Waiting for me, and I ran as fast as I could. The next thing I knew I woke up in the factory water tower with this blanket. I don't know why he didn't kill me. He certainly could have." She paused before conceding to say "My last name is Jennings. Jane Jennings."

"He would have drained your blood and killed you when you were no more use to him," Gold said. "That's the way vampires are. It's a miracle you escaped. Almost nobody does, although we know a few people who did."

"That wire's probably still at the motel. We didn't get a chance to lift one coil," Jane said. "I won't go back for it, not if the price is doubled." She smiled and giggled. "Somebody'll find it, sell that shit, make a nice payday. Buy enough drugs to get high for a while."

"We'll check out the motel tomorrow, even though Bo's gone," Gold said. "I don't think they'll come back."

"I'm in," Bargain said.

"They probably vacated the factory, too," Gold said. "But we'll explore. Maybe find that new angle you were looking for. Then, it's back to work figuring out where they are now."

CHAPTER THIRTEEN

Bo and Kazmer left the factory. Their sleeping bags and the tarp used to cover the van were rolled up in the back. It was still dark and Bo rode shotgun.

"Where is this new place you have in mind, Kaz?" Bo had been looking out the side window but now turned to Kazmer.

"You will see. I think it is a place better than the factory," Kazmer said. "Definitely better than the motel."

"I hope so," Bo said. "I was thinking of something gothic. Know what I mean? Old and spooky."

"I know. This is not gothic. It is another cemetery. An underground vault. It is dry. And there is a store across the street from the cemetery where I can get food. The store sells newspapers because I want to continue my study of English."

"And I can keep up with what's going on in the world. That's important. Even for a vampire."

"Yes. I understand," Kazmer said.

"Can you see the vault from outside the cemetery? Where we'd go in and out?"

"No, Mister Bo. It is away from the street in an old section. It does not appear to have many visitors."

"How do you find these places?"

"I am always looking. You never know when we must move again."

"My memories of cemeteries are not good, Kaz. Especially after the last one."

"I can look for another place. One you will like better. I will—how do they say?—peel my eyes for another place."

"Let's leave this city. Really, I want to go home. To where my family lives, the place I grew up before I went away to college."

Kazmer took a suck on his cigarette. He took his eyes off the road for a moment to inspect the ash on its end. He released the smoke and said, "What if someone sees you? Someone who remembers from before? You disappeared from university when the mistress brought you here to the West Coast. You are a missing person." Kazmer looked worried and tapped off cigarette ash on the van's floor. "I saw stories in the newspaper about missing people. It might cause trouble if you are seen. Identified. Everyone would want to know where you were all that time. It is almost a year. It will be difficult to answer."

"No one will see me in the middle of the night, Kaz. That's what I'm thinking. I'd like to see my home. See how my parents are. I know some places that will give us protection during the day. This time I'll find a place for us to stay. It's my old stomping grounds."

"It will be better to remain silent than stomp," Kaz said.

"You always know best, Kaz."

"I will stop for a sandwich and gasoline for the van. We will leave while it is still dark," Kazmer said. He waved a hand. "Maybe you can feed tonight before we go."

"We'll see," Bo said. "I would like to get that girl back. Have some companionship for the ride. I came so close. I wonder where she is?"

Kazmer shot Bo a glance. "She is trouble. She is like Lisa. Strong. Thinking all the time. She got away on us. Lisa got away on Lazlo and me when we brought her from the East Coast. Fought like a tiger. This other girl was trouble, too. A criminal. You could never take an eye off her. Always have the eyes peeled. At least Lisa was a good person. I'm happy she and her baby got away."

Bo smiled. "Yeah, Kaz, but you don't understand. I wanted sex with that girl."

"I know about sex. You will have others, Mister Bo," Kazmer interrupted, one of the few times a Shadow would dare to interrupt his master. "You will see. You might find a pet like you were to the mistress. Over the years, you will have hundreds, thousands of women. It is the way of the vampire."

"Right now, I'd be happy to have one, but I wouldn't want to put someone through what I went through, Kaz. I would want someone willing. Another Shadow. Someone I could turn eventually. Someone who would want to be turned. I'd sit that girl down and explain everything."

"What about me?" Kazmer said, slowing the van to enter an all-night convenience store with gasoline pumps.

"Sex? I don't think that's possible, Kaz. Not with you."

"Not sex." Kazmer's voice rose. He gripped the van's steering wheel. "To become vampire. That is what I want."

"Don't worry, Kaz. You're first on my list. Who knows, maybe someday we'll have our own colony. You might have several women to make you happy."

"That's right. Who knows? Several women? That would make me happy." Kazmer relaxed to reflect on that idea.

Bo pointed a finger at Kazmer. "What I would do is make sure the girl knew all about being a vampire. I'll explain everything before I change her. She would never see her family or friends again. She'll never take a human life. I would explain the—"

"The powers you have now?"

"Yes, but I would also explain the thirst. The terrible thirst that consumes me every waking moment. That is the curse of the vampire."

Kazmer grunted. "It is a good curse to live forever."

"If I had it to do over, I would have made sure I died back at the colony before I was turned. This is no existence. I would have let those kid vampires tear me apart. I would have offered my blood to any of the undead. I am not happy, Kaz. If I could, I'd step out in the sunlight. I'd burn up in seconds. Be gone. I wouldn't care. But that terrible vampire disease won't let me do it. I've already tried. It stops me. If I could find the Brethren, I'd knock on their door, let them fill me with arrows until one hit my heart. No pain they could inflict is worse than this thirst."

Kazmer eased the van up to the pumps and stopped. He looked at Bo. "When you feed, doesn't the disease reward you? Doesn't the hot blood taste good? Does it not satisfy you?"

"Not for long, Kaz. Not for long. The thirst rages back. It is always in the back of my throat. That is all I think about."

"Doesn't the hunt, the kill, give you pleasure?"

"No. Not at all," Bo said.

"Over time, you will learn to control the thirst. So the mistress told me. There are times the thirst might put you in danger. Demand to be fed, like when you are in a crowd. You will learn to put the thirst down..."

"Suppress," Bo said.

"Yes," Kazmer said. "You must suppress the thirst until you can find one victim alone. Then strike."

"I can't see it working, Kaz. I have no desire to live through the centuries. To kill to preserve me. I can't imagine it."

"It will come, Mr. Bo, I think. Give it time. If you had an older vampire to guide you, as is done in a colony—"

"Well, I don't. I don't want one."

Kazmer grunted, slid from the van's driver's seat, and walked slowly toward the store. After Kazmer pumped gasoline, got food, and ate, they set off toward Bo's home, another long drive.

THE WHITE VAN crept along Particle Street. Bo gave Kazmer directions. The night sky had turned purple. Dawn approached. Finally, Bo instructed Kazmer to pull to the curb. The van engine idled. Bo looked out the passenger side window.

"This is it, Kaz. This is where I grew up. My bedroom was in the back."

"It's a nice home," Kazmer said. "Clean. Beautiful lawn. You were rich."

Bo smiled. "Not really rich. The place has no flowers, though. My mom always planted flowers. Now the beds are just mulched. I see weeds, too." Bo turned to Kazmer. "Tomorrow, I want to go to the library. Look through the newspaper files."

"You might be recognized."

"I don't think so, Kaz. I've been gone almost five years, between college and the West Coast. Anybody who'd remember me would be away at school. Gone from here. The library at night was never a place to hang out. I should be okay."

The sky lightened. A glimmer of orange appeared where the sun rose.

"You should get in the back, Mr. Bo, or you will burn."

"There was an abandoned movie theater downtown. We should be able to stay there today. Maybe find a better place tomorrow."

Kazmer pulled out and followed Bo's directions. It seemed strange to be back in the town he had called home. So much seemed different, even though most of the old businesses remained. The old theater and its marquis loomed ahead. Even in the near dark, the large black letters announced a broken promise.

R OPENIN SOON

"It hasn't changed since I was in high school," Bo said wistfully. "I spent a lot of time here when I was a kid. After the multiplex opened at the mall, it got all the new movies. These guys showed older ones. The ones you might have missed the first time around. But then the streaming services killed this place. Ended up killing the multiplex, too. The Roxy here ended up showing a lot of soft porn, T&A stuff, and B horror movies. You could buy a ticket for a horror movie and stay for the next feature, which might be porn. The owners were old and had a bunch of kids working here not much older than I was. They didn't care what you watched or how long you stayed. They were doing homework or watching the porn themselves. But they always had an endless supply of stale popcorn."

"I don't understand the big sign," Kazmer said, pointing to the marquis.

Bo spelled out the words with missing letters. REOPENING SOON.

"I understand. What is T&A?" Kazmer said.

"Tits and ass, Kaz. Not hardcore but just enough to give a kid a thrill."

Kazmer smiled. He pulled out his tobacco pouch and rolled a smoke. "I like popcorn, even if it is a little stale. I might like T&A, too."

"You see the second exit door along the side of the theater?"

Kaz nodded while he licked the paper.

"There was a trick to opening the door from the outside. Everybody knew it. It might still work. That will get us in."

"I'll find a place to park the van," Kaz said, "Then come back. Will you take the sleeping bags?"

"Sure, Kaz. Say, these are a lot better than hauling around a casket.

Kazmer grunted. Bo climbed into the van's back and pulled out the sleeping bags, slipped from the van, and jogged down a trash-strewn alley between the theater and the next building. He reached the second exit door, inserted his strong fingers between the double doors, and pulled. The doors separated a few inches. With his hand inside, Bo pushed up on the bar lock and the door opened enough to squeeze inside. He looked back toward the van and smiled. Kazmer pulled out.

Bo WAITED inside the exit door in the dark. A sliver of light came through the crack, growing stronger as the sun rose. Bo stepped away from the light. Eventually, Kazmer tapped at the door and Bo let him in.

"This is where I spent a lot of my childhood, Kaz. What do you think?" Bo smiled, proud of their new digs.

"I think it was nicer then," Kazmer said, taking the last drag on his cigarette. "Probably beautiful."

"It was, even though it was already getting shabby when I was a kid. It's very ornate. Don't you think?"

Kazmer grunted. "Ornate. That is a good word I will remember and try to use."

The large theater's seats were arranged in a crescent across the first floor with wide spaces between the rows. Here and there plaster had fallen from the rococo ceiling with its faded gold and red trim and smashed on the floor. The once-plush red seats were covered with dirt and debris. A movie screen hung above a wide, silent stage in the front, where raucous vaudeville acts performed during the 1920s. Kazmer used a flashlight to illuminate the floor as they walked toward the stage. He panned its beam over the dusty and threadbare crimson drapes hung at both sides of the screen and the decorative box seats that were arranged on both sides of the stage. Water dripped from a hole in the roof and filled an orchestra pit, where a piano and chairs floated.

"What a shame," Bo said. "If I had the money, I would restore this place, no matter what the cost."

"More T&A movies?"

"No, Kaz. I'd restore it just for the memories."

"Kazmer grunted. "Good memories are nice to have."

CHAPTER FOURTEEN

When the vampire disease woke Bo after sundown, Kazmer was already up. He sat near Bo's sleeping bag on a dusty balcony theater chair, his legs extended in the wide aisle, the remains of his meal on the floor. He had propped open a rear door that still allowed in enough light for him to scan a newspaper. Kazmer was alerted to Bo's rising by the sleeping bag zipper opening. He handed Bo a section of the newspaper as Bo approached.

"Really, Kaz? You gave me the classifieds."

Kazmer looked up from the comics. "You said it is important to read the whole paper if you want to understand today's world. To make my English better."

"True, Kaz. True. You like the comics?"

"I like the drawings. I can read what the little people say, but I don't always see how it is funny." Kazmer frowned. He put down the newspaper and pulled out his tobacco, rolled a cigarette.

"Yeah," Bo said, looking toward the ceiling, as if looking for an answer there. "With comics, there's a lot of play on words."

Kazmer frowned, paused his pour of tobacco on the rolling paper, and slid his eyes toward Bo. "I don't understand *play*."

Bo laid a hand on Kazmer's shoulder. Kazmer looked up. "You already know that sometimes words have more than one meaning."

"Yes."

"So, when a character in the comics uses a word with the wrong meaning, or a different meaning, the reader finds that funny. It's a play on words."

Kazmer finished his misshapen cigarette, and lighted it. Shrugged.

"Surely you and your brother told jokes in the dialect you talked in," Bo said. He squeezed Kazmer's shoulder, and the man winced, almost dropped the cigarette in his mouth.

"I know jokes," Kazmer said. He smiled. "My brother Lazlo knew many jokes. Some were about sex. He told them because I liked them, too."

"You'll see, Kaz." Bo smiled at his pupil. "As your understanding of English increases, you will find things funny in the comics. Keep reading. Someday, I will hear you burst out laughing. The other thing that will happen is that you will like certain comics more than you like others. They will be your favorites. You'll make a connection."

"It is a long journey to understand a new language," Kazmer said.

Bo opened the newspaper Kazmer had offered him and scanned the ads. "I don't think I'll be looking for a job any time soon. Now wait." Kazmer looked up from the comics. Bo continued, "Here's one. Nightwatchman/security guard. Qualifications? High school diploma and 'have the ability to stay awake all night.' Flexible hours. Other duties as necessary. What do you think, Kaz?"

"For me?" Kaz looked incredulous.

"For me, Kaz. You could drop me off after sundown and pick me up before sunrise. Flexible hours"

"No. Not possible."

Bo danced around and flapped the newspaper open and shut

like a bird's wings. "I always wanted a job. Now's my chance. *The job is in the hospital.* I'll bet they give me a uniform."

Kazmer grunted. "Too many people work in the hospital, even at night. Doctors, nurses. I know."

"You don't get the point. I'd have access to blood. Bags and bags of blood. No more killing. And then there's the lab. Vials and vials of blood. Gallons of blood. What do you think they do with all the blood that's no longer any use? They take a vile and test a drop." Bo stopped his dancing and stared at Kazmer. Waited expectantly.

Kazmer pulled the half-consumed cigarette from between his lips and released a lung full of smoke. "I don't know. I don't think it is an idea."

"I'm sure they dump it, Kaz. They won't save it. If they did, the hospital would be filled with blood. There'd be no room for patients."

Kazmer scratched his beard stubble. "Hospitals are big places. Who knows where they keep blood."

"I would find out, Kaz. I'd reduce the stockpile. There'd be no reason for a new wing. I'd save the hospital millions. They might even give me a seat on the board of directors. We'd have to meet at night, of course, to accommodate my schedule."

Kazmer grunted.

"I can see it now, Kaz. I'd make my rounds every night. Stop at the nursing station to yuck it up with the nurses. Make them coffee. Blur to Dunkin'. Get them sweets."

"They would notice how pale you are." Kazmer shook his head and sighed. "They would have you admitted. Find out you are dead. Have no heartbeat. This is not a good idea. Not an idea at all, Mr. Bo. It will only bring trouble."

"We'll get makeup, Kaz, to make my skin darker, more natural looking."

"More alive?"

"That's it. Now you're getting it. We'll get some—I think they call it foundation. You apply it evenly to hide imperfections."

"Your skin has no imperfections. You are young vampire."

"The foundation will make my skin darker. I won't be unnaturally pale."

"You will need a shower before we shop for makeup. Before you go to work."

"Again? Already?"

Kazmer nodded.

"We'll get a room, like we did before. Then we'll shop."

"I will get the van. It is down the street. We will have to move it anyway." Kazmer stubbed out his cigarette butt. Ground the remaining tobacco between his thumb and index finger. He walked up the aisle slowly toward the back of the balcony, stopped, and turned around. "This *foundation*," he said slowly, with care. "Is it like the foundation you build a house on?"

"You could say that." Bo smiled.

Kazmer thought. His eyes lifted and scanned the dark ceiling for a moment. He burst out laughing. Slapped his knee.

"What is it, Kaz?"

Kazmer composed himself. Returned Bo's smile. "Foundation. That is funny. We should make a comic."

Bo and Kazmer rented a room and showered. Sprayed themselves with Ax. They returned to the van, drove back downtown, and cruised the business district until they passed a women's attire shop. Kazmer parked the van, and they walked back to the shop. It was late in the business day. The cosmetic counter was to the left of the front door. A woman behind the counter greeted them.

"I need some foundation," Bo said. "To make my skin appear darker. Just a little. More natural."

"I see," the woman said. She pursed her lips. She stepped back as if to show her tight-fitting royal blue dress. Her perfume confused Bo's senses.

Kazmer cleared his throat and appeared uncomfortable. He looked around the store, focusing on three mannequins nearby in a group.

Bo bit his lip. The employee crossed her arms. Waited. Kazmer raised an eyebrow toward the dummies. Feigned interest in the slim, headless figures with sparkling white veneers.

"Well," Bo said finally. He raised a hand to his chin and pushed his face to the side until it showed in profile to the woman. "I have a skin problem. The...dermis is pale."

"Very pale," Kazmer added, showing concern.

The woman flashed her eyes toward Kazmer and stepped closer, leaning over the counter. Returned her gaze to Bo. Squinted. "I can see. Yes. Are you this pale all over?"

"Unfortunately, yes," Bo said, matter-of-factly. "But my face seems to be the palest. I was thinking a foundation might help."

"It would help," the woman said, equally matter-of-factly. "Is your skin sensitive?"

"It is," Kazmer interjected.

Bo and the woman stared at Kazmer a moment before she continued.

"If your skin is especially sensitive, the foundation might aggravate it. Cause a reaction. You should ask a dermatologist."

"I did," Bo said. "I told him the paleness concerned me, socially, and he recommended a foundation."

"Over the counter?"

"Of course."

"In that case, you can use one of these," the woman said. She sidestepped a couple of paces and opened her arms with palms up to show an array of cosmetics."

"Do you plan to use this foundation all over?" the woman said. She closed one eye as if winking.

"No. No. Just on my face and neck."

"The condition is already getting better," Kazmer said, making another rare foray into a vampire's business that was strictly prohibited from a Shadow. Apparently realizing his mistake, he looked toward the floor. Blushed.

"I understand," the woman said.

"Could you recommend a...shade?" Bo said.

A second woman behind the counter sidled up to the clerk. Kazmer stepped away. Showed renewed interest in the mannequins. Touched the fabric on one of the dresses.

"Let's see, the woman said. She pulled out several containers and laid them on the countertop. She reached across the counter and ran her fingers through Bo's hair. Both women seemed to show an interest in Bo, despite his apparent skin condition. It was the allure of the vampire disease caused in humans. "We'll have to find a color that matches your hair," the first clerk said, "or it will look fake. Know what I mean? You don't want it to look like makeup."

"Do you plan to wear this foundation when you go out?" the second woman said. She raised a jar toward Bo's ear. "Like when you go out on dates?'

"Mostly when I go to work."

"Where do you work?" the first clerk wanted to know.

Kazmer returned slowly to the group.

"What do you do?" the second woman said, raising another color to Bo's hair.

"Nightwatchman," Kazmer interjected.

"That's not right," Bo said. He shot Kazmer a look. "Actually, I'm on the security force."

"Ohhh," the women cooed.

The first woman in the tight blue dress said, "My BF is an RN at Valley General. Is that where you work?" She brushed the back of her fingers against Bo's cheek. Her hand recoiled immediately. "You're cold."

"That's part of the condition. Cold skin. My hands. My face. That's all, though."

Kazmer stepped away again. This time in the opposite direction.

"Cold hands, warm heart. Isn't that what they say?" the second salesperson chirped. She raised her hand toward Bo's face. Bo dodged it like a boxer. "I suppose it's better than having a fever."

"True. Because you'd never know when you're really sick," Bo said.

The women and Kazmer laughed. Even Bo chuckled.

The first clerk raised another color. "I think this might be the best. Not too dark and it seems to match your hair." The woman slid a mirror across the counter toward Bo, and all four inspected the color. Even Kazmer pursed his lips and nodded his approval. The second woman convinced Bo he needed lipstick to prevent his lips from looking too pale against his darker skin. With the makeup purchase completed, Bo and Kazmer returned to the abandoned theater. With the aid of Kazmer's flashlight, Bo applied the foundation to his face and neck and to the lipstick around his mouth.

"How does it look, Kaz?"

"I don't know much about makeup," Kazmer said, raising his hands. "The mistress never used makeup. The blood she drank fixed her skin."

"That might be true, but she had a darker complexion in life than I did. She might have been pale, but she was not as pallid as I am. I think this looks good."

Bo said it was necessary to try out the makeup in public. He had never made it to the movie with the vampiress the night he was mortally wounded by gunfire. Now, he and Kazmer would go. They agreed on a comedy.

Kazmer was hungry. Therefore, the boys stopped for fast food and ate inside. They both ordered cheeseburgers, fries, and soda. There was a small crowd eating in, while a constant stream of vehicles circled around the drive-thru. They heard orders barked from outside via the intercom. Bo passed food toward Kazmer, sliding drinks, sandwiches, and sacks of fries across the small, uncomfortable booth they occupied. No one seemed to notice Kazmer did all the eating. A casual observer might have thought the men ate at the same pace. Their eyes might have paused on a young man with streaked, caked makeup and lipstick, but no one commented.

The theater was rather new, part of the remodeled video plex at the mall outside town. However, the floor was sticky and there was a faint odor of marijuana in the air, as if it got caught inside the air conditioning and recirculated along with the smell of popcorn and the theater's other stale smells.

After they bought tickets, Kazmer used the bathroom. The two extra-large sodas he had drunk worked on his kidneys and filled his bladder. Bo waited in the lobby near the doors of their theater entrance, holding Kazmer's popcorn and another soda. From across the lobby, Bo zeroed in on three college-age toughs. All athletic looking. Bo knew the type. He had not been a fighter in high school and occasionally had to weather the abuse of bullies. One of the trio sighted Bo, put his elbow in his friend's ribs. The second whispered to the third and motioned with his long chin toward Bo. The three chuckled and slowed their pace. They scanned Bo, head to foot. They carried no concessions toward the theater. Bo thought they were the type who would make endless trips back and forth to the lobby to buy food and drink after the movie started. Bo looked away toward the bathroom exit, hoping Kazmer would return. The last thing Bo wanted was a confrontation with the trio in a crowd. He might be identified. Surely, multiple people would record his image on their cell phones. It was a long walk back to the white van that also would be identified. He should go into the theater and get a seat. Let Kazmer find him. After all, Kazmer had driven across the country at least twice in the last year. The crowd was scarce. Bo would be easy to find.

The men approached. Bo looked toward the bathroom exit. No Kazmer. He poked an index finger through the popcorn's top layer. The men sniggered.

"Yeah, it's fag night," one said. The biggest guy pursed his lips and kissed the air. The third laughed. Made a motion to swat the popcorn from Bo's hand but came up short. They all laughed more.

Bo didn't feel fear. At one time, as a human, he would have feared them. Perhaps he'd move to another theater, and watch a movie he didn't care to see, as long as he had tickets and *they* weren't inside. Kazmer exited the bathroom. Gave his hands one final wipe on his hoodie front. Smiled. Waved at Bo. The trio retreated as Kazmer joined Bo.

"I like to sit close to the screen," Kazmer said, taking the popcorn and soda from Bo's arms.

"How about halfway back," Bo countered. "You can see better."

"Very well."

"If you want to sit close, we don't have to sit together, Kaz."

"We sit together. Halfway back. See better."

The theater was dimly lit. The screen was dark. Bo shot a glance to the side and saw the trio in the last row. From somewhere the HVAC system clamored, pushed air. Kazmer counted the rows as they moved down the center aisle.

"It doesn't have to be exact," Bo said. "*About* halfway. It's not a literal thing."

Kazmer grunted. "I should have smoked outside on the sidewalk."

"You can wait, Kaz. This movie will be funny. You don't want to miss anything. We can talk about it later."

"If you want. Talk about what?" Kazmer moved his popcorn from one arm to the other.

"Talk about your favorite parts. The funniest things that happened."

"In here," Kazmer said, moving toward the seats. "Exactly half-way. How far in?"

"About half."

From the back of the theater, a voice rang out, "It's date night."

Kazmer stopped. "What's that," he said.

"A couple of assholes," Bo said. "Find a seat."

Bo moved in a few more steps and sat down. Kazmer plopped down beside him. The theater darkened. A coming attraction blazed across the theater's screen, followed by a warning about no smoking and being courteous to other movie fans. Bo found the darkness comforting, although the loud volume bothered his hypersensitive hearing. It was something he didn't expect. Bo didn't notice the three men move from the back of the theater to three rows behind them until the giggling started. They threw popcorn occasionally that sailed over their heads or stuck in Kazmer's long hair.

Kazmer released a low, barely audible growl. He reached inside his hoodie. Bo knew he was going for the stiletto knife he always carried. "Exit over there," Kazmer whispered, inclining his head toward Bo, motioning across the theater with his popcorn bucket.

Bo placed his hand on Kazmer's, which was tense on the armrest. "Let it go, Kaz. They'll stop when the movie starts."

"How do you know?" Kazmer turned his head toward the trio. They laughed. Made kissing noises. Several people around the theater made shushing noises. The trio fell silent. Bo patted Kazmer's arm and moved his hand off the armrest. The movie started and the theater was filled with music and actors' voices.

The movie had everything one would expect in a modern comedy. There was the *couple*, played by handsome and beautiful actors. The couple each had zany friends—the guy who thought he was smart but wasn't—and some dopey friends. One was always high, one was a nerd, one was gay, and one was a lady's man who never managed to hook up. One was fat. The women were just as preposterous. One was man crazy but couldn't make a connection. One was studious and always managed to think their way out of problems, wore large glasses, and seemed always to carry a book. One was a klutz who fell often but never was injured. One was fat. They sailed, drove, and swam from one party to another, whether it was in a swanky mansion or a basement club. Both venues were filled with gyrating bodies and loud music. The *couple* made love, fought, broke up, found new, vapid partners, and eventually got back together. In the meantime, all these people had run-ins with the law, gangsters, drug dealers, and a mad scientist. As expected, there was a happy ending. Bo and Kazmer laughed, and some scenes were so funny they wiped tears from their cheeks. There was even a smattering of applause as the credits rolled. The lights came up, and as if on cue, the giddy crowd rose, gathered their possessions, and headed for the exit. Bo and Kazmer stood and stretched their legs, although the muscles in Bo's corpse needed no stretching. Kazmer gathered his empty food containers.

"We will talk about this funny movie," Kazmer said. "You made a good choice, Mr. Bo."

They turned to leave and found themselves facing the trio three rows behind them in an empty theater. The young ushers had yet to return with their garbage bags to collect trash left behind before the next show.

"Mr. Cute and Mr. Ugly," the biggest man sneered. "Out on fag date night. I want to see you kiss before we let you go."

"We not like that," Kazmer said. He patted his hoodie, where the knife was concealed inside.

"We don't want any trouble," Bo said. He showed no emotion. He felt his fangs extend; his claws grew. He licked his lips.

"Check out the tongue on the dude," the smallest man said. "Stick it out again. It's some kind of deformed."

"Put it in your friend's mouth," the smaller man said.

The third man chuckled.

"Put it in his ass," the big guy said. He smiled and turned to Kazmer. "Pull down your pants and let cutie with the makeup lick your ass."

Kazmer grunted. He reached for his knife. Bo blurred and raked his claws across two necks. He grabbed the big man, punctured his neck with fangs, and drank greedily. The two others grabbed the gaping wounds in their throats and choked on blood.

They crumpled to the floor between the rows of seats, twitched, and gurgled. Bo pulled his fangs from the big man's neck, threw the body away like a ragdoll, and slurped up the blood on his face with the long, vampire tongue. Kazmer had out his stiletto knife now. Looked at Bo. Pursed his lips.

"You are fast, Mr. Bo. I think you inherited some of the mistress's traits when she turned you. You are as they say, advanced in the vampire world."

"This time I left blood for the police to find. I didn't drain him."

"That is good, Mr. Bo."

They exited the theater and crossed the lobby. Kazmer deposited his cup and popcorn bucket in a trash can. They were outside on the sidewalk when the first blood-curdling scream came from inside.

CHAPTER FIFTEEN

Kazmer moved the van several times a day, choosing vacant lots, alleys, and back streets where he imagined it would go unnoticed. He didn't mind walking, even if it involved a hike of several blocks. He changed the license plate every other day to one of a dozen he had in a box in the van's back compartment. Kazmer always approached the van warily when he wanted to move it. He walked around the vehicle, examined it for damage, while he scanned the area for anyone who might be watching him. There could be police, criminals, even worse, the Brethren. He tried to be cautious with all his movements.

Once inside the van, Kazmer rolled a cigarette out of the wind that sometimes scattered his tobacco. Once satisfied with his handiwork, he lit it, inhaled deeply, felt the rush of nicotine to his brain, and exhaled slowly. Meanwhile, he checked the surrounding buildings and parked vehicles. One could not be too cautious. Kazmer started the engine and let it warm for a minute or two. His eyes moved from window to window, mirror to mirror, making a final check. Finally, he pulled out, proceeded slowly ahead. Before

Kazmer returned to the theater to pick up Bo, or move the van to another location, he drove a complicated path, often circling blocks, doubling back, making sure he wasn't followed.

One evening after returning to The Roxy after parking the van for the night, Bo said, "Again? We could park in the all-day lot half a block away. People leave their cars there for days, sometimes weeks. Nobody notices. Nobody cares. All you have to do is pay the fee at the end."

"I prefer this way. You never know when the Brethren are watching."

"Tell me something, Kaz. How many times have you lost your van? How many shoes have you worn out looking for it? How many miles have you walked?"

Kazmer paused for a moment, scanned the lobby's ornate ceiling, with its dangling shreds of peeling paint, as if calculating answers to all the questions. "I never lost the van, Mr. Bo."

"Never?"

"Never. That is my job. It is part of my most important job. Keeping you safe. Always having an...how do you say?...an escape route ready. One that will work for you."

"I believe you're overly cautious, Kaz. I really do. I'm not a child."

"You are in vampire years. You have much to learn. I can teach you so much. Only what I know. We should look for a colony where someone can train you in the vampire ways. The mistress would have been a good teacher. She liked to talk about the old times. She could show you how to use your powers to protect yourself. Most important, you must learn how to control the vampire disease. Otherwise, it will put you in danger just to be fed. It knows only hunger. Not safety. Do you understand?"

"No, Kaz, I don't."

"When the Brethren attacked our colony you were underground, hidden, changing to vampire. The vampires had the Brethren trapped inside the tunnel. My brother and me...I."

Bo nodded his approval and smiled.

Kazmer continued. "We were guarding Lisa and her man. The Brethren opened jars of virgin blood. The smell drove the vampires...how do you call it?"

"Ape shit."

"Ape shit?" Kazmer chuckled for a moment. "I like English. The smell of the virgin blood drove the vampires ape shit. The Brethren were trapped. The vampires could have kept them trapped. Let them starve to death. Have no...casualties in the colony. But no. The vampires went *ape shit*. They threw themselves at the Brethren to get the jars of virgin blood. The Brethren shot them with crossbows." Kazmer raised his arms as if shouldering one of the weapons. "They staked them with spears." Kazmer thrust his arms out, as if holding a lance. "When the vampires fell, the Brethren chopped them with machetes. Vampire blood was spilled. Not virgin blood from the jars. Some of the vampires were almost a hundred years old, but they could not control the vampire disease hunger. The disease sensed the blood and wanted to be fed the sweet virgin blood. The vampires attacked the Brethren, made themselves easy targets."

"And the vampiress? Eva?"

"She sensed the virgin blood way up on the wall in her crypt. Called the vampires to come back, but they charged up the tunnel to their doom. The Brethren waited. They were strong."

"And she...what did she do?"

Kazmer smiled and seemed to replay the episode in his mind. "She was many hundreds of years old. She learned how to control the vampire disease thirst. She had fought the Brethren many times over the centuries. She knew the virgin blood was a trick. Nun's blood collected from convents around the world."

"Like the Red Cross?" Bo interrupted.

Kazmer nodded. "The Brethren have many friends around the world. As the vampires are secret, so are the Brethren secret. I believe she thought the Brethren might have a special trick for her.

One she had not seen before. One that would kill her, too. So, she dug into the soft dirt inside her crypt." Kazmer moved his hands like a dog paddling water. "She decided to wait for the fighting to be done. Wait for the Brethren to leave."

"Then what?"

Kazmer shrugged. "Who could have guessed? The crazy man with the Brethren blew up the colony. There was an avalanche. The house on the hill where you and Lisa got showers and used the bathroom caved in, slid down the hill, and burned up. My brother Lazlo was killed by the Brethren, was buried in one of the crypts when the place exploded. After everyone was gone, I waited on the hillside for you and the mistress to dig out. The mistress never came out. I think she is dead."

"Really dead?"

"Really dead. The way a vampire dies. Forever."

Bo scratched his chin. "So, the mistress is dead?"

"I think so."

"She tucked her tail between her legs and hid underground to avoid the Brethren."

Kazmer looked incredulous. "There was no other way. After the colony vampires were killed, the Brethren outnumbered her. She could not escape outside in the daylight."

"She buried herself."

"Yes."

"How could the explosion kill her? Rip her apart?"

"Maybe. Yes, but her powers to get better are strong in a vampire so old. I think a large rock or a wooden beam crushed her heart, the same as driving a stake through it." Kazmer bumped his fists together and grimaced, motioning as if to snap a twig in his hands.

"I hope she's gone," Bo said, wistfully. "Forever. I haven't heard her in my head like I did." He patted the side of his head.

"That could be a sign," Kazmer said. "She might be dead. Or

she might not want to communicate." Kazmer scratched his cheek. Added wistfully, "You might be strong enough that she has no control over you anymore. Time will tell."

CHAPTER SIXTEEN

Goldenrod got a text message from Persimmon. "Persimmon got a dead junkie too, down the street, around the corner. In an abando. Third floor. She's calling 9 1 1."

"Tell her to wait," John Bargain said. "I want to do a vlog. I'm behind. I have an audience. You can come."

"I don't know that I want to," Gold said. She lowered her cell phone. "I sent her the message to wait."

"These drugs are a real problem. I want to do something downtown. Show what it's like to live on the street. Die on the street. I said I'd take you on a vlog. You wanted to come along."

"Not this one," Gold said. "I don't want to be identified. I don't think it's right for you to ID a dead person."

"I won't ID you, the dead junkie, or anyone we talk to. I'll blur the faces. I can even change your voice if you want to say something on the video. You can hang in the background. If you happen to step into the frame, I will edit you out. You can see the final vlog before I release it."

"All right."

Gold texted Persimmon that she and Bargain were on their

way. It was a short walk a block down the street, a right turn at the corner, and a half block on the left. There were a number of abandos on the way. Each had a date in chalk on the threshold. The sign the Brethren had checked the buildings for vampires on that day. Of course, that didn't mean a vamp couldn't take up residence that night. It was a place to start in their search for Bo and the missing vampiress. Brethren members had made friends in the police department. They inquired about unusual cases that did not make the newspapers or websites. Some Brethren scoured newspapers and true crime websites, ones that posted the latest grisly crimes, the unexplained, accounts of missing persons. They expected Bo, as a new vampire, would be sloppy in his killing sprees, unable to squelch his rage, his new thirst for blood. The vampiress would be more meticulous. She would better hide her murders. She knew the Brethren watched for any indication she and other undead were at work in the city.

John and Gold picked their way along the filthy sidewalk, stepping over garbage, skirting junkies passed out on the pavement, or dipping. The days were getting warmer. Today wouldn't be the scorcher of full summer, but it would get hot. The city's rank smell already rose, carried on a constant breeze. A row of abandos—all condemned—were lined by brightly-colored tents or lean-tos made from tarps. The gutters were filled with trash and sodden paper plastered to the concrete. The homeless asked for money with raised palms, hollow eyes, mouths with decayed and missing teeth, rotted by the drugs that held them in their grip.

Bargain videoed the scene. Some homeless eyed his camera suspiciously. A few looked like they wanted to steal the device, but it seemed they knew they didn't have the strength to run very far with it. Perhaps they knew a beating would follow a grab-and-run. After collecting video and the street sounds, honking horns, sirens in the distance, and people shouting Bargain narrated as he panned the camera this way and that.

"Bargain Videos with you again, after a short hiatus. No, it wasn't a vacation per se. It was just a recharge of my batteries after some trying days. Now, however, I'm back. I'm back with a vengeance. Today I'm with my friend, who asked to remain nameless." He panned the camera toward Gold, who covered her face with her hands, then swatted at the camera.

"Get that out of my face," Gold hissed.

"My friend is a little touchy about having her picture taken, so that's why her face is blurred out," Bargain continued. He chuckled. "It's not that she's gross. She is actually quite beautiful, stunning even, as you can see from what you saw that wasn't blurred. Who was it who said, '*Mercy!*' I think Roy Orbison. Anyway, we're walking down Barber Street. There's a lot of homeless, a tent city that strings out for blocks along all these abandos. Here's a guy out cold on the sidewalk, either passed out drunk or shot up with tranq. One thing is clear. It's never too early to be passed out drunk or shot up. It's a way of life on the street. Living from one fix or bottle to the next."

Bargain panned the camera down and across the body slowly. "I'm blurring out the faces again to protect the people involved. Plus, I don't want some of these goons coming after me or suing my ass. My friend thinks that's funny. Be careful what you say, or you will find yourself back in the video. By the way, that is not the first time an obscene gesture has been turned on me. But you can see nobody is looking out for this guy. Somebody has turned out his pockets looking for money or drugs. He's on his own."

"I don't like his color," Gold said. Her Nike and slim yoga-panted leg entered the frame to nudge the man below a knee. He roused briefly and slipped back into his coma. "At least he's still alive," she added. "For now."

"This guy could use a haircut. I don't want to be disrespectful to the incapacitated, but if there are any barbers in training who want to get some practice, this is the place. Barber Street. Get it? Barber Street? Haircut? My friend didn't think that was funny, either, although she laughs at most of my jokes. There you go. I got a smile. That made my day. I can tell you honestly, there doesn't appear to be a legit barber on Barber Street. In fact, I don't think there is anything legit on this street. Meanwhile..."

"Hey, sport, be a pal," said a white junkie, young, very thin, wearing a dirty wife beater. He held up a scrawny arm with a dangling rubber tourniquet. "Do the working man a favor. Tie this off for me. I got my needle ready. I need another hand."

"Oh, no. Sorry, bro," Bargain said, backing away, keeping the man and his arm ravaged with infected holes, in the frame. "That needle could be your executioner," Bargain said. "I won't be the one to pull the lever."

"Come on, be a sport," the junkie whined. "I know it got some tranq in it, but that's okay. This is good stuff. I got it off my regular dealer. He wouldn't give me any bad stuff."

Even with a gimble to steady the video, the camera moved back and forth, as Gold pulled Bargain away from the junkie. They crossed at the intersection, waited halfway across the street for traffic to pass, and continued down Fountain Street. One driver blared his horn at the couple. Bargain continued his vlog. "Nothing like a horn toot like that you don't expect to restart your heart. Remember, I'm not responsible for broken eardrums."

"Asshole!" Gold added.

"That's my girl. Tells it like it is."

Bargain panned the camera forward. Persimmon and Old Harriet stood in the distance. "What a coincidence," Bargain continued. "I got two more friends down the street. Real friends. At some point, we'll do lunch. I might be persuaded to drop a tip if somebody else picks up the tab. Anyway, I have more blurring to do back in the *studio*.

Persimmon stood with her hands on her hips. She did not look happy to see Bargain's camera.

"Turn that damn thing off," Old Harriet hollered. "I'm persona non grata."

Bargain switched the camera to his face. He smiled. "We'll take a short break. There might be a brief word from my sponsor if I can find one."

Persimmon frowned as Bargain and Gold approached. "Okay, I'll blur you guys out." Persimmon lowered her head and looked at Bargain over the top of her sunglasses."

"Even better, I'll edit you two out. Easy-peasy." Bargain smiled.

Persimmon returned a smile that was less than genuine. "Once again, John. I want none of the Brethren in your videos. The undead have more friends, more connections than you can imagine."

Bargain started his video again when he and Gold were inside. "We're inside an abando—that is, an abandoned building. They're famous for attracting the homeless, drug users, and even drug sellers. They are a place to squat to keep a roof over your head until you get chased out by the city, or the owner, or another squatter with more muscle. I thought this might be a place to explore to let you see what these dumps look like. The lighting might be a little funky, but remember, these places have no electricity, no water, and no heat. Most of the copper wire and plumbing have been stripped out—stolen—and sold by anybody trying to make a fast buck. That's why you see holes in the walls and ceilings.

"You can see these rooms have a lot of trash. This was probably an apartment building at one time. The homeless moved in and moved out. They carry a lot of junk with them, especially the mental ones. It often gets left behind. Up here's a missing window. You might be able to hear the wind coming in. It stirs up dust. I can smell it. Very unpleasant. My friend over here agrees. This is a good way to get—what do you get from working in coal mines"

"Black lung," Gold answered.

"There you go. The lady is a great repository of knowledge. First in her class. She's holding up two fingers. Second in your class is nothing to sneeze at. Actually, she did just sneeze. Don't know if you could hear it. You can't make this stuff up, folks. Now she's holding up the middle finger. I get the point.

"This is the second floor. Looks like Godzilla was here. Tore a toilet out of the floor and smashed it in the hall. These rooms, as you can see, are equally full of trash, junk, you name it. Another broken window. I know one thing, I wouldn't set up a tent next to the foundation down on the street, especially if I knew how bad these windows are. A good wind and you could have glass raining down on you. No tent will stop that. You'd be sliced and diced. Third floor coming up. These steps are a killer. Maybe this build-ing'd still be running if there was a working elevator in it. It sure wouldn't hurt."

Bargain swiveled the camera to record himself. He made a face, pinched his nose, and spoke in a nasal voice. "Oh, God! You don't need a guy named Hamlet to tell you there's something rotting on the third floor. Have we nosed out Polonius, dead behind the wall-paper, a sword through his guts? I don't think so. That is foul. I'm going to breeze through these rooms to get to the source and then get the hell out of here. Yes. That's me choking on the smell. It's intense. Oh, God! You're looking at it. There's a dead body in here. More blurring to do. What a shame. You can see a needle on the floor. And maybe a bag of dope. I'll zoom in. My lungs are going to collapse. My nose just fell off my face. Thank heaven for small favors. And there goes my friend. You're in the video, dear, like you didn't want to be. It's not my fault. There she goes, marching across the room to examine a corpse. It's Mrs. Sherlock Holmes. No wonder your husband was a dope fiend. You being a necrophiliac. Now she's squatting in front of a dead guy. I don't know why I'm telling you this, because you are watching it unfold. You are hereby banned from my bed...until you shower. Ohhhhhh. She's exam-ining the body. The smell is intolerable. Anybody have a magot you want gagged? What's about to happen? A postmortem or necro session? It's your call."

Gold turned suddenly. "Shut the fuck up and get Persimmon up here. And turn off that damn camera. This junkie's been drained."

CHAPTER SEVENTEEN

The night after the movie at the multi-plex, Bo and Kazmer returned to The Roxy. Bo blurred up to the balcony, where they had made their camp. He sat in a theater seat and held his head in his hands. Kazmer joined him after the steep climb.

Bo looked up at Kazmer as he approached. He still held his head in his hands, as if he had a terrific headache. "I killed again. I said I wouldn't do it. I'd get a job at the hospital. Drink the blood in the lab. The old blood they wouldn't use for transfusions. I had a plan, Kaz."

Kazmer sat next to Bo. He smoothed his hand over the once plush fabric on the seat next to him. "Killing is part of the vampire life. You will get used to it...eventually."

"I don't want to get used to it. I am not a murderer. Vampire, yes. Murderer, no. I don't want to be a vampire."

"Those men were not good. They make fun of us. Say we are gay. Good people are—what is the word?—tolerant."

"Good people are tolerant, Kaz. You're right. What if they weren't bad people. Maybe they were wrong, confused. That's no reason to kill them. All three. Maybe they were just friends out blowing off steam. I couldn't control myself. It happened so fast."

"They were blowing off more than steam. I believe they would have harmed us, if they could. Harmed other people, if not us. They were bad. Would have ended up in prison."

"That's better than being dead," Bo said, turning to face Kazmer. "There should have been another way. Something that didn't involve death. We could have talked, explained. You and I were friends the same way they were friends. Going to a movie." Bo sat up straight. Shook his head. "There must be a way. I didn't ask to be like this. 'Please, Eva, make me a vampire, so I can live forever and kill people. Good and bad. Whoever comes my way. So I can live like a rat in abandoned buildings and cemeteries.'"

"Imagine living forever. That is a long time. It is a tradeoff. You might live in a place like this and..."

"Stink like a rotting corpse."

"But you never will be sick. Never have even a cold. You will survive. You would have the time to go everywhere in the world. Meet people you could not have imagined. Make many friends."

"Watch them all grow old and die."

"I am learning English. You could learn many languages, if that is what you wanted. You like to read, Mr. Bo. Just think how many books you could read. You would see the world change. You would have...wisdom."

"I'd trade it all for a natural life, Kaz."

Kazmer started to roll a cigarette. "I would trade places with you in a minute. Give you my life to become a vampire and live into the future."

"I'd take that trade, as long as I don't have to smoke that tobacco," Bo said.

Kazmer smiled and lit his cigarette, blew a stream of blue smoke into the air above their heads. "Lazlo made me my first cigarette," he said, examining his misshapen handiwork. "It was long ago. I like this strong tobacco. Lazlo was a good brother. I miss him. He taught me how to make cigarettes. Soon I could make them better than he could, and when he wanted to smoke I rolled two, one for him and one for me."

When he looked at Bo, Kazmer's eyes were watery. He sighed. "It is lonely without my brother. Since we were boys, we did everything together. We shared our chores. We worked together in the mines. Got strong from hard work. We met the mistress by mistake."

"Accident?" Bo asked.

Kazmer thought for a moment, as if he ran any number of words through his mind. "Yes. We met her by accident. We had been drinking in a tavern. Drinking away our paychecks, as most single men did. We were a little drunk and walked down a narrow alley. We thought it was funny we could not walk in a straight line and bumped into each other and the walls. There was an argument ahead of us. Two men...cornered."

"Yes. They had her trapped?"

"Yes. She was cornered, as I said. The light was low. There were shadows, but we could tell she was young. She was dressed like a servant, maybe out on an errand late at night. I looked at my brother. He looked back. The girl didn't scream, didn't fight. She let the men push her around. They laughed at her. Talked obscenities. She did nothing. One grabbed her from behind. The other tore her dress up here." Kazmer raised his free hand to his neck, closed his meaty fist, and yanked it down. He paused to take a drag on his cigarette and held the smoke in his lungs a long time, as if remembering the story that happened long ago, before releasing it slowly above his head into the dank theater air. "Lazlo and I pressed ourselves against the alley wall so we would not be seen. We didn't want any trouble. It didn't take much to get into trouble with a girl. The men did not see us, but the woman did. She smiled. The man in front hit her in the face for being so..."

"Insolent?" Bo offered.

Kazmer thought for a moment. "Yes. She was insolent," Kazmer said, pointing his cigarette at Bo, "But his hand made no mark. He hit her again. This time it was harder. Still, the punch made no mark. The man looked at his hand. There was blood on the knuckles. His own blood. The men stopped. Stood there. The woman laughed. It sounded hollow like her body was an empty barrel. Then, from nowhere, there was a man with the three of them. He did not run. He did not walk. He did not drop from above. He was there! Before the men could scream or call for help, the man and woman grabbed the two criminals and opened their necks, drank their blood in front of us. They made big gulping, sucking noises. They drained all the blood. They smiled at each other and dropped the bodies like they were trash.

"Lazlo and I were so scared we could not move. We knew what vampires were from the legends, what the old people told us since we were children. But we never saw one or even knew someone who saw one. The vampires came down the alley to us in a second. They were in one place, then the next. The woman pressed herself against me. She was beautiful, but I could feel she was stronger than any man, even Lazlo. The woman licked my face with her tongue. It smelled. *They* smelled of death. We smelled the men's blood they drank. I was ready to puke. To faint.

"The mistress said, 'What have we here? Dessert?' in the old dialogue our grandmother taught us when we were boys. The dialect we used to talk to her. Lazlo said in the same old dialect, 'We are your servants, Madam.' The vampires looked at each other and laughed. On that night we became vampire Shadows. It was the only decision to be made. If we did not pledge our loyalty, they would kill us. Drink our blood. If we betrayed them, they would kill our entire family, down to the youngest child. Drink all their blood. That is how it happened a long time ago."

"Kaz, after all you have seen and done, this is what you want to be—a vampire?" While Kazmer formed his answer, with considerable thought, Bo continued. "It might look attractive, but what if you don't like the future? What if the world finds out about vampires? Suddenly believe in their existence. You would be hunted like an animal, without mercy."

"That is why most vampires stay together in colonies. How do you say it, there is safety in numbers. The colony can be no bigger than the food that can be taken. Everyone inside the colony must be careful. Guard against being found. Follow the rules."

Kazmer stubbed out his cigarette and ground the ashes and few remaining tobacco flakes between his thumb and index finger, where there was a callous from the heat and friction.

Bo stared at Kazmer for a long moment. "You've killed many, Kaz?"

"Yes. Many."

"Does it bother you to kill?"

"No. Life in the old country was tough. You had to look after yourself. I looked after Lazlo, and he looked after me. Now this country is tough. If you want to survive, to protect your colony from the Brethren, you have to be ready to kill. That is the way it is. Sometimes, other people get in the way. Learn too much. Then they must be killed."

Kazmer had his tobacco out and was in the middle of rolling another cigarette. He spit tobacco flakes from the last smoke while he concentrated.

"So, you weren't a virgin when you met Eva."

Kazmer chuckled. "No. Lazlo and I spent our money on women and drinking when we were young. Our blood was not special to the mistress, the way your blood was. When we joined the mistress and her brother we had to reform. Control ourselves. We went to town meetings to learn what was going on. To see if anyone talked about the undead. That way we could tell the mistress." Kazmer finished the cigarette, inspected it, and pulled a lighter from his pocket. "Do you want to tell me about your brother?"

"No."

"It's painful. I understand," Kazmer said.

"The thing about little brothers is that most of the time they are a pain in the ass. They follow you around, like when you want to go to the pool and watch the girls. Or, when you go to the pool to watch girls they go through your personal things at home."

Kazmer smiled. "I was that younger brother. Lazlo always said he would take me on the mountain and feed me to the wolves."

"Did it stop you?"

"Of course not."

The master and Shadow laughed.

"Really, my brother was a cool kid. He was cooler than I ever was. More popular. A good student. He was too young to hang with me and my friends. He always asked a million questions. He was annoying. He slowed us down." Bo paused for a moment to watch the smoke rings Kazmer blew. Finally, he continued. "When we were young, my parents said he always imitated me. Whatever I said he would repeat. He sat or lay the same way I did. I couldn't stand it. He thought it was funny. There were times I remember hating him, but there were good times between us. When we were alone. He'd ask me advice, especially about girls. It was funny. He'd hear stories in school and want to understand. Make sure he knew what was true. There were things he didn't want to ask our parents."

Bo paused again. "When I was getting ready for college, he found new friends. Got mixed up with drugs. No one noticed. The focus was on me going away to school. He slipped to the wayside. I was at college when he was found dead. Homecoming football game. Under the bleachers with a needle in his arm. Him and another kid. Overdoses. The other kid survived. I planned to come home that weekend and go to the game. See my old friends. But there was a party and I stayed at school. If I had come home, he might still be alive."

"That is a sad story," Kazmer said. "I am sorry."

"I'd like to see his grave. I haven't been back since the funeral."

"We can go," Kazmer said. "Tonight. Now. You can give me the directions."

———

THE MAIN GATE to the cemetery was closed for the night. Kazmer pulled the van along a stone wall on the exterior. It was a rural cemetery with virtually no traffic on the roads at four am. It was a cloudless night. Balmy. A full moon and the stars lit the ground enough for Kazmer to see without a flashlight. They found a smaller gate to the cemetery hanging open and walked through it. Bo led the way. He followed the asphalt drive through the oldest section with its high, ornate stones. Some graves had statues of angels, or mourning women dressed in robes. They passed a row of mausoleums on the left.

"You know the way?" Kazmer said, barely above a whisper.

"He's buried with my grandparents."

"Everyone together. That is the way it should be."

Bo remained silent.

"This is a beautiful cemetery," Kazmer said, as if noticing the grounds on a tour. "New by European tradition. Well kept. Look. The grass was just cut," he added, as if amused. "It sticks to my shoes."

They left the road and passed through a section of ground-level gravestones and toward the back of the cemetery. They crossed another asphalt drive, wide enough for one vehicle. Bo pointed. "See that tree that looks split?"

Kazmer grunted.

"It's over here. Behind the tree, five graves in." Bo walked on. Stopped suddenly.

"Can you read the names? I can't see in the dark," Kazmer said.

"Of course," Bo said. "That's my grandparents, Nan and Pap." Bo pointed at the gravestones. This is my brother and next to him..." Bo paused for a moment. "Is my mother."

CHAPTER EIGHTEEN

Persimmon sprinted up the stairs from the exterior to the abando's third floor. John Bargain and Goldenrod waited at the landing. They told Persimmon what they had found. The wind howled through a broken window down the hall. It helped move the stench of death around the floor. Old Harriet made the slow climb up and joined the group.

"One thing's for sure," Old Harriet said, between puffs. "Climbing steps will never become habit forming. At least for me." Since her beehive hairdo was singed twice in fights with the undead, and as a result resembled a melting ice cream cone on her head, leaning precariously, Persimmon had Old Harriet's hair cut shorter and more stylish for a woman her age. Old Harriet was thrilled with her new look and often paused to see her reflections.

"You didn't tell me the junkie was drained," Persimmon said to Old Harriet, after inspecting the body. "This is important."

"After we spread out, I smelled the junkie first, then when I saw him with the needle and the dope on the floor, I was sure it was an OD. I've seen a lot on the street. OD'd myself a few times." Old

Harriet was not contrite. "He's a real stinker, and I didn't want to get up close and personal with him."

"We'll *all* have to take a closer look now," Persimmon said. "John, I want some more video and still shots, especially of the neck wounds. And I don't want to see any of us in your shots. Blur or no blur."

They approached the corpse that sat on the floor, legs straight and spread slightly. Back against the wall. The head was inclined on the right shoulder. The milky eyes stared. The mouth hung open as if in mid-sentence. Folded hands rested on his lap. The visible skin was mottled.

"Poor thing," Old Harriet said. "The aftermath of drugs."

"This one was murdered," Persimmon said. "You could call drugs a contributing factor. That's what brought him here." She pointed at the exposed neck's left side. "This is what killed him. See the puncture wounds?" She touched the body. Gave the left thigh a squeeze.

"He's as dry as Old King Tut," Od Harriet said. "He was somebody." She raised a hand to her mouth.

"Drained of blood," Gold said. "Just about every ounce."

The Brethren backed away a moment and Bargain approached to video the corpse. Then he took still shots of the face, the neck wound, the hands, the mottled flesh. Persimmon and Gold moved closer to the body, squatted, and swatted at the flies that swarmed around the corpse. Bargain and Old Harriet moved back to the door.

"It's enough to ruin a girl's appetite," Old Harriet said, with a head wag. Bargain agreed.

Persimmon palpated the corpse's neck near the wound. Looked at Gold. "Very neat," Persimmon said. "The bite is right on the jugular."

"An experienced vampire," Gold added. "No torn flesh. Right to business. The incision is so clean it's easy to miss."

"I wonder whether this guy had already shot up before our

vamp arrived. Maybe he was already unconscious. Either way, he was an easy target." Persimmon wiped a forearm across her face. Then chased a fly.

"It's hard to say," Gold said. "Naturally, none of us are experts when it comes to drugs, but he had a lot of infected holes in his arms."

Persimmon and Gold looked toward Old Harriet. Persimmon motioned for her to come over. Old Harriet groaned. Walked across the room. "What do you think, Harriet?" Persimmon asked.

Old Harriet bent over, ready to pick up the needle.

"Careful," Gold said. "The police might dust it for prints, this whole place, depending on how *interesting* this guy proves to be. He might have had warrants out."

Old Harriet dropped to her knee. Studied the syringe. She looked up at Persimmon, and Gold, who had stood. "This looks new," Old Harriet said. "Never been used. It might be one the city gives out to junkies. Anyway, there's no spoon, no lighter to cook the fix."

Persimmon reached down and patted a front pocket. "Feels like a lighter. Maybe a spoon, too."

"That about explains it," Old Harriet said. "He found a nice, quiet place to shoot up. Was just getting his stuff ready when whoever surprised him. I don't think he was unconscious."

"He was livin' the dream, and then the vamp arrived," Gold said.

"I'd say the vamp put the needle in his arm for show," Old Harriet added, looking toward the group.

They moved downstairs and into the daylight. Persimmon used a burner cell phone, one of several she had, to alert police about the body.

"Downtown air isn't clean, but I'll take it over that third floor," Bargain said.

Persimmon and Gold discussed the corpse upstairs. They didn't think Bo could find the jugular, make such a neat incision, hit the vein directly with his fangs, and leave virtually no blood spilled. Enraged by the vampire disease thirst, Bo would attack the victim, tear open the neck, feed on the spurting blood, and in the process make a mess of the body and the surroundings.

This killing had the markings of a surgeon. There was only one conclusion: Eva, the ancient royal vampire, had survived the attack on the undead colony and the explosion that leveled the hillside.

THE FOUR RETURNED to the Brethren stronghold in the ranch home on the city's outskirts. Several patrols were still searching for evidence of the undead. Some Brethren were doing household chores or out shopping. One car was in the garage for maintenance. All vehicles had been gassed up. Everyone took a turn, even Persimmon, their leader, at the mundane tasks of maintaining their group. Still, other Brethren hunkered over newspapers and computer screens, searching for oddities that might not catch the attention of most people. Periodically, the Brethren broke away from their tasks and collaborated with the others. Some newspapers —even larger ones—were down to publishing a few days a week. Anything to save money. Although older people still preferred to hold a newspaper in their hands, and clip articles for friends and family, younger readers embraced technology and searched for news on their phones or computers. Therefore, most of the Brethren toiled over screens.

Sometimes, several Brethren found the same strange news items. There was an early morning car accident, apparently involving one damaged car, totaled, and left abandoned in the middle of the street. There was no evidence of another vehicle or anything that collided with the vehicle. Although there was heavy blood loss at the scene, there was no driver. Police claimed no person so severely injured could have walked from the wreck. Hospitals had no records of an injured person brought in by ambulance or a Good Samaritan. The most interesting detail was that the accident occurred near the explosion and avalanche that occurred a few days earlier.

Then there was the missing teenager from the valley, who went out before sunrise to feed animals on the family farm. It was something she did every day. She disappeared before breakfast, leaving only her boots in the field near the road. The animals in the barn were agitated but none were harmed. The girl was an honor student, popular in her senior class, and president of the high school's Future Farmers of America organization. She never caused her family any trouble. She didn't even have a boyfriend.

Then there were the three young men murdered in the Multiplex movie theater. While the theater emptied after the movie, two had their throats slashed by a sharp instrument. The third had his neck ripped open. Again, although there was a large amount of blood spilled at the scene, the third body's massive loss of blood could not be accounted for. After Persimmon and her group returned to the Brethren stronghold, it was clear that Eva had drained the junkie downtown and Bo killed the others.

The murders at the movie complex occurred in Thaxton, a small town in Ohio. It got Persimmon thinking. Bo might have moved. The vampiress, too. It was not uncommon for a few vampires to move into a town, decimate the living, and move on. Persimmon had an idea. She called Lisa Van der Meer.

Lisa answered with the sound of a baby cooing in the background. "Is this a bad time? Persimmon said.

"Not at all. I'm putting Sherry down for a nap. I saw it was you calling. Any luck?"

Persimmon was blunt. "We think Bo and Eva survived the attack, judging from murders we've seen locally. We don't think they are together, yet."

"Yet?" Lisa said. Persimmon heard her patting the baby's back. Just had supper, Persimmon thought. Then the baby burped.

"I bet that felt good," Persimmon said.

"Now she might take a nap."

"Did Bo ever mention his hometown, when you were held by the vamp?"

"He did, several times. He worried about his parents. It was in Ohio, but I don't remember..."

"Thaxton?"

"That's it. Thaxton was the place. Why do you ask?"

"There was a triple murder in a theater in Thaxton. There was only a squib online, but it sounded like the work of an inexperienced vampire. We might check it out. Not all of us though."

"And Eva?"

"We're still looking. I don't think you have any need to worry. I hope she has moved on. All the Brethren agree at some point she will link up with Bo, whether he wants it or not."

"How would she find him if he's on the move?" Lisa said.

"It's a vampire thing. She had a strong connection with Bo and Kazmer. She might look for them. There's not much loyalty among vampires, but with Bo it's different."

The baby cried.

"I'll let you get back to work," Persimmon said. "At some point, we'll swing back east. I want to see that baby."

CHAPTER NINETEEN

Bo Bentwood knelt by his mother's grave, placed a hand on the sod, which had just started to green, as if he could feel a message from below. He looked up at Kazmer. "I had no idea this happened. Just last winter." He looked back at the ground. "I wonder what happened."

"I am sorry. It is difficult to lose a parent. Lazlo killed our father after he beat me unconscious. We never knew what happened to my mother. She was already gone."

"Could she still be living?" Bo asked in a low voice.

"I doubt it. She would be quite old. I don't know exactly. To be honest, it would be better if she was dead. Life was hard where we lived. I'm sure your mother had a good life."

"I don't know, Kaz. She lost two sons. One to drugs. The other just disappeared. Maybe that was worse than drugs. Not knowing what happened. At least they had a grave to visit. I thought about contacting her and my father to let them know I was still alive, hoping they could keep it a secret. But how would I explain all this." Bo stood and raised his arms in front of him. Let them fall to his sides. "Mrs. Bentwood, your son is alive and, yet, he is dead. He has no heartbeat. He doesn't breathe like a normal person. He kills and drinks blood to survive. He is cold when you touch him. He might stink like the corpse he is unless he just showered. And if he is hungry enough, he might kill you, too."

"That would be hard to tell," Kazmer said, his gaze lowered to the tombstone, a wistful look on his face. "It might be harder to believe."

"You know, Kaz, this was a shock, finding my mother dead. Buried here. I feel like I should cry and throw myself on the ground. But I feel nothing. No remorse. Just hollow. I want to cry, but I have no tears. I don't know that I can cry."

"So it is with the vampire disease. The undead show no emotion, I think is the word. They only can feel rage. Thirst. Self-preservation." Kazmer paused for a moment. Patted his hoodie pocket. "Mr. Bo, would you mind if I smoked?"

"Go ahead, Kaz. If it will make you feel better."

"This visit to the cemetery has made me sad," Kazmer said, reaching for his tobacco. "It makes me think of my family and the old country. I feel sorry for you, too."

"You are sad, and I feel nothing. How my mother—and father—suffered when my brother died. They blamed themselves for not noticing the changes he went through. The new friends, the secretiveness, his grades that slipped. That all came out later. After the funeral. They could hardly function for a long time. Really, they were never the same again."

"I would be sad if I lost you, and you are not my true son," Kazmer said. "But you are like a son." Even in the near dark, Kazmer managed to roll a misshapen cigarette and light it.

"You'll have to teach me how to roll them, Kaz. Then I can make you a smoke when it's dark."

Kazmer smiled. "That is all right. I like to roll my own. It gives me a chance to think."

"About what, Kaz?"

"Things."

"Maybe I should start to smoke."

"It is not good for your health."

They shared a glance and chuckled.

Bo DECIDED to look up his mother's obituary in the local newspaper in the public library. However, he knew the staff there would remember him. Therefore, it fell on Kazmer to do the research. Bo told Kazmer where to go and what to do after he got through the main doors. Kazmer wore a new outfit, including a hoodie. He had shaved with difficulty inside a motel room where they had cleaned up. His left cheek and chin still showed blade abrasions from chopping through his tough beard. The library was rather new. No columns or high ceilings. Once inside, Kazmer approached the main desk, where a middle-aged woman stood, checking through returned books. She looked up and smiled. Asked if she could help him.

"I am interested in looking at the newspaper from February 12th for an obituary," Kazmer said in his methodic best English.

"Do you know our computer system?" She waved a hand holding a pen toward a table with two computer monitors and keyboards."

"No," Kazmer said, lowering his head sheepishly. He ran through the directions Bo had given him. The phrases he had suggested. "I am not computer...how do you say it?"

"Literate," the woman offered, grinning.

Kazmer twisted his lips into a frown. "I am computer illiterate."

"Of course." The woman smiled. "Let's see if I can help." She walked around the desk and toward the table. Kazmer followed. "Do you have a library card?"

"No, but I would like to get one. I like to read, especially the newspaper."

"Excellent. We can get you a card after we're done here."

"Thank you, madam. You are very helpful."

"It's my pleasure. I'm not accustomed to dealing with such polite people."

"Everyone should be polite. It would make the world a better place."

The woman smiled again and sat at the desk in front of the keyboard. Kazmer stood at her side, bent over slightly to watch. Her fingers flew across the keys. She looked up. "Here is the newspaper site."

Kazmer had pursed his lips and raised his eyebrows. "It's really easy to find when you can type that fast. As they used to say, like the hammers of hell. No disrespect intended."

"None taken," she chuckled. "Sometime when you come in, I'll show you how to use this system. That way you can look up newspaper articles, see if we have a particular book, and whether it's here or out. It saves a lot of time. Nobody looks in the stacks anymore, until they know exactly where to go." She raised a pointed finger. "There is something to say about looking in the stacks. I have found many an excellent volume by accident."

"I see," Kazmer said. "I think I would like to look in the stacks someday. When I have more time."

"After you have a card, you can borrow books, take them home to read in the comfort of your home."

"Yes. *Home*," Kazmer added after a long pause. "I would read in comfort."

"Exactly. Now what is the name you're looking for?"

Kazmer referred to his slip of paper again. It had become wrinkled in his hoodie pocket. He turned it over in his beefy hands and then upside down. He cleared his throat. "The name is June Bentwood." He looked down at the librarian.

"Did you know June? She was a friend of mine. She was a volunteer here and a great reader."

Kazmer paused a moment, his lips parted slightly, looking for the words. "I am getting this information for a friend."

The librarian's fingers flew over the keyboard again. She pointed at the monitor with an index finger, without lifting her hands off the keyboard as if she was ready to type some new request.

Before Kazmer could train his eyes on the screen, she said, "June died of Covid, I believe, in the hospital."

Kazmer looked back at her.

"It's not in the newspaper," the librarian said, "but I heard through the grapevine that she had a heart issue no one knew about, not even her, something to do with a valve. She was devastated by the loss of two sons only a few years apart. Then Covid hit her." The woman pulled her hands from the keyboard and folded them on the tabletop. Her mouth made a tick to the side. Her neck pulled slightly, too. "I knew both boys, of course. Was a visitor in their home, many times. And they were in my home. The whole family."

"We think my brother had Covid, but he would not go to the doctor," Kazmer said. He returned his eyes to the monitor's screen, and read slowly, silently, while his lips moved.

"Did your brother recover?" the librarian asked.

"Yes. He got better. He was a strong man."

"*Was?*"

"He died later. In an accident."

"I'm sorry."

"I miss my brother. We were close." After a short pause, Kazmer said, "May I get a copy of this article? For my friend."

The librarian made a few quick keystrokes and stood. "It will print out over there." She pointed back at her desk. In the distance in the library as quiet as a tomb, a printer whirled to life.

Kazmer followed the woman back to the main desk. She retrieved a single piece of paper from the printer tray and handed it to Kazmer. "Thank you again, madam," Kazmer said and bowed slightly.

"You're welcome, I'm sure," she answered with a smile. "Do

you want to get your library card now? It will take only a few minutes."

Kazmer's eyes darted back and forth. "I'm afraid I will get a parking ticket. I should have put money in the meter. Next time."

"Sure. Well, look for me and I'll show you the central card catalog on the computer. It's easy, as I said. And I promise not to type too fast."

CHAPTER TWENTY

THE NEXT EVENING, AFTER SUNDOWN, BO AND KAZMER returned to the Bentwood's neighborhood. Kazmer got fast food on the way and used the bathroom. He slurped his coffee while he drove, smiling at the aroma in the steam that rose from the paper cup. He parked the van down the street from Bo's home and opened his hamburger and fries. Kazmer complained that whoever packaged his meal did not include the extra ketchup he requested. Bo smiled, thought Kazmer could make a meal on ketchup, slipped from the van, and pressed the door closed quietly.

Bo wore a hoodie with the hood up to conceal his identity and his pale face. He walked along the sidewalk toward his old home, his hands jammed in his pockets. It was about 10 p.m., not late enough to be too conspicuous or to raise suspicion. After all, he might be out on an errand, returning home after visiting a neighbor, searching for a pet that got away.

His street was quiet. There was no traffic. It was "garbage night." Trash cans were lined up at the curb for collection early in the morning. How he had hated the noisy trucks, their engines, the hydraulics that compacted the trash, the workers jabbering back and forth, the empty, tossed cans hitting the ground. All he wanted was that extra hour of sleep before school. He hoped he wouldn't encounter a resident bringing out trash. After all, if you wheeled out cans too late, it would set off the neighborhood dogs. Possibly cause people to see what they were barking at. They'd scan the streets for a moment, either peering around curtains or stepping outside on front porches to see what the matter was and check the weather.

Bo did not fear meeting another person. He could walk down a city's worst streets without a worry. Criminals could not deter him. Bullets would not stop him. Neither did he fear the Brethren. He had not encountered them yet. He knew their crossbows were lethal. But they were mere humans. Any dozen of them would not be strong enough to subdue him. He could blur and attack them, slashing with his sharp claws. If they had crossbows and weapons, if he felt endangered, he could blur and be far away in an instant.

The only thing that concerned him was being recognized. It would be difficult to explain his sudden appearance after a year's absence. Where have you been? What have you been doing? Why didn't you contact your family and let them know you were all right?

What would he say?

I was held captive by an ancient female vampire, who kept me in shackles, who raped me inside her casket and drank my blood, who kept me in a weakened state so I couldn't escape, who could read my mind, who turned me into a vampire after I was mortally wounded by gang bangers on a shooting spree. Who would believe him, even with the proof he no longer had a heartbeat, no longer breathed, was cold to the touch, could extend fangs and claws at will, constantly thirsted for human blood, could not tolerate the sun's direct rays, would burn to ashes if he did. What had happened to his college friends, Ridge and TJ? They disappeared. I can tell you. They were hung upside down and drained of blood until their bodies were desiccated, and shrunk to the sizes of children. Then there were the murders. How many were there to date? Seven. Lucky seven. They were slashed, bitten, and drained. What a story! Worthy of a great horror novel or movie. And every word was true.

One more thing concerned Bo as he walked the last few feet to reach his boyhood home on the quiet, small-town street. How many doorbells with cameras were recording his every step? How many motion-sensor lights were ready to snap on?

He lowered his head and continued. He hoped not too fast to raise suspicion, and not too slow that it would appear he cased the homes for a future break-in. Some homes had multiple cans out for collection. That meant a big family lived there, where someone always would be home. Then there were the houses, like his father's, that had one can at the curb with one small bag inside. It was a sure sign that an elderly couple or one person lived there. Or, perhaps, someone who spent part of the week on the road or always ate out. An easy target because the house was empty for hours at a time.

Bo left the sidewalk at the corner of his father's property and walked on a diagonal over the thick, manicured lawn toward the dark living room window. His father had talked about having a security system installed when Bo went away to college, but it was never done, at least to Bo's knowledge. Bo's father was the type of guy who fixed the barn door after the horse got away.

Bo approached the home, squeezed between ornamental bushes, and peered into the dark living room. A light in the kitchen provided limited illumination through the doorway into the living room, casting shadows from the furniture across the floor. Everything inside appeared the same as it was when Bo lived there, except for a new, larger flat-screen television mounted on the wall. The afghan Bo's mother threw across her legs while she watched TV was folded neatly and lay at the end of the sofa, where it always had.

Bo moved across the front of the house, rounded the corner,

avoided the hose caddy on the side, vaulted silently over a four-foot-high chain link fence, and continued to the back of the home. A sensor light snapped on when Bo crossed the back of the house. He ducked out of sight below the deck. He noticed immediately the deck needed cleaning and fresh stain. That had become his job over the years. Bo heard a kitchen chair scrape over the floor. He looked above the deck floor and saw his father peer out the window over the kitchen sink.

What had caused the light to turn on? Your dead son haunting you? More likely a raccoon crossed the yard on its way to the curb to peruse the trash cans for a meal. His father scanned the square of the illuminated yard.

Bo believed the deaths of his brother and mother and then his strange disappearance had been hard on Dad. His face was sallow and more lined. His hair was grayer and thinner. His eyes sunken and forlorn, as if accustomed to grief. He could be a vampire himself, gaunt, gazing from his castle battlements over the moat, waiting for a victim to arrive in the night. The light blinked off and Dad turned from the window. After a moment, Bo heard the kitchen chair scrape on the floor again, starting and stopping twice as he pulled himself back to the table. Bo abandoned his hiding place and moved undetected by the light sensor to the kitchen window. There was always a dead spot the light sensor did not reach. His father sat at the kitchen table, his head bowed over a bowl of ice cream and the local newspaper.

Bo watched his dad inside the quiet house, dipping a spoon into the cold dessert. Between scoops he scanned the newspaper, sometimes following a line of information with an index finger. Eventually, his head rose, and he scraped the remainder of his melted ice cream from the bowl into his mouth. He checked the time on the microwave oven above the stove. Then he stood and seemed to sigh. Before he turned toward the sink, bowl and spoon in hand, Bo blurred away. He startled Kazmer when he appeared suddenly at the van's passenger side door. He opened the door and climbed inside.

"You weren't gone long," Kazmer said. He stabbed out the remains of his cigarette on the steering wheel, started the engine, and pulled out.

"I saw my father through the kitchen window," Bo said.

"Was that good?"

"No. He looks older. He's grieving, I believe."

"He has gone through a lot in the last few years. The people he would have depended on now, at this age, are gone," Kazmer said in a low voice.

"I wish I could do something. I don't know if he would understand if I told him I'm *alive*. Even if I didn't mention the vampire *thing*. How could I explain where I've been? I couldn't see him in person. I doubt he could keep my existence a secret because he'd be elated I'm back."

Kazmer drove back toward town and The Roxy. Bo was silent and watched the view out the side window. Kazmer pulled to the curb a block from the theater. They got out, made sure the vehicle was locked and started a slow walk back to the theater, hoods raised. The streets were quiet. No cars. No foot traffic. That's how it was in a small town. Apparently, someone forgot to roll up the sidewalks. Kazmer waited at the corner in the shadows under the theater's marquee.

Bo slid down the alley, checked the surroundings, forced open the emergency exit door, and stepped inside. He whistled and Kazmer followed. Once Kazmer was inside, Bo used his strength to close and secure the door again. It was still dark, and they climbed to the balcony. Kazmer said he was tired and crawled inside his sleeping bag. He was soon asleep. Bo sat on a dusty theater seat, put his head back, and scanned the ceiling. Chunks of plaster had fallen. Paint hung in long, thin strips like fly paper. Bo wanted to help his father, but the terrible thirst in the back of his throat consumed him.

He knew he needed to feed. Upon inspection, the flesh on his hand and arm sagged. He felt his face and realized he must look older than his father. He could think only of feeding. Bo imagined the woman he kidnapped from the motel. He wanted her back. He wanted to spread out his sleeping bag and have sex with her on the balcony landing. He imagined her scent. How could he find her? His father would have to fend for himself for the time being.

CHAPTER TWENTY-ONE

It was early morning, just after dawn. Persimmon bent over a map of Ohio spread out on the kitchen island in the Brethren's rancher stronghold, tapping a pencil on a specific location. Other vampire fighters crowded around her. Coffee was brewing. She blew at a strand of long, dark hair that fell over her forehead. The hair, which had escaped her ponytail, came back immediately, and she pushed it off her face behind her ear. One could practically see the wheels turning. The tapping increased in frequency, like a little drumbeat, and slowed. The location she studied was covered with graphite points.

She looked up and scanned the faces around her. "Who wants to go to Thaxton?" she said. "Road trip."

"What they got in Thaxton, Ohio?" Mellow Yellow asked, raising an eyebrow. "Anything good to eat, like the world's best cream puff?"

Persimmon smiled. "Not that I know of. But they do have a vampire that's already killed three people. Maybe more by now."

Mellow Yellow, a mountain of a man, looked at the ceiling a

moment as if pondering the question, stroking a wiry beard. "I'm in. We'll work on the cream puffs later."

Persimmon flashed a smile at him. Looked at the others surrounding the island. "As you know, we're chasing Bo Bentwood, a newbie vamp who's not too careful covering his tracks. I believe he'll be easy to find if we can get to him before he gets uncomfortable and leaves Thaxton. It should be an in and out."

"We're in," Overboard George said, pulling Mad Maggie to his side, and circling an arm around her shoulder. Maggie wagged her head in agreement. "I could go for a cream puff myself."

"We know Bo," Mad Maggie said. "We can recognize him in a second, even in a crowd."

"There aren't too many crowds in Thaxton." Persimmon chased the strand of hair off her face again. It slipped forward every time she inclined her face toward the map. "It's a small town, maybe thirty thousand people. It's like a lot of places, mostly in decline."

"Sounds a lot like where I grew up," Old Harriet said. "Thaxton? We knew Bo when he was human. That doesn't mean we'd show him any mercy. Count me in. I've never been to Ohio."

"We need only a few Brethren for this trip," Persimmon said, still fighting the wisp of hair. "Most of us will remain here and search for Eva. I hope to bag one of the vamps, either Eva or Bo, before they can link up. That's what they will probably do at some point. Then they'll be more difficult to find. They could go anywhere. Who else? I have room for two more."

"How's the pizza in Thaxton" John Bargain asked.

"I didn't google *that*," Persimmon said. "I'd imagine about as good as the stuff we get around here."

"Okay. As long as it's not worse. I'll go, if I can do some vlogs." Bargain spread out his arms. "My salivating audience awaits. I can see it now. The Great Pizza Quest."

"Alright," Persimmon said slowly, staring at Bargain, "as long as you don't record the vamp or any of us. Got it?"

"Understood," Bargain said with a smile.

Goldenrod stepped up to the island. "I'll make sure he stays in line. I've become his wingman."

"Be ready in an hour," Persimmon said. "Pack for a light mission, but don't skimp on the ammo. You never know what we'll find."

"What about *her*?" Old Harriet said, motioning down the hall to a room where they believed Jean was still sleeping. "Those vampires are sex fiends. If Bo has the hots for her, maybe she could lure him in."

"Like a decoy?" Persimmon asked.

Old Harriet crinkled her eyes and smiled. "Exactly. Like a wooden duck bobbing on a pond."

Persimmon thought and blew at her errant strand several times. "It's not a bad idea," she said finally. She looked at Gold. Gold nodded in agreement. "We'll take her only if she agrees to go. Wants to be in on the kill. I don't want to keep an armed guard on her twenty-four-seven. That could expose us. She must follow our rules."

"Who knows," Old Harriet said, raising a finger. "She might make a good addition to our group of vampire exterminators."

Persimmon chuckled. "Yes, Old Harriet. Who knows? We leave in an hour. Everybody knows the drill. Leave your will and any special instructions here. Just in case."

Fifty-three minutes later, the Brethren left their stronghold in two SUVs. They communicated between the vehicles with walkie-talkies. Gold and Overboard George took the first leg of the long journey to Ohio.

Old Harriet sat in the first vehicle's back seat. She groused that it was too bad Del Hatch wasn't with them because he always had a serious supply of snacks on board. They hit the interstate and drove east. Old Harriet enjoyed the ride, scanning the greening scenery.

"I forgot spring was here. I like the view. It would be a lot nicer if it wasn't for all that trash along the highway. People are pigs. They don't deserve nice roads. Pretty scenery."

After several stops to eat, stretch their legs, and gas up, the Brethren reached the outskirts of Thaxton the next morning. They were all tired. Old Harriet slept through most of the night. They exited the interstate and traveled on a secondary highway where the speed limit was lower. Persimmon was driving again, now in the lead SUV. Her GPS app wanted them to exit at the next intersection. Two blocks later, the local fire police had the road blocked by two old geezers in yellow vests.

Persimmon rolled to a stop and dropped the window. "What's the problem, gentlemen," Persimmon asked.

"Got a shooter in Burt Grimes Elementary. You'll have to go..."

"What!" Persimmon roared. "My kid's in there."

The distraught-looking man with a neck of stringy cords started to point toward the detour, but Persimmon roared off, leaving him to choke on a lung full of fumes. Gold took off in the second vehicle, despite the codger's protests. Persimmon followed the trail of flashing lights. Fire trucks, ambulances, and police squad cars were staged in case they were needed. Any number of emergency personnel tried to flag her down, but Persimmon roared on. She spotted a mostly deserted parking lot ahead, entered it, and squealed to a stop. "Stay here!" she commanded, exiting the door. "Get a new driver ready to go."

Persimmon sprinted to the row of entrance doors. She felt the .9 mm on her hip, concealed in a holster inside her jean belt. A man next to the doors tried to stop her and waved his arms. "You can't go in there. A man has a gun."

"I'm the substitute they called." She tugged on the handles, going down the line of locked doors.

"You can't go in there. It ain't safe."

Persimmon stopped, faced him, and pulled out her pistol. "I can shoot my way in."

"Don't do that, ma'am. I'll have to clean up all the glass. Go down two more doors. That one's open for the police," the man pointed. "But I warned you."

Persimmon followed the man's instructions. She moved down and tugged on the door handle. It swung open in her grip. She slipped inside, letting the door bang shut. The man followed her movements from the outside. She sprinted up six steps to the main floor and stopped to decide whether to continue up when she heard a series of shots to her right. There were officers on both sides of the hall hunkered in the deep door wells to classrooms. She ignored the officers as they hissed for her to get back.

One grabbed her arm when he saw the pistol. "Get back!" he ordered.

"I'm with homicide," Persimmon snarled and escaped his grip. She flipped open her jacket lapel as if to show a badge when more shots rang out. Bullets slammed into lockers down the hall. She pulled the jacket closed before the officer could see anything. "What's going on."

"The kids are locked in the auditorium. So far, nobody's been wounded. The shooter's trying to get in. Right now, he's focused on Clausen, who's pinned down across the hall in the boys' bathroom. You ought to have a vest."

"You're right."

"It seems like he has a bag full of ammo. He's in it for the long hall. Wants to do as much damage as possible before he goes out." The cop's face glistened with sweat. He rubbed his finger across his mustache as if it suddenly bothered him.

Persimmon sweated, too. She found it hard to swallow.

Three quick pops rang out.

"I need a cold drink," Persimmon said with a smile.

The cop wiped his brow. "It's hot in this vest."

"That's why I left mine in the car."

"If you want a drink, there's a bar down Vernon Street." The officer pointed with his thumb.

"I'll meet you there after we take down this fucker." Persimmon stepped away from the cop. Moved to the hall's center.

"Hey! Hey! Get back here," the cop hissed. "He can see you."

"That's what I want." She winked at the cop. "What's the name of this place"

"The school?"

"The bar."

"O'Toole's."

"Meet you there later, alligator."

The officer looked on in disbelief. "After a while—"

Persimmon walked away, her gun at her side.

The shooter poked his head around from the auditorium door well. Police fired a half dozen rounds at him. The shooter ducked back. Children shrieked inside the auditorium's double doors. Persimmon not only had the attention of police officers, who called at her to retreat, the shooter saw her as she walked across the hall, kicked spent bullet casings out of the way, and stopped at a row of lockers. The shooter poked out his head from safety and pulled back immediately as if Persimmon's sudden appearance was a trick. She stood calmly, like an Old West gunfighter. The shooter popped out and back several times over half a minute. He didn't give police the chance to get off any shots.

"Put your gun down and come out," Persimmon called. "We won't let you take any of our kids."

"Fuck you," the shooter returned. He took half a step forward; his gun was already raised to fire.

Persimmon's gun hand flew up. She shot. The back of the shooter's head blew across the auditorium doors. The shooter crumpled to the floor. Persimmon holstered her gun. Returned down the hall. Officers ran toward the fallen man. Persimmon sprinted toward the stairwell.

"Hey!" the sweating cop cried as she passed.

"Got to take a wicked piss! See you at O'Toole's!" Her voice receded down the hall.

That fast, Persimmon was gone. Outside in the sunshine, she told the man at the door the incident was over. Just as fast, Persimmon got picked up, and the SUVs booked it out of the parking lot.

"What's wrong with you?" Gold blistered over the walkie-talkie.

Persimmon sank into the passenger side seat. She took a water bottle from Old Harriet, screwed off the top, and took a long drink. She picked up the walkie-talkie from the consul and replied, "This world has more than one kind of monster. Now there's one less."

CHAPTER TWENTY-TWO

The Brethren checked into the La Di Da Motel in Thaxton. It was the only place to secure rooms in town and—never a palace—was threadbare and home to a few permanent residents who appeared down on their luck. They mostly sat outside their rooms on folding chairs, filling ashtrays on the ground. One worked on his car, never bothering to close the hood or put away his tools. A growing viscous puddle spread from the oil pan to a drain nearby. The sidewalks were cracked and choked with weeds. A pool behind the building was choked with leaves and slimy water. The surface scum appeared thick enough to walk over. A sign on the fence around the pool said KEEP OUT.

An old man played solitaire on the front desk, his cards, brown and oily, looked as old as the motel. A portable television played inside a small, cluttered partially visible office behind him.

Persimmon ordered four rooms side-by-side and plunked down cash. That raised the man's eyebrow and produced a smile. He had stringy, gray hair, fly-specked glasses, and yellow teeth. He said the management didn't tolerate wild parties. When asked where there was a good place to eat, he scratched his beard-stubbled neck, as if it might be a trick question or there were many fine restaurants in town.

"You like barbecue?" he asked after a long moment, thrusting his oddly shaped head toward Persimmon as if her answer was a condition to secure room keys.

"Sure do, if it's good," Persimmons said.

"Then it's Porky's. Just down the road." He pointed in the direction with a crooked index finger. He looked Persimmon over and added. "It's not far, but you'll probably want to drive. They got a huge parking lot for such a little diner."

"Do I need reservations?"

"At Porky's? Nah."

Persimmon collected the room keys and her receipt, which was printed on an old adding machine and initialed by the clerk. "You staying long?" the man asked. Both bushy eyebrows were raised this time. "Got to arrange the maid service, you know."

Persimmon smiled. "Not sure. It could be anywhere from one night to a week. We have some business in the area."

"Oh?"

"Our business."

"Just thought I might be of help." It was his turn to smile. He looked sheepish for a moment.

"I'll let you know. We have several appointments already. Might need to set up some more." Persimmon spun on her heels and left the motel office.

Back at the cars, Persimmon handed out the keys. Overboard George and Mad Maggie in one room. The next was John Bargain and Gold. Persimmon and Jane would bunk together. Old Harriet got her own crib. Mellow Yellow had decided to remain on the West Coast.

They inspected the rooms, which all smelled musty. Old Harriet was thrilled to have her own room. She invited everyone to convene with her. "Hey, Old Harriet, you don't have a TV,"

Bargain said. He pointed to an empty stand, dust-covered, missing the television.

"I knew having my own room was too good to be true." Old Harriet frowned. Dropped on the bed with a sigh.

"We'll see about this," Persimmon said. She marched back to the office. The clerk looked surprised when she entered suddenly. "Need more towels?" He grinned.

"One of our rooms is missing the color TV you advertise." Persimmon gave him the room number.

The clerk frowned. Looked around the room, as if there might be a collection of TVs available. He poked his head into the office and swore under his breath. "I'll bring one right over. Give me a minute. I'll have to plug it in and make sure it works. I might need to adjust the color."

Persimmon returned to Old Harriet's room. She no sooner closed the door than the clerk knocked. She held the door open while he struggled in, bouncing off the jambs, and placed the television on the dusty stand. He sweated and was out of breath. He laughed giddily while the seated Brethren watched him connect the television plug and cable wire. After he caught his breath, he turned on the television.

"There you go," he beamed. "All fixed." He looked at the Brethren as if he were an appliance salesman expecting shoppers to be impressed with the latest set. "The color looks good, too."

"It's not even a flat screen," Old Harriet groused.

"It's all we have. Anything else you need, just give me a yodel." The clerk apologized and bowed several times as he backed out of the room. Old Harriet followed him out and locked the door. She returned to the television to turn it off. "Say, this thing is warm already.

"That's the set he had playing in the office," Persimmon said. "What's he going to watch?"

"Who cares," Old Harriet fired back. "Serves him right for being a cheapskate."

The Brethren got down to business. They spread out in Old Harriet's room and sat on the beds and two chairs available. "Do we want to involve Bo's parents, the Bentwoods, in our search?" Persimmon asked. "I can't imagine getting intel from them and using it to stake their son. Slam, bam, thank you, ma'am."

"They might not know anything," Bargain said, looking around the room.

"But, if Bo's in town, he might have made contact," Old Harriet said.

"We could do a little fishing," Bargain said. "We could say we're doing a documentary on missing people. You have Bo and his friends, Ridge and TJ. All missing."

Persimmon cleared her throat. "Police back east have listed his friends as murder victims, even though there were no bodies ever found. They worked off DNA on bloody clothes found in After Dark's basement," Persimmon said. "Bo is still considered *missing*. There was no trace of him."

There was a long pause. Everybody thought, looked back and forth among one another as if looking for answers. Bargain and Gold traded smiles. "Let's try the documentary angle," Gold said. "JB and I will contact Bo's parents. JB knows all the technical terms for filming. If they ask questions, nobody can BS better than he can."

Persimmon looked around the room at her fellow vampire fighters. "Let's do it."

Overboard George picked up the room's telephone. "Free local calls," George said, smiling, pointing at a sign taped on the wall. He opened the scuffed desk, where he sat and pulled out an ancient, dog-eared telephone directory from the drawer. He slipped on his readers and opened the book, flipped the pages backward through his thumb, turned a few pages forward slowly, and traced names with an index finger down one column and up another. Overboard

George frowned and pushed the glasses back on his nose. "Here we go, Arthur Bentwood. There's also a Jerry Bentwood." His serious face scanned the Brethren. "Different addresses. Both are here in Thaxton. Even though this phone book looks as old as the Dead Sea Scrolls, old folks might still have landlines. Who says we start with Arthur?" George looked around the group again.

They all agreed with a nod or raised hands.

"Good choice," Bargain said.

"Ask for the old lady," Old Harriet said, with a wag of her head. "She might be more forthcoming. Men usually don't like to talk on the telephone, especially to strangers."

Overboard George bit his lip, found the telephone number again with his finger, and punched it in. He handed the phone's receiver to Gold, the closest to him.

"Thanks," she mouthed silently. The group suppressed chuckles.

Gold scanned her friends. Someone picked up the phone. "Bentwood."

"May I speak to Mrs. Bentwood?" Gold nodded toward Old Harriet.

Old Harriet smiled and winked at Gold.

"Who's calling?"

"Is Mrs. Bentwood available?"

"Who's calling? My wife has passed."

"I'm sorry, Mr. Bentwood. I didn't know."

"Who is this?"

"My name is Kelly Gold." Gold shrugged. "I'm a producer for BBC America."

Bargain sniggered. Persimmon elbowed his ribs.

"You have the wrong number," Arthur Bentwood said.

"Sir, do you have a missing son?"

There was silence. Finally, Arthur Bentwood said, "I do."

From there, Gold winged it. She told the old man she was working on a documentary about missing young people in America.

Gathering stories and evidence. She said she got Bo's name from his university. Gold said her research would determine whether the documentary would be completed and broadcast. She asked for a few minutes of his time for an interview. Bentwood seemed skeptical. In the end, he agreed to meet Gold and her cameraman, but he didn't want them in his home. They would meet tomorrow afternoon at Porky's.

PORKY'S WAS NOT the kind of place that would impress a first date unless you were a local and had no other place to go. It was just as seedy as the La Di Da. Just the type of joint where the motel clerk would feel at home. In fact, John Bargain imagined him seated at the old bar, hunched over a draft and a bowl of stale beer nuts. Strips of duct tape coming undone at the edges covered rips in the threadbare carpet, especially around the entrance, where countless steps and the weather had ruined it over time. Ceiling fans overhead squeaked and swayed as if they were caught in a storm. The Brethren found the food passible the day they arrived. Barbecued pork or chicken arrived in plastic baskets with sides of fries and slaw. The coffee was good. The desserts under plastic, domed lids looked inviting. Old Harriet was impressed the most and smacked her lips as she ate. She was having the time of her life hunting vampires.

Arthur Bentwood arrived at the restaurant ten minutes early. He declined lunch. Gold and Bargain sat over coffee at the back booth they requested, to the waitress's chagrin who talked under her breath about the extra mileage to the location they picked. She knew Bentwood. Touched his shoulder. Asked if there was any *news*. He shook his head and she walked away after leaving him coffee and refilling the two other cups. Bentwood was amazed at Bargain's camera.

"The clunky old ones carried on the shoulder are dinosaurs,"

Bargain laughed. "There are a lot of retired cameramen with bad backs and shoulders. This is the future."

As Bargain recorded the conversation, Gold explained the proposed documentary. There was still a lot of work to be done before the evidence was pieced together and broadcast. During a break for coffee refills, Bentwood said he saw a story online about people disappearing out west in national parks.

"We have a man on it," Bargain interrupted suddenly. "Even as we speak, Del Hatch is exploring the Pacific Northwest for Sasquatch."

Bentwood twisted his mouth. "What's a Del Hatch?"

"He's a legend," Bargain said, smiling. His grin turned to pain after Gold kicked him in the chin.

Gold shot Bargain a look, cleared her throat, and continued. "The most difficult question I have to ask you, and apologize for it, but it's something we ask everyone. Have you heard from Bo? Has anyone seen him around town, especially recently?"

Bentwood looked stunned. "What kind of question is that? I'd never keep such a thing secret." He was already sliding from the booth. "This interview is over. Don't contact me again." He walked away and waved to the waitress.

"Well?" Gold said to Bargain.

"You kick like a mule."

CHAPTER TWENTY-THREE

The snap Del Hatch heard from his perch in the Pacific northwest, three miles west of base camp, caught his attention immediately. His eyes flicked but his head didn't move. He knew it was a dry stick snap. The question was, what made it? He ended his satellite phone call abruptly, whispering his goodbye to John Bargain and laid the instrument on the ground next to him. Dressed in a ghillie suit to hide himself, Del brought out his camera that was secured inside the suit, moving an inch at a time to avoid detection. After the camera was out, he felt the .9 mm pistol on his hip. Whatever made the noise might be a cougar or brown bear. He hoped it was a Sasquatch prowling around in daylight. Del didn't want to shoot critters; he preferred snapping their photographs.

Next, he pulled out his aerosol can of Sasquatch sex pheromone. He had bought the spray online from a couple who made a variety of canned scents at their home in Morris, Pennsylvania, up in Tioga County, not far from the New York state border. The grinning couple appeared genuine, Del thought, seated on a comfortable-looking sofa, a Springer Spaniel on each side of the couple, their products lined up on the coffee table in front. Del could only imagine how they canned various scents from doe, elk urine, etc. Actually, he couldn't imagine how they captured the odors. Especially the Sasquatch sex pheromones. Perhaps they used chemicals that came close and had a laboratory in their basement. Did they try it on each other? Maybe that's why they grinned in the online photograph—got a snoot full just before the shutter snapped. The pheromone spray was on sale, a BOGO. Del figured he couldn't go wrong.

Although he didn't know whether the Sasquatch spray would give Bigfoot a boner, he had evidence the stuff confused vampires. On the night he was left to fend for himself in the old cemetery on the West Coast when he had his ass parked on a mausoleum roof near the vampire entrance to their main underground lair, he sprayed a mist of the stuff over his head, fearing the vampires might identify his human scent. The vampires were confounded by the Sasquatch sex pheromone odor and couldn't identify it when they emerged from the mausoleum. Rather than investigate the scent, they blurred away to hunt for new victims, fresh blood.

During the seconds after he heard the stick crack, Del reasoned that the sex pheromone—if it worked—would scare off any predator, other than Bigfoot, which he was after in the first place. If it didn't work, it still might confuse a cougar or brown bear enough that it would decide to take off rather than face the stinker that made the smell. Moving like a chameleon, Del pulled out the spray can from his belt loop, transferred it from one hand to the other, and continued the long, painful process of raising the can outside the ghillie suit. He was excited; his respiration came in short breaths—in through his nose, out through his pursed lips.

The forest was quiet. Too quiet. Nothing stirred. Not a squirrel. Not a bird. Not an insect. Which Del knew was unnatural. Even a chipmunk made a raucous when it ran through dry leaves. Whatever stepped on the stick apparently had frozen in place, just as cautious as Del.

It's probably nothing. That's what I'm thinking. It'll be worth a good laugh back at camp. I just hope I don't piss my pants before I find out what's behind me. The initial sound came from behind him and to his right. After he had the spray in front of him, Del started the slow process of turning his head to where the sound had come from. After a minute of chameleon-like moves, Del reached the maximum he could turn his head. He moved his shoulders next, trying to increase his range of vision.

There was another crack. Same as the last one. This time it was closer, he thought, directly in front of him. Time for action. Del raised the aerosol to check the spray direction. He couldn't see well through the ghillie suit face mask. He pressed the button. The spray hit his eyes. Del howled through the surprise and pain. Something behind him bolted and ran away across the ridge. Del blinked repeatedly. He cursed. Despite the blurred vision, Del stood and spun around. Everything appeared in shadows. Whatever animal had been there was gone. Del saw small blurry hoofprints dug in the pine needle floor. *Had to be a deer. Nothing else. Booked it out of here real fast. No way it was a Squatch.*

Pain seared Del's eyes and cheeks. He grabbed his water bottle and poured its contents over his face and eyes. *There should be a warning on the label. Don't spray near the eyes. This shit's better than mace.* Del sat down again, squinted, and blinked, but his vision remained blurry. He made out the large tree in front of him, maybe ten yards away. Beyond that, the terrain moved downhill. It had been a wicked climb. His hamstrings and thighs burned when he finally flopped down in front of another large tree he thought would give him cover from the rear. *My sight will come back. It must. Just wait it out. Otherwise, I'm going to have a hell of a time getting back to camp.* Del rested his back against the tree. The forest floor of pine needles provided a comfortable seat and a pleasant aroma. The forest remained still. He tried to calm himself and breathe slowly, deeply. He stared into the distance. Occasionally he blinked or squinted, hoping to see an improvement in his vision. There was none.

He looked to the right and back to the left. When he tried to focus his eyes forward, he saw something move toward him. It came uphill walking on two legs. Del couldn't tell who it was or how far away it was. It was a dark, blob-like figure. No details were visible. It wound its way back and forth up the hill. It didn't walk in a straight line. It appeared on one side of the big tree in front, disappeared behind the tree for a moment, and reappeared on the other side. Slowly, it grew larger but was still blurred. *What the hell? It can't be, but it is. Well, folks, I think there's a Squatch in these woods. Waited my whole life for a glimpse of the big guy, and now here I am—finally watching him and I can't see. Look at him move. He's doing the alley-oop on me, looking out one side of the tree and then the other. Typical Squatch behavior. Read about it a million times. Appears rather small, but there's nothing to use as a reference, especially when everything's blurry. Could be a juvenile. Must have smelled that spray. He's curious. What are you doing out here by yourself, little fellow or little girl? I don't think it can see me, or smell me yet. Hope it won't be too disappointed. Maybe I'll just sit here and see what happens.*

The figure continued its climb uphill. Del couldn't tell whether this was a small Squatch hiding behind the tree in front of him, poking its head out one side and then the other to sneak a peek, as anecdotal accounts claimed about Bigfoot, or was it a large animal still many yards down the hill. Del squinted, blinked, and closed his eyes for a few seconds at a time. Was his vision any better? It was. Slowly, his depth perception came back. The figure was not close but down the hill. It did not growl, as Del first imagined, but it cursed. After a few more blinks his vision came into focus.

"Del, you big prick! Can you hear me? Where are you?"

Del recognized the man. It was Sam Barber. Not the composer, but the butcher turned Sasquatch researcher.

"Up here," Del waved. "I'm in a ghillie suit."

"I see you now. We have an emergency in camp."

"We have an emergency here," Del countered. He removed the

fabric head hood. "I sprayed myself in the eyes with this Sasquatch sex pheromone." Del offered the can to Barber as he reached him.

"That wasn't too smart," Barber said. "Don't get any friendly ideas."

"I didn't say it was smart. Just a mistake."

"Look here," Barber said, rolling the can in his palm to read the directions. "*Avoid contact with eyes.*" Barber was a pudgy man, balding, having trouble catching his breath after the climb. He had stripped off his jacket and tied it around his waist.

"What's the problem at camp?" Del showed concern.

"Doc Melvin thinks Benny has acute appendicitis. Ben's in a lot of pain. They already took him back down to the hospital in town."

Del twisted his mouth. "Doc's not a real doctor."

"He's the closest thing we have." Barber raised his hands in frustration. Dropped them to his side. "That's why he's called Doc. Anyway, we decided to break camp.

"No," Del said. "Not so soon."

"We figured it wasn't worth it with Ben and Doc out. Who's goin' to fix something that breaks without Doc?"

Del dropped his eyes to the ground. Looked up after a moment. "I suppose you're right. Benny's the cook and Doc's the fixer. It's better that we break camp. Del smiled while he was quiet for a moment. "I might be able to get a few licks in on a vampire expedition."

"A what?"

"Vampires are just as real as Bigfoot."

CHAPTER TWENTY-FOUR

There was a tap on Old Harriet's motel room door. She looked up from a Travel Channel program on alien sightings. "Come in," Old Harriet answered weakly. Persimmon opened the door, slid through, and closed it behind her.

"I thought I heard you go out," Harriet said. Just as she returned her gaze to the television a commercial came on. Old Harriet turned down the volume and focused on Persimmon.

"I'm back now." Persimmon held one arm behind her back.

"Got something?" Old Harriet craned her neck and swayed side to side a bit to see what Persimmon hid.

"It's nothing."

"Must be something."

"Oh, this? It's just a little something I picked up." Persimmon produced a small cake from behind her back, resting on a palm. "All they had was chocolate with peanut butter icing."

Old Harriet's eyes lit up. "You know that's my favorite." She held out her arms to accept the cake. Persimmon handed the cake over, and pulled paper plates, forks, and a knife from a bag in her waistband. She slid next to Harriet on the bed.

"This is all for you, Old Harriet. It's only a small one."

Old Harriet stripped the safety seal off the container and worked on removing the clear plastic top. The top disengaged with a loud crack. "Looks like one of the UFOs I just seen on the TV," she said pointing at the muted television.

Although Persimmon declined a piece, Old Harriet insisted she have a slice as she cut the cake, the tip of her tongue exposed at the corner of her mouth. "What's the occasion?" Old Harriet wanted to know, sliding a wedge of cake on a plate, handing it to Persimmon, and then sucking icing from a knuckle.

"I thought you could use a lift," Persimmon said, "and peanut butter icing is a surefire remedy."

"You're right," Old Harriet said. "The last few days have been tough." She scooped her own slice onto a plate and dug a fork in immediately, lifted the rich cake to her mouth, and savored the taste."

"Feel better?"

Old Harriet smiled. "There's more," Persimmon added. She ran to the door, reached outside, and brought in a half gallon of milk. "Ice cold."

Old Harriet beamed and accepted a plastic cup of milk. Persimmon poured one for herself. "Want to talk about it?" Persimmon said, after sampling the cake and washing it down with a swig of milk.

"It's nothing," Old Harriet said. She inspected her fork. Licked icing off the plastic tines.

"It does matter," Persimmon insisted. "You're part of *our* family now."

The women stared at each other for a moment. Old Harriet placed the plate on her lap. A tear welled in her eye. She raised her hand and pressed her thumb and index finger together. "I came this close to going back to the dope. Left to myself, downtown, I could have found a dealer in a minute. Bought all I needed for a fix. It was a struggle. Even though I don't have a driver's license, I could have taken one of the vehicles. There's always a way to get dope."

"Are you okay now?"

"Every day's a struggle." She held up her fork, a wedge of cake balanced on it. "This helped a lot. Thank you."

Persimmon placed a hand on Old Harriet's thin shoulder. "That's what I'm here for."

Old Harriet swallowed cake and looked toward the ceiling. She spoke as if talking to herself. "If I knew I could get some of the old dope, the brown heroin, I'd sell this cake and your car parked at the curb for a fix." She directed her gaze at Persimmon. Both their eyes filled with tears again. "I'd find a sweet box like Overboard George had back in the day, haul it downtown, and go back to the streets. *If I could get some of that good old brown heroin. On a bad day, I'd settle for some tranq."

"Staying sober seems to be working for Overboard George," Persimmon said.

"George has Mad Maggie. They lean on each other," Old Harriet said. She took another forkful of cake and a drink of milk. "Maggie helps with George's urges for dope. He helps keep her mind straight. I talk to Bad Nelson once in a while. He's sober since he went back east, but he has Megan and her boys. They depend on him now. He got a job." Old Harriet smiled. She wiped her eyes. "He's still nutsing around with his potato guns. He wants to make a compact edition that shoots faster stakes. I got nothing. Nobody."

"That's not true, Old Harriet. You have all of us." Persimmon said. She spread her arms and hugged Old Harriet for a few seconds. "You can talk to any of us."

Old Harriet shook her head. "I don't know. I think the Brethren tolerate me, an old woman, because I came with the rest from the East Coast and now you feel sorry for me."

"That's not true and you're not that old."

"I never really fought no vampires like the others."

"You were with us when we stormed the vamp colony on the West Coast. You used your machete on them."

"That was a good time." Old Harriet smiled. Sniffed.

"You and Mad Maggie chopped Fagan to pieces. You two killed their colony's leader."

Old Harriet smiled. "It was Del Hatch who pulverized Fagan with that BAR." She held an imaginary gun at her hip as if spraying bullets around the motel room. "Cut him to ribbons. Then we came in with our machetes. Cut him up good. The funny thing is he never showed any fear, even while we were dismembering him, limb by limb, hacking him apart, and he couldn't do anything to escape. His arms and legs were gone. I kept a foot on him so he couldn't roll away. He just glared at us. All that hate."

"That's how vampires are, Old Harriet. If you're with us when we find Bo, you can't show him any mercy. Not for a second. No matter how you *felt* about him when he was human."

"I understand," Old Harriet said. Her face showed resolution. "I'll imagine Bo's my first—and only—husband. I wouldn't show him any mercy if I had him in my machete's striking distance." She imitated a chopping motion with her hands. "My old man was abusive, all right. Knocked me around silly, but we were both drunks. He tended bar for a guy so this fellow could go home for a few hours and see his old lady and kids eat supper. The owner went out one door and I came in the other. The old lad fed me free drinks while the owner ate his supper. I staggered home about the time the owner came back. The old boy'd come home after the bar closed, after he was pickled, find me drunk—when he was the one who got me that way—and knocked me around. Bruised me up with his fists. Black eyes, fat lips, concussions. He dished it all out. When I had enough, I didn't go to the bar one afternoon to get soused. I packed a bag and hit the streets. After a few weeks on my own, I took up with a man everybody called Bunny. I never knew what his real name was. He had white hair and kept it tied in a bun on the back of his head. It looked like a rabbit's tail. We lived in a little commune in a tent made from vinyl tarps strung through the trees near a stream. You could only see the tents from the highway overpass. By the time you saw them, you were over the bridge and the tents were out of sight again. Nobody went to the trouble to roust us out of there. It wasn't accessible unless you knew the path to get in and out. We didn't bother nobody, so we were left alone."

Old Harriet smiled again. "Bunny was a kind man. His hands were soft. He didn't punch me. He liked listening to the water gurgling in the stream. He even made a little waterfall out of rocks near our tent. The waterfall was about a foot high, but the noise the water made going over it was comforting. I remember him standing in the water, bent over, placing his rocks just so. Bunny said he didn't need music when he heard the noise of that water and the birds in the trees. With the little money we had he bought suet cakes and hung them in wire cages in the trees to attract songbirds. I was happy for a while. Didn't have to fear getting knocked around. But Bunny didn't have much drive. The only time I ever saw him work was when he fooled around with that waterfall. When he found a rock he liked and placed it just so on the stack of rocks he already made." Old Harriet stopped for a moment and raised a finger to make her point. "Bunny was the one who introduced me to H. Before long I was addicted. We shared needles because Bunny said we were like husband and wife. I was cute back then. Younger"

"I'm sure you were," Persimmon said. "And you still are."

Old Harriet took on a sour expression. She sniffed, cleared her throat, moved her empty paper plate, and licked-clean fork to the nightstand. "We didn't have a radio. No electricity. Saw a newspaper once in a blue moon. We only knew what other people in the commune told us. They only knew what other folks told *them*. It was called *word on the street*, even though we didn't live on no street. Everybody was happy. Everybody was a user, but what was nice was nobody got knocked around. One day everybody said there was a storm brewing. That was the word on the street. Bunny and the other men made sure all the tarps were secure. I stand corrected. That was the second time I saw Bunny work. We could see water in the stream had risen. We settled under our tarps waiting for the rain that was coming. Some people hunkered down together. The wind picked up and flapped the tents so that you couldn't hear the water anymore. The birds took flight to who knows where. Nobody knew it was a hurricane coming. Bunny got agitated. He didn't like stress. Couldn't stand the wind. He shot up. OD'd. We didn't have Narcan back then. There was nothing I could do except try to bring him out of it. The hurricane tore through our camp. The tarps came undone and sailed away in that awful wind. Like kites they were. The stream overflowed its banks. Destroyed Bunny's waterfall. There was a flash flood. I found out later it was predicted, but we didn't know it was coming. It carried the camp and us away. Bunny floated away in the muddy water, torrents of it, along with some of the other folks, and I couldn't hold on to him. A few of us who could swim made it to the new shore, which was much removed from the original bank. We climbed out, dazed, and went our separate ways. I never knew what happened to Bunny and the rest of them—who lived and who was swept away."

"I'm sorry, Old Harriet," Persimmon said. She took Harriet's hand.

Old Harriet sniffed again. "It was a long time ago. I lost everything I owned, which wasn't much, and could fit in a few shopping bags. Except one thing." She paused a few seconds. "I didn't lose my addiction. I went back to the streets and lived that way until I got involved with fighting vampires. Best thing that ever happened to me. Imagine a vampire being a good thing."

"I'm glad you're with us," Persimmon said.

Old Harriet placed her free hand on Persimmon's. "I was happy back then, all those years ago on the stream bank, under the flapping tarps and next to the gurgling stream and the little waterfall. Swatting mosquitos all the time." She looked at Persimmon. "Now I realize I'm happy again."

CHAPTER TWENTY-FIVE

Bo spent the night sprawled on a balcony theater seat with his legs stretched out in front. He chewed on a thumbnail, a habit from his life as a human. While Kazmer dozed blissfully nearby in a seemingly dreamless sleep, Bo pondered his own future. How could he adapt to this new world? In truth, the world had not changed that much in the last few weeks, but Bo had. Reluctantly, he had given up what was left of his family, forsaken school, his friends, even his beloved Dodge Charger with the Hemi under the hood, which now sat in his father's driveway, covered to keep off the elements.

He had gone off the grid with a crazy European murderer who catered to his every whim for the vague promise Bo would someday turn him into a vampire. A man who had left a trail of murders across the globe, a man who considered killing a human no more than squashing an insect. Bo would have preferred to lie in peace near his mother and brother in that quiet corner of the cemetery. That was where he belonged. Rotting in a grave. Tree roots would invade his casket, attach to his corpse in great spidery bunches and consume his flesh. Insects would gnaw on his bones while they crumbled. As the years passed, there would be nothing left of him, after the skull and femurs decomposed. They were usually the last bones to be returned to the earth.

It was difficult to concentrate on the future. The back of his throat and the back of his mind were consumed by the vampire disease's demand for blood. There was no avoiding it. Bo needed to feed. His other desire was to have sex with the girl he found out west at the deserted motel. If only he had more time with her. He remembered the smells of her skin and hair. The delightful feel of her warm body when he carried her through the dark motel. If they had had sex, Bo thought she would have enjoyed it enough to stay with him instead of fleeing. Kazmer claimed it was too soon for him to take a pet, the way Eva the vampiress had taken him. Kazmer said some vampires took several partners over time who they some-times shared with other vampires. Bo found the idea of multiple sex partners intoxicating.

However, he would have to have his first tryst before he thought about multiple partners. The smile on his pallid lips faded. His anemic face drooped. Bo's thoughts were consumed by blood. The vampire disease forced on him visions of blood, rich, oxygenated blood, torrents of it. Blood fell in waterfalls before his eyes, sluiced and boiled in a great river that extended for miles in both directions as he stood on a riverbank. He smelled the rich, iron aroma. His mouth grew slack. He drooled. All he had to do was kneel and lap up the river. He imagined the hot elixir coursing down his throat instead of the slash through the earth. The taste would slake his heated throat. Stop the pounding in his head. He could divert the entire river through his mouth. It would never fill him. With his thirst for blood quenched, Bo could return to thoughts of the young woman, but he realized that even as he consumed the entire river of blood, sucked the gouts and pools from the banks and riverbed, the thirst would return. It would never be satiated.

Bo moaned.

Hours of darkness remained until dawn. Bo blurred from the theater. He stopped long enough to force open the emergency exit door and close it after him. He arrived at the Thaxton Memorial Hospital four blocks away in a second. The thirst for blood consumed him. He stopped outside the hospital near an ambulance that had just unloaded a patient. The EMTs were busy resupplying the bandages, gauze, bloodlines, nasal cannula, syringes, and bags of plasma they used.

"Five bucks says he makes it," one EMT said.

"I'll take that," the second EMT said. "I hope he does, but there's no way he survives a gunshot like that." The man counted through a drawer of items that slid into the side of the ambulance bay. "Who'd want to be a vegetable? He's a goner."

Bo stood outside the ambulance's open back doors. *The guy is dying. He's in pain. On his way to being a vegetable. I could help him on his way. Eliminate that pain. Not to think of the suffering his family will go through caring for a vegetable. The family would thank me. The victim would thank me. And I would feed.*

Bo raced through the emergency room doors before they slid closed. He would be on camera. He tried not to look at the ceiling and give the camera a better view of his face. He kept his hooded face turned toward the floor. Looked through the tops of his eyes. The waiting room had a smattering of people scattered around slumped in chairs, some leaning on palms. They appeared to be tired of waiting for their turn, their chance to see a doctor.

A heavy-set nurse came through double doors to the left, scanned a clipboard, and called, "Jackson? Henry Jackson?"

A lean black man stirred at the end of a sofa. "Henry?" The nurse nodded her head, looked at the clipboard again, and scrutinized the man as he struggled to stand. "Henry?" she asked again, still nodding her head.

"I will be when I wake up," the man said in a soft voice. The nurse came forward and offered an arm for support.

"Ah, hah, we caught you napping," the nurse said, smiling.

"Been here a while," the man said.

"I'm sorry, Henry." She started to guide him toward the doors she had just come through. "We had two emergencies. Another one just rolled in. You're going to see a PA instead of a doctor."

"At least I'm seeing somebody."

In the distance through the doors' small windows, Bo saw a gurney rolling down the hall. Even at this distance, he smelled a trail of blood in the air. His lower jaw quivered. His fangs pressed through the gums. The back of his throat was on fire.

The old man's knee buckled. He started to go down. The nurse caught him with her free hand. He grabbed her other arm. The clipboard clattered to the floor. During the instant all eyes in the waiting room turned to the chunky nurse and slight black man executing a pirouette, one of them by accident kicking the clipboard away, Bo blurred through the doors unnoticed and caught up to a female paramedic and male nurse propelling the gurney down the hall as fast as they could walk. The two showed surprise at Bo's sudden appearance at the gurney's side. Bo looked at the man on the gurney. A kid, really.

"Gunshot?" Bo asked.

"Who are you?" The paramedic demanded.

"You shouldn't be in here," the male nurse said. "You'll have to go back to the waiting room."

Bo stared at the paramedic, then the nurse. They returned his gaze and slowed the gurney until it stopped. They stood silently as if waiting for instructions. Bo's mouth quivered again. The paramedic had her period. The odor of her blood, mixed in the air with that of the kid on the gurney, was intoxicating. Bo looked at the injured kid. He was unconscious, lying on his back, supplied with oxygen, a breather covering his nose and mouth, and lines of plasma and saline punctured his already riddled body. His torso was patched up in blood-soaked bandages and wrapped in gauze like an Egyptian mummy.

Bo looked at the male nurse. "Where do you keep the blood?"

"The lab," the tall man said, as if in a dream. He pointed down an intersecting hall.

About halfway down Bo saw a sign that stuck out from the wall above a door. LABORATORY. The female paramedic followed the nurse's finger as if in a trance. Bo walked toward the lab. The nurse and paramedic shook off their lethargy and continued pushing the gurney toward an examining room. Bo stopped outside the lab and pressed his palm against the door. His claws were extended. The thirst in his throat roared like a blast furnace. He imagined he could breathe fire like a dragon. He closed his eyes for a moment. *I must control this urge, or I'll slaughter everyone in this hospital.* He took hold of the door handle, opened it, and pushed. The door glided open silently. He stepped inside and let the door swing closed. A man and woman sat in recliner-like chairs donating blood.

The woman perked up immediately and smiled. "I'm donating for my sister. She has an operation scheduled for tomorrow. They don't think she'll need it. This is a precaution."

Bo nodded. Smiled. The woman's voice roused the man. He looked at Bo. Nodded. "Me too. Just for shits and giggles in case my sister-in-law needs some vino in her veins." He jerked his thumb toward the woman in the other chair. "Her sister. Say, you look like you could use a bag of blood yourself. Never saw anybody so pale. They got a freezer of frozen stuff in that locker." He jerked his thumb at a dark door labeled FREEZER.

"You alone?"

"The attendant—" the man started.

"Technician," the woman added, smiling.

"Went to the can, I think," the man continued. "Should be back any minute."

Bo smiled. Checked the freezer. A fine mist flowed out when he tugged open the door. Bo pulled out two frozen pints of blood in thick plastic bags. He laid them on the counter. Bo took hold of the woman's bag of donated blood and massaged the nearly full container between his hands.

"You a doctor?" the woman asked.

Bo tore the bloodline between the bag and the woman's arm and tied off the line on both ends.

"What's going on here," the man barked as Bo reached for his bag, cut the line, and tied off both ends in a second.

"Emergency!" Bo said. "Hold down the fort for me."

The astonished couple looked on as Bo gathered up the blood—warm and frozen—and stuffed them inside his hoodie. He blurred from the room and down the hall. He was through the waiting room before the double doors banged off the walls as he went through, giving everyone a start inside the cavernous area. The exterior sliding door was already open, just beginning to close, when Bo blurred into the night. He didn't go far. He settled into the corner of a building obscured by bushes. Before he settled on the newly spread mulch, Bo sucked greedily at one of the bags of warm blood. He drank the second pint just as fast. He stretched out his legs. Let his back and head find the bricks behind him. There was nothing like the taste of warm, human blood. For the moment he was satisfied.

CHAPTER TWENTY-SIX

Members of the Brethren sat or stood with a copy of the Thaxton Chronicle spread on a bed in Persimmon's room at the La Di Da Motel. This bed had become the spot where all important decisions were made since the group arrived in Thaxton. Some Brethren faced the newspaper so it appeared upside down to them. Persimmon tapped an index finger on a front-page story they all had read. They scratched their heads, pulled their chins, wrinkled their brows, or scratched their cheeks, but there was no mystery.

Persimmon stood, scanned the faces around her. "It looks like our Bo is hungry." Grunts and head nods agreed with her. "Typical dumb newbie vamp antics. He can't control the disease that rages through him."

There were a few chuckles among the group. The newspaper account told the story of a young man who entered Thaxton Hospital emergency room and stole four pints of blood—to fresh pints as they were being donated—and two frozen points from storage. Then he fled from the hospital on foot. The story hinted at cult and gang activity, but Police Chief Warren Meyer discounted both claims. He thought it was a prank.

Across the newspaper's front page, just under the banner, were three photos of Bo, caught on closed-circuit cameras, with him entering the hospital's ER waiting room, walking down the hall to the examination bays, which was off limits to the public, and leaving the hospital looking considerably heavier than when he entered. A hood obscured most of Bo's face. The CC photos' grainy appearance did not help matters. All that was visible in all the photos was a whisp of light-colored hair that stuck out over his fore-head. The story further said a glitch in the camera recording made it appear the thief disappeared for brief periods while he moved inside the hospital. In addition, witnesses who encountered the man could not recall details of his face, only that he was pale and rather handsome. Photos of the husband and wife donating blood during the robbery were buried on the jump page with the rest of the story.

"Well, we know Bo can blur," Persimmon said. "That's expected and would account for the so-called video glitches. The reason he disappeared from the camera—"

"Was because he disappeared from the camera," the group answered in unison. Persimmon smiled. The Brethren sniggered.

"I wonder if Bo can mez yet," Persimmon said, becoming serious again, raising an eyebrow to Overboard George.

"I say he can mesmerize the general public," Overboard George said. "You Know Who's blood turned him into a vampire."

"That ancient bitch," Old Harriet snarled. "I got a special edge on my machete to whittle her to the bone."

"With Eva's blood in his veins, I'll bet Bo is well ahead on the vampire learning curve," Overboard George said. "We can't take him for granted. Not for a second."

"That's right," Persimmon said. She looked around at the faces in the group. "If you encounter Bo, be cautious. Call for backup before you make a move. Don't try to stake him alone. He's not your typical newbie undead. If he spots you, walk away, as if you didn't see him."

"Be nonchalant," Old Harriet said, with a wag of her head. "That's the way I play it."

"And what if we spot Eva?" Persimmon said.

Old Harriet stepped forward. "Same deal. Nonchalant. And call me." Old Harriet raised her new cell phone toward the group. "I'm open for business."

Everyone smiled at the old woman.

"One more thing," Persimmon said. "We must get somebody in that ER today and nose around. See what happened that wasn't in the newspaper."

"Nonchalant," Old Harriet piped up.

"Got you covered," Goldenrod said. She shouldered through the Brethren, pulled a knife from her pocket, opened it, and sliced the outside of her left thumb near the knuckle. She covered the wound immediately with a cloth. "Three stitches. Maybe four. Easy-peasy. No washing dishes for a while." She looked from face to face while she wiped blood from the blade. "So, who's driving me to the ER?"

John Bargain was out the door with Goldenrod. He drove his car with Gold next to him and Old Harriet in the back. "Will you still be able to hold hands?" Old Harriet wanted to know with a grin.

Gold turned to face Old Harriet. "I don't plan on *this* slowing me down," Gold said. "It's just a nick. I'm due for a tetanus shot anyway."

"Don't know if I ever had a tetanus shot," Old Harriet mused, and returned her gaze to the city passing by. "Had a mean cat once. The damn thing bit me. It was a comfort, though, when it wasn't so wild. When we were both lonely." Old Harriet was quiet for a moment but then perked up. "Look at that! A Roxy theater. We had a Roxy in my hometown when I was a kid. I spent many an hour there watching sci-fi movies and eating chocolate bars."

Bargain stopped the car. Looked at the old theater and its crumbling marquis. "That might make a great vlog. Wonder if we can get inside." Horns honked behind him, and Bargain pulled away. It was mid-morning when they reached Thaxton Hospital. A few patients were already signed in and sat in the waiting room, holding painful body parts. Most were accompanied by solicitous friends. After Gold checked in, showed the nurse at the desk the bloody rag around her thumb, and explained the *whoops* that caused her injury, she joined Bargain and Old Harriet in an odd corner of the waiting room. Old Harriet soon drifted outside and headed for another door up the sidewalk marked Admissions. Old Harriet went inside and followed a sign for the Waiting Areas. She stood at the back of the carpeted room with its comfortable-looking furniture. About half the seats were filled. Sitting as close to the reception desk as possible, the couple from the newspaper article sat side by side. Old Harriet watched them for a moment then meandered up and down a few rows of seats before sitting next to the woman.

"I hope it's nothing serious," Old Harriet said, leaning toward the couple.

"We're waiting. My sister has..." the woman looked at her watch, "should be in surgery now." She returned Old Harriet's smile.

Old Harriet wasted no time. "Were you in the newspaper this morning?"

"Sure was," the man said. The woman nodded.

Old Harriet leaned closer. "So, what happened? He stole the blood right out of your veins?"

"Just about," the woman said.

"Not exactly," the man countered. "I knew that creep was trouble as soon as he came in, wearing one of those hood sweaters with the hood up. Especially when it's so warm."

The couple started talking at the same time. Old Harriet couldn't understand either.

"Wait! Wait! Wait!" Old Harriet said. "One at a time!"

The couple shot each other a hard glance. The man relaxed and sat back in his chair. The woman leaned closer to Old Harriet.

"What terrible pictures that newspaper photographer took. I looked a mess."

"They do it on purpose," Old Harriet said. She put a palm on the woman's forearm and smiled. "Tell me what happened."

The woman looked around furtively and began her story. They were at the hospital to donate blood that would be used in the event her sister needed a transfusion. If the blood was not needed, it would be returned to the blood bank to help other patients. The technician left the room. "My guess was he had to use the can," the man offered. "Then the thief entered. Like it was timed."

"He had a wild look in his eye, especially when he saw the blood," the woman said. "He said one word—Emergency! That was it, but that one word sounded..."

"Hollow," the man finished. "Like he talked from inside a barrel. I told him there was frozen blood, too, never thinking he'd take our blood, but he moved so fast it was hard to imagine what he did at that moment. He cut the bloodlines, tied both sides off, and picked up the bags. He already took blood from the freezer before I got the words out. I pulled out my phone to get a picture of him, but when I raised the phone, he was already gone. I got a photo of the empty room." The man paused a moment. Stared at Old Harriet. "Let me tell you something. I'm no dunce with a camera." He clicked his tongue in his mouth.

Old Harriet pulled a folded photocopy from her tiny purse. Unfolded the paper. Showed it to the couple.

"That's him," the two voices chimed.

"You know him?" the woman added.

The man reached for the photocopy, but Old Harriet snatched it away, folded it neatly, and returned it to her purse. "I know him," Old Harriet said. "He's trouble. Stay away from him." Old Harriet stood, bowing slightly. "Thank you for the help. I hope your sister has a quick recovery." She returned to the back of the room and exited the door she had entered.

CHAPTER TWENTY-SEVEN

Bo blurred back to The Roxy, twelve blocks, in a matter of seconds. His vampire powers grew almost daily. He was no longer awkward blurring as he was on the night he emerged from the earthen bank and collided with a car. That female driver was his first victim. His powers of reasoning had increased. He was able to control people in the hospital with his mind. He wondered whether they remembered their encounters with him.

He slowed to human speed within a half block of The Roxy. He walked the remaining distance cautiously, ever vigil, pried open the theater's emergency exit door, entered the building, and paused to listen a moment. He stuck his head outside to listen again, saw the first rays of sunlight cresting the horizon, splintered through tree branches in the distance. Bo ducked inside and secured the door.

He returned to the balcony, where Kazmer was still asleep. Empty cups, hamburger wrappers, flattened ketchup packs, and a few squashed french fries lay near him. His face showed the contentment of a full belly. Bo cradled the frozen bags of blood as if they were premature twins. By night they would thaw and provide him with a meal. Bo spread out his sleeping bag in his usual place on the balcony floor and crawled inside with the frozen blood. He pulled up the zipper to cover his face. Before he slept, he had an idea that made him smile—like an old west stagecoach robber, he would drain the local blood supply before moving to new territory.

Unlike humans who could have troubled sleep, vampires didn't dream. They fell into a near-paralyzing coma during daylight hours, instinctively rising as the sun's last rays slipped below the horizon. However, vampires could be roused from their comatose condition during daylight hours and move around inside out of direct sunlight. Whereas humans could dwell on any number of problems that interrupted their sleep, vampires entered a thoughtless void where they remained until sundown, when they woke, neither refreshed nor troubled. Vampires only sensed their desperate need for blood.

As evening arrived, Bo unzipped the sleeping bag. He turned to see Kazmer in his usual seat, a new pile of trash at his feet. The hamburger wrappers were replaced by cardboard boxes that contained roast beef sandwiches. Empty french fry bags, ketchup, salt packs, and crumpled napkins were strewn about.

Kazmer grunted. "It is night already? Mr. Bo, you are my trusty alarm clock." The big man grinned. He licked the remnants of his meal from his fingers.

"Kaz, it looks like you're eating well."

Kazmer pulled the last licked finger from his mouth with a resounding pop. "I didn't know your town had a roast beef restaurant. I found it today. Very good."

"It must be a new spot. It wasn't here when I was in high school."

"No gristle. Meat was very tender. The girl at the drive-thru gave me extra ketchup and napkins, just like I ordered. I gave her a nice tip. She was surprised."

"Did you ask her out?"

Kazmer shook his head. Looked at the floor. "No time for girls. This one was too young."

Bo grinned at his friend. "You will have time, Kaz. Eventually."

Kazmer picked up his trash, squeezed it to a minimum size with his powerful hands, and shoved everything into the largest takeout bag. He patted his stomach and smiled.

"Take a seat, Kaz. I have a plan."

Bo produced the frozen blood bags from his sleeping bag and offered them to Kazmer, who took them reluctantly, placed one under his arm, and moved the other back and forth between his hands to give each a moment of warmth. Kazmer set down the bags on a theater seat. Rubbed his hands vigorously. Then the big man sat down. Meanwhile, Bo started his tale of the hospital visit, the snatch of four bags of blood—two fresh and two frozen. Bo said he planned to hit the hospital again, as well as mobile blood drives across the city. Fresh blood would be consumed immediately. Frozen pints when they thawed. If a scene got hot, they would move somewhere else.

Bo and Kazmer realized a nomadic lifestyle was part of being undead. It would be possible for Bo to blur in and out of hospitals and blood drives virtually unnoticed, certainly unrecognized, fill his hoodie with blood bags, and disappear. Perhaps he would devise a special bag to carry or garment to wear, perhaps insulated, to transport the purloined pints. Bo grew excited and animated, throwing his arms about as new ideas formed. From his seat, Kazmer pursed his lips, grunted, or nodded as the story was unveiled. Finally, Bo finished and dropped into a seat near Kazmer.

"What do I think?" Kazmer said. His head dropped toward his shoulder and straightened. "I never heard such a plan from a vampire." He raised his forearm and extended an index finger. "Most vampires want to kill their prey."

"That's out of the question, Kaz. I don't care what most vampires want. I don't even *want* to be a vampire. You know how I feel about murdering humans."

Kazmer continued. "Most vampires like the chase. The hunt. That is what I know from my..." he thought a moment, looked toward the ceiling, and pronounced the word slowly, "ass...o... citation with vampires through the years. I believe the vampire disease is somehow satisfied with the kill, the release of certain chemicals associated with the death. Chemicals are released in the blood of the victim when bitten. The disease—"

"Fuck the disease!" Bo slammed his fist down on the theater seat armrest. It splintered under the force and raised dust into the air. "How can I control this disease if I follow its every whim? I want to be its master!"

"It was just a thought, Mr. Bo," Kazmer said, sounding contrite. "If the disease is satisfied, it might not make you so thirsty. But I wouldn't know."

Bo stood, blurred around the theater several times until the threadbare stage curtains swayed and released a shower of dust on the old stage. He returned to his seat and stared at Kazmer. "Well?"

Kazmer scratched his temple. Took the audacity to look Bo in the eye, which was generally forbidden in vampire/Shadow relations. Kazmer parted his lips, hiccupped after his fatty meal, and looked quickly at the floor. "I think your plan might have...what is the word?"

"Merit."

"Yes. Merit," Kazmer said, pointing a greasy finger at Bo, returning his gaze back to the vampire. "It might work. If police get suspicious after a time, we can move to another city. Eventually come back, maybe, when the blood supply is up. Carrying sleeping bags is easier than moving caskets. I will not have to bury bodies."

"It will be easier on you, Kaz. I'm thinking of you, too."

"I hope so. Let's—as they say—give it a whirl."

CHPATER TWENTY-EIGHT

Eva, the ancient vampire, who was born in the Middle Ages as a minor nobility and turned to vampirism at the age of twenty, dug toward the surface through the remains of the vampire colony Del Hatch had destroyed with explosives. She had remained underground for unknown days in fear the Brethren waited to stake her on the surface. Through the millennia she learned to control the vampire disease and its raging thirst. That control allowed her to suppress the disease and extend her heightened senses to protect herself. The disease could put her in danger, risk being extinguished, to slake its thirst.

Even underground she could hear bugs, worms, and vermin scratching their way through the loose dirt. The explosion collapsed the vampire's main vault, caused a landslide on the hillside, and resulted in the collapse of the old house the undead used as part of their base. Eva moved slowly, cautiously, not wanting to produce a sudden sinkhole on the surface that might alert any nearby Brethren. She wormed her way through the soil to within a foot of the surface. There she waited for sundown. She slept for part of the day, waking shortly after nightfall. She began to inch toward the surface.

Eva listened intently and smelled the night air on the exterior. Satisfied no humans were present, she emerged on the bank about halfway between the top and the cemetery below. Charred remnants of the old house lay scattered along the hillside. Excavating equipment sat in the cemetery, waiting to clear the mausoleum and graves covered by the avalanche.

Eva still wore the tight jeans, western shirt, and cowboy boots she wore the night Bo was shot at the mall. His dried blood, smeared with dirt, still covered the shirt and jeans. She brushed dirt from her clothes and hair. Then she sat on the dirt, removed her boots, and shook out more dirt. Hiding underground was nothing new to Eva, digging like a mole in the early hours of the day to avoid sunlight, peasants with their crosses and pitchforks, and even soldiers when they were not battling one another among the small countries that dotted Europe's landscape during the Dark Ages. She and her brother Gerrard often found it necessary to dig underground to avoid the ever-present vampire hunters emboldened by daylight. Even then the Brethren were organized and a formidable foe.

With moonlight, starlight, and her incredible eyesight, Eva examined Bo's blood on her sleeve. Raised her arm to sniff. The sweet smell of virgin blood still lingered. She dropped the arm into her lap. *My little rabbit. Did you survive the Brethren attack? Did Kazmer survive with you? Are you walking this world with powers you cannot fathom? By now you are no longer a virgin. Your blood would have no more allure to me as it once did. Still, I miss you, little rabbit. I even miss the nonsense human boys think of when I plumbed your thoughts with my mind. Do you hate me for turning you when you pleaded to die? Or, when we meet will you embrace me and thank me for opening a universe you could not have imagined as a human?*

Eva used her vampire mind's power to call Bo over the distance that separated them. She waited for an answer as if she had just tapped out a distress call on a radio, but there was no acknowledgment as there would have been when Bo was human. She commanded Bo and he obeyed. He would undress and crawl into her casket, unwilling but ready to pleasure the vampiress. A mere thought from Eva would make Bo offer an arm, a shoulder, a leg to be bitten and his sweet blood sucked. Never enough to cause death. Just enough to keep him too weak to attempt an escape. To keep his mind malleable. A mental order from miles away would cause Bo to get in his car and drive to her location. Was Bo dead? Killed in the explosion that obliterated the vampire colony, or had he escaped? Was he already too far removed for her to make a connection? Or had he already developed the power to block her call?

If Bo had died in the explosion, his corpse would have been rotting if he had not yet turned at the time of his death, and she could detect the gases released. Eva walked back and forth across the bank, top to bottom, testing the air with her acute sense of smell. She abandoned caution and the possibility the Brethren might be watching to determine Bo's outcome. She was relieved she could not detect Bo still in the ground when she finally reached the cemetery floor. There was time to think about Bo later. She had to feed first.

Eva blurred to a rundown section of the city. There were rows of abandoned buildings on both sides of the street, a tent city, and sidewalks lined with boxes and shelters made from vinyl tarps and plywood scraps. The streets smelled of garbage and human excrement. The gutters were clogged with trash. Unable to reach storm drains, water with swirling oil stood in pools after a recent rain. Nothing new to Eva who had lived through the Middle Ages.

She could have pulled any junkie from his or her box or tent and drained the man or woman on the sidewalk. Even though such an action might go unnoticed, she knew she had to be more discreet. The Brethren would be on notice for murders that involved puncture wounds and the unexplained loss of blood. She fought against the thirst that raged in her throat. She fit in among this streetscape. Dirty, disheveled, her skin slack from malnourishment. She appeared no different from any street junkie. Although she was considered tall in her human years, now she was about medium height, thin. She walked along the street slowly, ever mindful of the surroundings.

She feared only the Brethren and their crossbows and stakes. Junkies who sat or lay on the sidewalk, reclined inside their shelters, stared at her. Some asked for money, drugs, or sex. She smiled in reply. Ahead a man weaved along the sidewalk. He had a pronounced limp and was bent at the waist.

The man walked beyond a break in the tents, climbed the steps of an abandoned building, and pushed open the door with difficulty. He turned to look out the door window. Eva paused on the sidewalk, looked up at him, and smiled. The man smiled back. Indicated with a jerk of his head that she should follow him. He moved away from the window.

This should be interesting, Eva thought. What was his plan? An attack. An offer of drugs and sex? Whatever the motive, the man would supply a meal. Although tainted with drugs, Eva imagined the man's hot blood coursing down her throat. The vampire disease raged inside her. She climbed the exterior steps and pushed open the door that had proved difficult for the man. She closed the door behind her. He had gone from the vestibule with its ornate floor tile that extended halfway up the walls and climbed the stairs to the upper floors. She heard his slow, measured steps in the stairwell. Eva followed the sound.

He reached the second floor, paused a moment, and continued down the hall. His shoes crunched on fallen plaster and kicked an occasional wooden lath. He paused again before climbing to the next flight. Eva shook the handrail at the bottom. She wanted the junkie to know she followed him. He continued up the steps, slower now. Eva wondered whether he was tired or wanted her to catch up. She quickened her pace. He had reached the third floor, walked toward the back of the building, and pushed open a door with creaky hinges. The thirst in her throat raged. She could take it no longer. She blurred up the remaining steps, down the hall, and embraced the man. He had already laid out his drugs, his spoon, and his lighter below the room's window.

"Ow!" the man complained. "You like it rough."

Eva sank her fangs into his neck. Ages of practice allowed the teeth to find the large vein and puncture it precisely. Eva tightened her grip, paralyzing the man with its ferocity. The vampiress's eyes glazed over. She sucked the warm blood. Its taste cascaded down her throat and cooled her thirst. She paced herself with long mouthfuls. Her lips tasted the sweaty, dirty skin on the man's neck. She sensed the junkie's terror. His inability to move. Enjoyed the movement of his flailing arms. His eventual surrender. Eva was intoxicated. She sucked until no more blood was available. The veins collapsed. She released the suction on his neck with a pop. Eva moaned with pleasure. The junkie's jaw was slack. His eyes stared. His face showed a look of contentment as if he were at peace. The vampiress ran her fingers through his greasy hair, let his body slide down her arm, and seated him in front of the window. The contents of his drug kit lay in a neat row at his side.

With the pleasurable feeling of a heavy meal, Eva paused to scan the room with its dusty floor, peeling paint and wallpaper, and stained ceiling. A sag above indicated loose plaster that was ready to fall. Eva dug her claws into the bulge and pulled down a section of the ceiling. Plaster and lath clattered to the floor. Dust filled the air. Eva stood for a moment under the hole in the ceiling and then propelled herself into the crawlspace above, barely large enough for her to crouch in. She landed cat-like on the ceiling joists. Her sudden movement raised more ancient dust. The buildings were constructed with no firewalls, which would allow her to move among the buildings if an escape were necessary.

Satisfied with this escape route, Eva returned to the room with the body and inspected a closet. It was small, but sufficient for her to sit in a corner and rest during the day. She pulled the closet door closed. The newly ingested blood had already turned her slack skin back to its youthful firmness and beauty. The junkie's body might go unnoticed for a week.

Her lips parted and she spoke, "Bo. Where are you?"

CHAPTER TWENTY-NINE

OVER THE NEXT WEEK, BO BLURRED, SAUNTERED, CAJOLED, and intimidated his way through Thaxton and surrounding hospitals and blood drives. He and Kazmer scanned the newspaper for blood drive announcements, whether they were in a traveling Red Cross Bloodmobile, a school gymnasium, or a church social hall. Sometimes Kazmer waited down the street or around the corner from the target, making and smoking his rank cigarettes one after another. Occasionally, Bo ventured out at night alone, when the target was close and blurred back to The Roxy with his liquid loot. The thieves had a special cooler and ice to keep the blood cool. Soon spent blood bags formed a growing pile on the theater's balcony. Each sealed bag had two neat punctures.

Bo found the nocturnal forays exhilarating, testing his ever-growing vampire powers. It was like hunting prey. He and Kazmer selected a likely target, gleaned from newspaper columns and advertisements or even public service announcements heard on the transistor radio Kazmer bought and played at low volume day and night. Kazmer liked to have extra batteries handy. A second target was chosen, in the event Bo found the primary target too crowded when he arrived.

There was the evening a blood drive at his former high school attracted Bo. A high school service club was the sponsor. The gymnasium was the location where sign-in tables, cots, chairs, and a table with plates of cookies and a tray of orange juice in cups were arranged under a backboard. A steady line of donors threaded from the entrance to the hardwood floor when Bo arrived. He blurred to the top row of bleachers and hid behind a banner.

Among those willing to offer an arm to be tapped were teachers and classmates he knew. Bo imagined a high school reunion would be in the planning stages by now. A reunion he would not attend. As he watched the traffic in, the registrations, the donors lying on cots, and the tapped leaving after helping themselves to energy-restoring cookies and juice, Bo decided to wait an hour until closing to make his move. The number of donors and volunteers would diminish. Bo blurred along the top row and down the bleachers against the far wall. He executed a handstand on the railing, some-thing he never could have accomplished as a human, and swung into the locker room's doorway. He executed this move so fast that no human eyes detected it. His passing did, however, rustle pennants on the wall and release their dust into the air.

Out of sight from the blood drive, Bo walked down the steps to the locker room. Inside it was dark. The air was heavy and smelled of disinfectants and a multitude of shampoos and soaps. One of the shower heads dripped a steady beat. A teacher's office and locked closet for sports equipment were at one end of the locker room; steps to the gymnasium floor were at the other. Nothing had changed. Benches and hooks for clothes sat across from the show-ers. Sneakers, towels, gym shorts, and socks lay scattered on the floor and benches or were draped over the clothes hooks.

Bo peered into the office—the door was locked—and noted the messy desk with papers, logbooks, whistles, baseballs, and various sports gewgaws. A stack of baseball bats leaned against one corner.

A bag full of soccer balls stood in another. He wondered whether some of the junk remained from when he went to high school some four years earlier.

Bo crossed the locker room and exited via the steps to the high school's main floor with its offices, classrooms, and auditorium entrance. A few low lights were scattered along the hall's length. Bo blurred up the steps to the school's top floor, halfway down the hall, and stopped suddenly at a locker built into the wall with others. It was his locker, 3-357, from senior year. He pressed his palm on the cool metal. Wondered who claimed the locker this year. He looked up and down the hall, and saw many similar lockers. Across the hall was his best friend Billy Holland's locker. They were in the same homeroom. How they conspired before class at Billy's locker. That's where their crew, Jimbo, Kenny, and Phil, met to talk about girls and make weekend plans. Bo couldn't help smiling. Billy went to state to major in English, Kenny joined the Marines, and Phil the Air Force. Even as a human, he had lost touch with them.

Jimbo was killed in a car accident a week after high school graduation. Bo remembered the funeral, closed casket, and hot temperature. His hands sweat so much he feared he would lose his grip on the casket handle. He and his buddies, the pallbearers, traded nervous glances as they hauled Jimbo's casket from the hearse, across the cemetery among the gravestones, and through the green grass. He worried their grips might be slipping, too. Worst of all were the springy boards along the grave's length they had to traverse to place the casket on the shrouded device that would lower it into the concrete vault below. He hadn't expected that. It was like walking over a diving board. Before Jimbo's death, funerals with their stiff, unnatural corpses, and cemeteries freaked out Bo. He had been relieved the casket was closed. Social media said Jimbo was decapitated in the accident.

Bo returned downstairs. With the blood drive concluded, volunteers carried out blood bags in insulated coolers. They were placed in a van outside the gym entrance. Inside the school, they collected their paperwork, stripped the cots of sheets and pillow-cases for washing, folded cots and tables, gobbled the last cookies, and gulped down the juice. The blood left unattended in the van was easy picking. Bo collected an armful and blurred back to the Roxy.

Bo revisited the Thaxton Hospital twice, and cleared out the frozen blood supply while blurring. Meanwhile, hospital staff noted the blood loss. With their apparent malfunctions, the hospital's closed-circuit cameras near the laboratory were replaced. Then Bo hit two more blood drives, finding more easy picking with unat-tended blood donations while they were moved from inside to waiting vehicles. The plan was working. Bo remained well-fed. The vampire disease was held at bay. When blood drive officials alerted police there was a problem—someone was stealing blood—Bo and Kazmer would move to areas outside Thaxton. Bo had not found it necessary to kill.

One night, Bo lay on The Roxy Theater balcony floor. He had just drained a blood bag, sucked out as much as he could, even wrung out the bag with a twist to squeeze out every drop, and tossed it on the pile of other drained bags. Kazmer sat nearby with the transistor radio to his ear. Cigarette smoke curled around his head. The glimmer of a smile crossed his face. He enjoyed music. He inhaled one last time, stubbed out his cigarette, and crushed the few remaining shreds of tobacco and the rolling paper in his fingers. He balled up the paper his roast beef sandwich had been wrapped in, gathered the other packaging from his supper, stuffed it inside the takeout meal's largest bag, crushed it into a ball, and tossed it over the balcony.

"Hey, Kaz! Throwing stuff downstairs would get you thrown out of here when this place was running," Bo said.

Kazmer grunted. "Let them try."

Bo continued. "Then they closed the balcony. Wouldn't let anybody up here. They said it was unsafe, but everybody knew kids came up here to sit in the back row and smoke pot."

"I like my tobacco," Kazmer said. "It is strong. Has a good flavor."

"I hope it tastes better than it smells."

Kazmer grunted. Smiled. Raised the radio to his ear again.

"Kaz, I might go out."

Kazmer lowered his radio and turned to Bo. "Be careful."

"I won't be long. I want to check on my father. Maybe I will get a chance to see him through the window again. Who knows when we might have to move."

"That would be a shame. We have a good place to stay. We have a good plan to get blood. The roast beef restaurant is close. You have fed, and still there is blood here. I have never seen you look better." Kazmer smiled at Bo through the haze of his cigarette smoke.

"I feel good, Kaz. I've come to learn that a vampire doesn't feel much other than thirst. Still, it's the best I've felt in a long time. Hold down the fort while I'm gone."

Bo blurred away. He stopped to open and secure the theater emergency exit door on the alley beside the building. The last time he visited his home, Kazmer drove. Tonight, Bo blurred the distance. He was filled with blood and felt strong and confident. Bo slowed and approached his father's home cautiously. He wondered how many doorbell cameras recorded his movements. Bo approached the home and crept up the driveway next to the home. He scaled the fence, and slunk to the kitchen window where he had watched his father before, avoiding the motion sensors that turned on the backyard exterior lights. A small under-the-cabinet light shone inside the kitchen, offering a little illumination.

Bo's father was not in the kitchen. Other than the kitchen light, the entire house was in darkness. His father must have gone to bed early. Bo stood in the mulch, listening to the night noises. A dog barked in the distance. A roosting bird resituated itself in a nearby tree, hoping from one branch to another with a flurry of beating wings.

Bo looked through the kitchen window, letting his eyes fall on familiar items from his time at home. Despite the abundance of recent blood, Bo felt surprised something seemed missing from his existence as a recently turned vampire. *What is it? How did Eva survive through the centuries without such a sense of loss? How will I make it?* Bo pressed his nose to the glass. The double-hung window was open an inch on the bottom. *Mom was supposed to be the one who was bad at locking doors and windows. Maybe it was Dad all along.* Bo lowered his nose to the open space and sniffed. He smelled his father's scent and the old familiar home odors, all pleasant.

CHAPTER THIRTY

Jane Jennings stamped her foot. She stood across from Persimmon with a bed between them in Persimmon's room at the La De Da Motel. "You had to start somewhere. This is *my* somewhere. What about her?" Jane said pointing to Old Harriet.

"Old Harriet had some special knowledge," Persimmon said, just as defiant, "before she came to us. So did all the East Coasters."

Old Harriet watched the two women with a fixed gaze.

"*Famous Monsters of Filmland* magazine?" Jane barked. She threw up her hands as if in disbelief. "That's what they used as a guide?"

"You better believe it. I have an advanced degree at that," Old Harriet said with a smile, pointing her finger at Jane. "I know what I know when it comes to vampires. I fought them on the East Coast. Helped clean out a nest there. And I read Del Hatch's magazines cover to cover."

"And then it was more on-the-job-training on the West Coast," Persimmon said. "Old Harriet can wield a machete with the best of them."

"Damn right I can," Old Harriet added with a nod of her head.

"We followed the undead west. Mad Maggie and I killed the colony leader there."

"Then why can't I get some OJT?" Jane said. "If you don't want me, just say the word. You brought me halfway across the country with you, chasing a vampire, and now here I sit. The least you could do is give me some bus fare to the West Coast, or somewhere other than this god-forsaken town."

Persimmon blew the pesky hair strand from her forehead. She paused for a moment and then started. "We thought *you* might be able to attract Bo. Then *we* would corner him. That's why you're here."

"Bait?"

"Yes, because we believed he has a connection to you."

"A connection because Bo kidnapped me after he killed my friends?"

"That's how it works in the vampire world," Persimmon said, showing no emotion. "You were almost Bo's first real piece of ass. Almost. Even though he coupled with the vampiress countless times in the year she held him as a slave. He was a virgin. His blood tasted especially sweet to the vampire. It was intoxicating. That was his allure."

Persimmon approached Jane. "The vampiress is an animated corpse. In the vampire world, that sex didn't count, at least for Bo. He didn't remember it. He was sore the morning after, bitten, scratched, and bruised, but as far as he was concerned, he might have been hit by a train."

"Lucky for him," Jane said. She shivered and grimaced. "That's like real necrophilia."

"Indeed," Old Harriet added. "That's how the undead like it! The deader you are, the better they like it."

"But Bo won't forget you, Jane," Persimmon continued. She paused another moment to stare at the young woman, holding up her thumb and index finger pressed together. "You were this close to being his first. One that he would remember. Your scent should remain in his memory."

"Even though Bo is a newbie, I believe he can detect you, be able to follow a few molecules of your breath, your scent, on the wind. He was turned by a powerful vampiress hundreds of years old who would have all those powers at her disposal. He might have inherited some immediately through her blood he ingested, rather than taking lifetimes to learn them. We know a lot about vampires, their habits, their powers, but there are still things we don't understand."

"That's the way it is in the vampire world?" Jane asked, in a voice barely louder than a whisper.

Persimmon and Old Harriet nodded their heads.

"That's the reason we kept you cooped up," Persimmon said. "We wanted to fight Bo on our terms, not his. We didn't kidnap you. We wanted to protect you."

"He coulda sniffed you out, honey, and attacked when we weren't ready. You might have been defenseless," Old Harriet said. "This La De Da isn't exactly a stronghold. A mad mosquito could break in these rooms."

Jane looked at Persimmon, who nodded in agreement with Old Harriet.

"Then what must I do to get ready for Bo?" Jane said. "Teach me. I'll do whatever it takes to help kill that vampire. I won't feel safe until he's a pile of ashes. After he's done, I'll help you kill them all, wherever they are."

Persimmon shot an anxious glance at Old Harriet. After a thoughtful pause, Old Harriet looked over Jane, smiled, and nodded her head. "We can start with machete lessons. My room. Tomorrow morning. Be ready. This won't be no La De Da walk in the park."

After Jane returned to her room, Persimmon said to Old Harriet, "I hope this works out."

"I think she's already one of us," Old Harriet said with a wink.

THE NEXT MORNING Old Harriet and Mad Maggie began the machete lessons. Jane was surprisingly strong for a drug user. The first thing Persimmon said was that the Brethren did not tolerate drug use. Jane agreed. She said she had been scared sober. Jane was instructed how to hold the machete handle, lunge, strike, and disengage a deep thrust into the body so the blade did not get stuck. Jane learned quickly, and seemed to enjoy interacting with the women. By the end of the session, all three women were sweating.

After lunch, Overboard George brought in a stack of *Famous Monsters of Filmland* magazines with paperclipped pages about vampires and annotations he and Mad Maggie had added. They went through the magazine articles carefully. Persimmon followed along with the discussion, ensuring Jane the movies usually got it right when it came to vampires.

Jane became reflective when the magazine pages showed photos, along with stories, of a movie she had seen years ago. She cried and laughed when she recognized movies she had watched with her father when she was a child or ones that had given her nightmares. After dinner, the Brethren introduced Jane to the stake, how and where to strike, and how to impale and spin away from a lethal strike before the undead's body erupted in an all-consuming conflagration. The pirouette was designed to avoid the flames. Jane had taken dancing lessons as a girl and caught on quickly. She and Old Harriet joined arms and spun around the room at the end of the lesson, collapsing on the bed in hysterical laughter.

Tomorrow, the group would take a field trip, where Jane would learn to shoot a crossbow, the Brethren's preferred weapon for killing vampires. It was important to hit the undead with the first shot, Persimmon said. You rarely get a second one when faced with the vampire's speed and strength. You never wanted to take on a vamp alone. The most experienced Brethren, ones with many kills, would call that foolhardy. After the vampire was shot and slowed, the backups moved in to stake and chop at the body while the shooter reloaded. A second or third bolt from the crossbow, with stake thrusts and machete chops, might be necessary to finish the fiend. Even a new vampire like Bo would have incredible strength, and blazing speed, to fight or evade an attack. After the vampire knew he or she was a target, he would be difficult to find and might even become the aggressor.

Persimmon said even though Mad Maggie, Overboard George, and Old Harriet had known Bo as a human on the East Coast, and been friendly before he came under the vampiress's control, he would feel no affection toward them if they came face to face. They were enemies and would be slaughtered. Only Jane might survive, for a while, if Bo wanted to retain her as a sex kitten, a pet. He would rape her and drink her blood. In general, vampires held no tender thoughts, made no alliances, and provided no acts of kindness. The vampire's only compulsion was to survive.

Early the next morning, Persimmon, Overboard George, and Jane loaded a car and headed to the city, an empty lot between two abandoned buildings. Now the lot was a dump. They parked at the curb and unloaded the vehicle. The hood of an abandoned box truck parked against one wall served as a platform for their weapons. Overboard George drug an old sofa across the lot and stood it up against the opposite wall. That was their target.

"This takes me back a step," Overboard George said, as he returned to the group, brushing his palms together. He pointed toward the sofa. "There was a time not too long ago that I would have considered myself lucky to spend the night on that rat-bitten sofa."

Persimmon smiled. "Those days are over, OG. Just an old nightmare now."

Overboard George returned the smile. "Sometimes I think I'll find my life story when I open up an issue of *Famous Monsters of Filmland.*"

"Your story will be right next to mine," Jane said. Her eyes filled with tears.

They got busy with the crossbow training. It was still early for the homeless to move about on the street. The lot itself was too littered for tents to spring up. Persimmon and Overboard George took turns with the instruction. Jane held the weapon, and got accustomed to its weight and feel.

"You never, ever, want to turn this weapon toward something you don't want to hit, say, like me," Overboard George said. "You keep it lowered," OG demonstrated, "even when it's not loaded. It's good practice." Jane followed his instructions. "You never want to slice a finger by touching the bolt's tip or shoot yourself in the foot," Overboard George added. "It's been done by some pretty good shots."

Persimmon taught Jane how to shoulder the crossbow, aim, and fire. After Jane was sufficiently proficient with an empty crossbow, Persimmon loaded a bolt. Then they removed the bolt. Loaded and unloaded the crossbow repeatedly to accustom Jane to handling the weapon. Jane sweated.

"Don't worry," Overboard George said. "It'll come. Soon you'll handle a crossbow like you do a cell phone now. It'll be second nature."

Overboard George drew circles on sofa cushions with a magic marker. After he was safely behind the firing line, Jane shot. A bullseye. The group applauded. Jane grinned. She shot and reloaded time after time, producing a nice cluster of shots on the target.

When they finished shooting and had the vehicle packed, Overboard George was behind the wheel. He turned to Jane in the back seat. "Like it or not, you're one of us now."

CHAPTER THIRTY-ONE

Bo and Kazmer cruised the streets of Thaxton. It was an hour after sundown and the sky held a fading wan illumination. Kazmer always insisted on driving the van.

"It wouldn't hurt for me to drive once," Bo said. "I could command it, you know."

"I know," Kazmer said, shooting Bo a glance. A hand-rolled cigarette hung on his lip. Smoke curled around his head like a python, making him squint. "Do you have a license to drive, Mr. Bo?"

"I do, in fact. It was lost with my clothes on the East Coast. I had a car, too. It's parked in my dad's driveway."

"The car doesn't do you much good without a license. What if you are stopped by the police?"

"What if you are stopped by the police, Kaz. I've seen your license. It's a fake. John Wayne? Really? What cop would buy that?"

"It was my brother's idea. Lazlo liked John Wayne. This van is in another name."

"What name?"

"Moses Howard," Kazmer said proudly.

"The stooge? Now I've heard everything."

"Lazlo liked Moe, too."

"You should pull over and let me drive."

"Not a good idea," Kazmer said, squinting at Bo. "You had a fast car. I remember it. You might drive this van too fast. If you are pulled over, the police will find out you are a missing person, if you give them your real name."

"You are impersonating a dead man," Bo said. "A famous dead man at that."

Kazmer grunted. "What is better? To be missing or dead?"

"All right. Tell me this. What is your real name, Kaz?"

Kazmer was silent for a moment. He looked at Bo and back at the street in front of them. "It is Kazmer...Savoy."

"No, Kazmer. Your last name is not *Savoy*."

"It is the name my brother chose. When we came to this country we...found money. To be honest we stole money. We bought new clothes. We went to a restaurant called the Savoy Room. It was expensive. They treated us like kings. When we came out our bellies were never so full. Lazlo said we would take Savoy as our last name to remember what it was like to be kings."

"So, what is your real name?"

"We never knew our real name. We were orphans and moved around. Even with relatives, it was never nice. You, Bo, were the only one other than my brother Lazlo who showed me kindness when you made me a sling for my arm. I still have it." Kazmer smiled and looked at Bo.

"You like to drive?"

"Yes. Very much."

"Good. Then you can drive, Kaz. All the time."

They took a slow lap around the block to pass Bo's family home. The Charger was still parked in the driveway under a tarp. His father stood in front of the car, his hands on his hips, as if he expected the car to do something. If that car could talk. It had been dented by a mutated vampire, one of the so-called Whistlers that hunted for the vampiress and her brother Gerrard. Bo, as a human, had baled into the car just before the Whistler, hot on his heels, crashed into the passenger side door.

The car had been the wheels that transported Bo and his friends, TJ and Ridge, downtown from their frat house. As they drove past the Bentwood home, Bo's father turned his head and gave the white van a casual glance. It was too dark to see inside the vehicle. There had never been much traffic on the street. Perhaps that or the van's slow speed caught Mr. Bentwood's attention. As Bo watched, his father turned his attention back to the Charger. In a few seconds, the van moved up the street and turned at the corner. Bo and Kazmer remained silent.

Eventually, Bo said, "I should feed tonight. Want to swing by the hospital?"

"Again?" Kazmer had rolled a cigarette, steering with his knees, and lit it. He inhaled deeply, and released the smoke slowly through his nose. "Weren't we just there? Some night they will be waiting for you."

"And who would stop me, Kaz? The nurses? The doctors?"

Kazmer raised an eyebrow. "The Brethren might get a breeze of it. Missing blood in a news story will attract them to Thaxton if they are not already here. That's how they move, follow the strange news. News that might be made by a vampire. I watch the news, too, now that you have taught me better English. It might be time to move from Thaxton."

"Not yet, Kaz," Bo turned sideways in the seat to face Kazmer. "One more thing. You don't get a breeze of something; you get wind of something. There's a difference."

"Good to know," Kazmer grunted and pulled out. He drove toward the hospital.

"You don't have to like everything I do, Kaz."

"I don't like it when you take chances. It is my job to protect you."

They were silent again, the kind of silence that occurred when they reached an impasse. Although Bo could command anything and Kazmer would obey, Bo rarely forced his decision on the Shadow. They would fall into silence. Eventually, one would cave in. Usually, Kazmer would relent and do what he was told, or Bo would not enforce his edict. Kazmer would take the better option. They rounded a curve in the road when a van passed them going the opposite way.

"Turn around. Follow it, Kaz," Bo shouted. He spun his hands in circles to simulate what was necessary to make a U-turn. "It says Hematology Services.

Kazmer spun the steering wheel wildly. The van almost rolled. Kazmer straightened the vehicle, turned the steering wheel the opposite way, and pursued the van.

"What's hema?" Kazmer said.

"That means blood. You're a vampire Shadow and don't know what hematology is?"

Kazmer grunted. "That word is not in my English lessons."

"Force him off the road. That van might be loaded with blood."

Kazmer tramped on the gas and sped after the van. He swerved from side to side and came within inches of colliding with the van's rear bumper before backing off. He repeated the moves again and again. Kazmer forced the van down a side street where there was no traffic. The driver pulled to the side of the road, parked the van on a diagonal, and jumped from the vehicle. "What the hell is going on? This isn't a Brinks truck. I got no money!"

Kazmer pulled in front of the van to prevent the man from getting inside and speeding away. Bo was out of the white van before it screeched to a stop. The blood van's driver raised his hands in surrender. Bo ran to the back of the van, gripped the back door handles, and wrenched the doors open. One fell off its hinges and clattered to the ground. He scanned the interior and grabbed two insulated coolers. Meanwhile, Kazmer jumped from the white van to open the sliding side door. Bo threw the coolers inside the white van and returned to the shotgun seat. Kazmer was back in the driver's seat, had the van in gear, and pulled out, peppering the blood van driver, still with his hands raised, with gravel.

Kazmer drove. Bo hooted. He jumped into the cargo area, ripped open one of the coolers, pulled out several bags of blood, sat on the floor, and consumed the blood, one bag at a time. Bo checked the second cooler. More blood. He returned to his seat up front and relaxed with a satisfied look on his face.

Beads of sweat stood on Kazmer's forehead. "This was wrong. You will be identified. Perhaps there was a camera inside that van."

"That was great, Kaz. I thought the old guy would shit his pants. 'I *got* no money. This isn't a Brinks truck.'" Bo imitated the robbed driver with a laugh. "To me, it's better than a Brink's truck, Kaz. That was good."

"We should get ready to move, Mr. Bo. You and the van were identified."

"There are a million white vans. I'm not going anywhere." Bo was gleeful, clapping his hands.

THE NEXT MORNING, Kazmer slipped from the theater and walked the half block to Betty's Restaurant. He ate eggs, sausage, toast, and coffee at the counter. The early-morning clientele knew him as Al West.

Kazmer bought a newspaper, too, and perused it while he ate and listened to gossip. It didn't take him long to find the front-page story of another blood heist. Kazmer twisted his mouth and grunted softly as he read the amazing story. Betty herself refilled Kazmer's coffee. She rested the pot on the counter for a moment and leaned over.

"Isn't that a hoot," Betty chuckled. "What idiots. They hold up the blood van thinking it's a Brinks truck loaded with cash. Grab two coolers of blood and take off. What a surprise they got when they found blood instead of money."

"Amazing," Kazmer said. He looked up at the waitress. Raised an eyebrow.

"Take a swig," Betty said, smiling. "I'll top it off. I only got a little left in this pot. Next round you'll get fresh."

Kazmer complied. Betty refilled the cup to the top. "There's the hero," Betty chirped, pointing the now empty coffee pot to a booth where a crowd had gathered. "He was in the van when the thieves ran him off the road."

"Oh?"

That's right. Go over and listen. I'll reheat your platter.

"Get Ron a piece of pie," a man called from the booth. "Nothing's too good for the man that saved a heart and liver ready to be transplanted. You might not realize it, but you saved two lives last night, chasing those two hooligans."

"Maybe more," Ron piped up. "Don't forget there was another cooler of blood I wrestled from them."

"Tell us again, Ron. Start from the beginning," Betty called. "Al didn't hear your story yet." She slapped Kazmer's arm. "Go over and listen. It's a hoot. They say Ron's up for a hematology award."

"What is that?" Kazmer said. He looked over his shoulder at Betty.

"Never mind." Betty shoved Kazmer several times. "Go ahead, Al. Don't be shy."

Kazmer stood and hesitantly moved closer to the booth. The giddy men seated or standing, leaning over the table toward Ron, grinned, nodded at Kazmer's arrival, and made room for him. Betty brought Ron his pie. Ron slid his half-full coffee cup back over the tabletop toward her for a refill. Ron waited for the fresh coffee, then circled his finger around the other men's cups. Soon everyone had a refill, even Kazmer stood with a new cup and saucer in his hand. Ron waited for all the cups to be replenished, looking among the eager faces. He even locked eyes with Kazmer for a moment before moving on to the next man.

Kazmer breathed a sigh of relief. He hadn't been recognized.

Ron shoved a forkful of pie in his mouth, chewed, and adjusted his suspenders over his ample stomach before he began. "Well, these two goons forced me off the road on South Kensington last night. I was making the last run of the day. Cut me off. I had no choice. Almost T-boned me. They pulled across the front of my van."

Ron's arm worked in a sawing motion to simulate how he was cut off. The men around him nodded. "I got out of the van. 'What do you think you're doing?' I yell. By this time the goons are out of their van. The big goon, bigger than this guy," Ron said pointing at Kazmer, "hollers 'unlock the money.' Meanwhile, the other goon comes around the back of my van—I think he had a crowbar or something—and knocks off the back door. He starts stacking the coolers. Now some of them have blood and some have organs inside. I dodged the big guy, who seemed kind of slow." Ron tapped his temple with a finger. "I knocked the other guy back and started to unstack the coolers. He gives me a sucker punch I don't expect. Knocks me to the ground. He grabs two coolers and takes off. They throw the coolers in their van and away they go. I was still dazed. It took me a minute to compose myself."

"No way a sucker punch is fair, even in a robbery," Betty said, returning to slosh more coffee into cups. Her face was flushed. She was having the time of her life. Kazmer returned to his seat at the counter to finish his breakfast, which was now cold. He bought coffee to go and rolled up his newspaper before leaving. As usual, Kazmer left a generous tip.

"Have a good one," Betty waved her coffee pot, now empty again, as Kazmer left the diner.

Kazmer waved. "You, too." He smiled at Betty and the group of men.

CHAPTER THIRTY-TWO

While Thaxton laughed up its collective sleeve at the miscreant robbers who waylaid the hematology van, and accepted Ron's story like it was gospel, the Brethren had another idea. The thieves had not mistaken the van for a Brinks truck loaded with cash destined for area banks, nor were they after harvested organs to sell on the black transplant market. They wanted blood in clean PVC bags that were good for forty-nine days. Blood that could be readily stored and transported just as easily. Even the police didn't consider blood as a motive for the robbery.

It was all a mistake, Chief Ronald Holmes said of the heist, quoted in the morning newspaper. "The perpetrators most likely were hopped up on drugs, probably meth, which gave them some false courage. After they were inside the van, they misidentified the coolers and thought they had just hit a big payday. The driver, Ron Simpson, gave them a tussle. He was about to subdue them when one of the bandits delivered a sucker punch. Then it was lights out for old Ron. The perps fled the scene without first checking their take." To a reporter's question, Holmes said, "We have no idea what happened to the blood. Maybe they drank it."

Persimmon smirked after reading the quote. "It looks like Bo is still in Thaxton. How stupid could he be?"

"Probably an urge he couldn't control when he realized a van with blood passed him," Goldenrod said. "Maybe he smelled the blood. Take a look at this photo of Ron Simpson. The only thing he could subdue is a bowl full of potpie."

"I'd believe the story," Jane Jennings said, pointing to the newspaper spread out on Persimmon's bed in the La De Da Motel. "A week ago, I would have called you crazy if you told me a vampire stole blood on purpose." She paused for a moment and lowered her voice. "Then I met a vampire. Now I know a lot more about the undead."

"We'll get the bastard, honey," Old Harriet said. She put an arm around Jane. "You keep gripping that machete to make your wrist stronger. OG put a hellacious edge on the blade. Once you start chopping, you won't want to stop. Take it from me. Remember to spin out of the way, or you'll get your hair singed. I learned the hard way." Old Harriet delivered an imaginary chop to the floor and executed a pirouette between the beds. "Just like that honey. I don't expect Bo's demise will create much of a fire—not like an old vampire would. The other thing is don't stand around watching the fire. Another mistake I made. Get away. The innards are always the last to be consumed. In a vampire, they stink like hell. Could gag a maggot."

Jane smiled. "I don't know what I'd do without all of you."

"We feel the same way," Persimmon said.

KAZMER STROLLED DOWN the street to Betty's Restaurant. Bo was inside his mummy sleeping bag for the day up on The Roxy balcony floor. Inside the restaurant, the regulars greeted Kazmer, who waved back with a smile. He grabbed a newspaper from a pile on the wide windowsill and sauntered to his usual seat at the counter. Betty poured coffee and set it on the counter by the time he slid onto the stool. Ron was in his usual booth surrounded by geezers who wanted to hear his tale again. One took his coffee cup for a refill. Another moved two stacked saucers with the remnants of pie out of Ron's way. After everyone had settled around him, seated or standing, Ron began his story again with obvious pleasure.

Kazmer focused on the newspaper's front page. Ron's voice receded in the background. Another story about the robbery had little new information. It recapped Ron's adventure and reiterated his harrowing experience twenty-five feet away. Kazmer looked up from the newspaper. An old codger had pulled out a cell phone to record Ron's story. One fidgeted in the aisle, unsteadily positioning himself to take a selfie with Thaxton's new hero, the man who was ready to subdue two thieves until he was unceremoniously sucker punched. Ron could have inserted a shark into his much-told story, and no one would have noticed. The grinning, giddy cronies were interested in what they perceived as Ron's recent haircut and a new pair of suspenders. Ron made pregnant pauses while he raised his cup to slurp coffee. The gaggle of men leaned ever closer, and waited silently, anticipating the story to resume.

Kazmer returned to the newspaper. Betty delivered his sausage, eggs, and, toast, and refilled his coffee cup. She wiped the counter around his breakfast plates with a damp towel and leaned toward Kazmer. "What's your take on this?" She jerked her head toward Ron and his entourage.

Kazmer looked toward the men. "Ron is a popular fellow. I think he was lucky he wasn't killed."

Betty inclined her head closer. "Who would mistake a regular van for one of those big Brinks trucks that carry money? I don't care how many drugs they were on." She looked back at Ron for a moment and returned to Kazmer. "Ron's full of hot air. If I knew you better, Mr. West, I'd say he's full of bullshit. I think those thieves were after blood. They knew exactly what they were doing."

Kazmer left a wedge of toast hanging in his mouth, what had been a perfect isosceles triangle. "Really?" he managed to say between clenched teeth."

"Really," Betty whispered, nodding her head.

"Who would want to steal blood?" Kazmer said between chews.

Betty left her rag in a pile on the counter and wagged her index finger before Kazmer. "That is the question. Who would want blood?"

The men at the booth were laughing again. More cell phones were recording. Ron paused to smile for photos. Kazmer looked into Betty's eyes. "I don't know."

Betty refilled a coffee cup at the counter's other end. She returned to Kazmer. Looked around. Leaned over his plate. "I think there's a cult in Thaxton. One that does ceremonies that use blood. That's the ticket. The police chief has an eye on the cemetery. Somebody reported candles in a circle at an old mausoleum. There were pry marks on the door. Whoever it was couldn't get in. Some of those old mausoleum doors are strong. I saw on TV that cults like to use old bones *and* blood in their ceremonies. Maybe they thought they could get bones inside." She gave Kazmer a knowing smile. "What do you think about them apples, Mr. Al West?" Betty stood straight, topped off Kazmer's coffee cup from the ever-present pot she carried.

"No drugs, no mistake?" Kazmer said.

"Cults. That's what I say. You know Lydia?"

"Lydia?" Kazmer's lips curled down at the corners.

Betty looked at the wall clock behind the counter "It's too early for her. She's a skinny little thing. What they call a Goth."

"I know what Goth is," Kazmer said.

"Then you know she dresses in black. Even the makeup—eyes,

lips, nails. Well, she thinks the blood was stolen by vampires. She says there is a vampire in town."

Kazmer grunted. "No such thing." He stared at Betty as if hoping she would be convinced. "Only the foolish believe in vampires."

"That's what I said," Betty whispered. "Lydia works security overnight at the hospital. They even got her a black uniform. She says the security cameras they have act up in the ER and the hall leading to the laboratory. Images get blurry like something moved so fast it couldn't be recorded. The hospital wanted to ditch the cameras for new ones. The so-called *glitch* was only in a few of them. Lydia said, 'No. We gotta slow down the video speed.' The hospital said it has money it has to spend or lose. Some kind of grant. It's easier to buy a few new cameras."

Betty moved closer to Kazmer's ear. Her breath tickled. "So, Lydia takes the video home and slows it down on her computer. She's a smart cookie when it comes to things like that if you know what I mean."

"I know what a smart cookie is," Kazmer said.

"What do you think she finds?"

Kazmer's eyes rolled toward the ceiling and darted back and forth a few times. "A glitch?"

"No!" Betty wagged her head as if she believed Kazmer was not a smart cookie. "There was a man. A man who moved faster than the camera could record. That caused the blur. Try to top that. The nights the glitches appeared, blood was missing from the lab, where they keep it." Betty pulled back and smiled. "Of course, the hospital kept the missing blood all hush-hush. Now, I'll tell you something else you won't believe."

"What is that?"

Betty scanned the counter. Hurried off to fill another cup. In the meantime, Kazmer tried to finish his breakfast, scraped egg yolk on his fork, stuffed the last piece of toast in his mouth, and swallowed his tepid coffee.

This was bad news, Kazmer thought. The man in the video was Bo. If they identified him there would be a real problem. Kazmer never liked this plan of stealing blood. It was much easier to drain the blood from bums. A knot grew in Kazmer's stomach. Betty returned with her nearly empty pot and filled Kazmer's cup. She surveyed the restaurant. "Do you want to talk to Lydia? I can arrange it. She's busting a gut to tell her story."

"What's the rest of the story?" Kazmer said, sipping his coffee after blowing on the hot surface. He wondered why Betty would confide in him. Had she told others?

"The best part." Betty smiled. She inclined her head toward Kazmer. "Lydia knows the man in the video. She went to high school with him. Dated him once. His name is Bo Bentwood, and he disappeared from college on the East Coast. Just disappeared over a year ago. Everybody thought he was dead. Got mixed up with drugs or a gang. You know how it goes."

"I don't know how it goes." Kazmer stared. "I don't like gangs."

Betty stepped back. Frowned. She moved closer again. "This is hard to fathom. Lydia swore by her story. She knows security." Betty winked at Kazmer. "She says the man in the photograph is Bo Bentwood and it's not Bo Bentwood." The restaurant owner nodded her head knowingly.

"I don't understand," Kazmer said, twisting his mouth. "It is him, or it isn't him?"

"Lydia said it was Bo, only he was thinner and very pale. His skin was...what?...almost translucent, she said. I had to look that up in the dictionary. *Translucent.* She made photographs from the video—stills, she called them—and Bo Bentwood had fangs and claws when he raced down the hall." Betty stepped back as if to size up Kazmer. "What do you think of that? Fangs and claws."

"I don't understand. Why did you tell me this?" Kazmer raised an eyebrow at Betty. He wished he had a cigarette rolled and lit. He wished he was outside and walking away from the restaurant.

"You ain't like the other men who come in here. You're sensible.

Not like those clowns fawning over Ron." Betty wiped her hand across her forehead. "You look like you've been around the block a few times."

Kazmer shrugged. "I've been all over this city."

Betty laughed. "Thanks, Mr. West. I needed that 'All over the city.' That's a good one. That's exactly why I confided in you. You were able to handle the information."

"Really?"

"You always seem to say the right thing at the right time."

Kazmer thought for a moment. "Well, a friend is teaching me English. I always try to say the right thing." Kazmer was silent again. Then he added, "Has Lydia told anyone about her story?"

"Just me."

"And did you tell anyone about Lydia's story?"

"Just you." Betty raised an eyebrow. Smiled at Kazmer.

Kazmer felt the secret pocket he had stitched inside his hoodie. His razor-sharp stiletto knife was there. He fingered the handle for a few seconds and thought some more. What would Lazlo do? "I would like to meet Lydia."

"Done," Betty said with a smile. She slapped her hand on the counter. "I hoped you'd say that."

"I hope you and Lydia keep this story a secret until I hear it," Kazmer said.

CHAPTER THIRTY-THREE

Del Hatch finished off the last of the best western omelet he had ever eaten, sopped up his bacon grease with a corner of toast, and finished off his black coffee. He wiped his mouth with a paper napkin, returned it to his jumpsuit neck, and looked out the large window. They had broken camp yesterday afternoon, after one of his fellow Sasquatch hunters, Benny, came down with appendicitis. He had the organ removed last night and now recovered in the hospital.

Del had spent the night in a local motel. Bad weather was moving in. Nobody wanted to be caught on the mountain in it. High winds. Possibly a late spring snowfall. Del had lived through worse weather, but this system was unpredictable and might be especially bad. Del shook his head as if thinking to himself. This was prime Bigfoot country. Steep mountains. Valley streams and lakes. Lush vegetation. Animals galore. The perfect place to find and photograph the elusive animal.

Bigfoot had created a cottage industry in this sparsely populated area. The small town at the foot of the uninhabited and mostly inaccessible mountain range was dedicated to Bigfoot, gaudy with totem poles, and inflatable and wood-carved Sasquatches, some mean, some friendly-looking. There was a Bigfoot gasoline station and attached museum with hundreds of plaster cast footprints on display, blown-up renditions of the Patterson-Gimlin creature filmed in 1967, plus newer out-of-focus, obscured-by-trees photos of hairy beings captured by local shutterbugs, including the station owner. There was a Bigfoot market with various Sasquatch brand food items, tree knockers, stuffed toys, bumper stickers, buttons, bedroom slippers, fireworks, animals-in-distress calls, paperweights made from replicas of footprint casts, and everything you could ask for to foolishly go camping in the wild, uphill terrain. There were Sasquatches on the town's road signs and painted in crosswalks, not to mention Bigfoot billboards at the town's opposite ends. An annual Sasquatch festival inundated the town with giddy Sasquatch aficionados with fat wallets, eager to take selfies with festival speakers and unload their cash.

Del preferred the town trading post, where he had just finished breakfast. Although it had its share of Bigfoot gewgaws, it had a Native American theme. The gift shop had, among other things, beadwork and blankets made by local Native American artists. Del bought two saddle blankets—although he didn't own a horse or saddle—because they were so beautiful. He'd display them in his gun room back home.

The trading post also had some darn good grub. Del always left a second tip for the cook, who would poke his head from behind the grill to thank him. Del saluted back. He was already considered a regular, and the trading post owner, in his clean, white, long apron offered Del more coffee. He accepted with a smile and placed a toothpick between his lips.

"Great breakfast," Del said, with a wag of his head, as if still savoring the food.

"Thank you. That's what keeps us on the map amid all this." The man raised his arms, calling attention to the town. "You know. I shouldn't complain. The festival brings the town and the businesses, including mine, a lot of money. We're debating putting a traffic light at the main intersection. It would be a big deal, but I say what will we do? Turn it off the other fifty-one weeks of the year?"

"Progress isn't always a good thing," Del said.

"Exactly. Then you have the tourists bringing or buying too much gear to haul up in the mountains, where they get lost. Get spooked. Shoot at everything that moves."

"Know what you mean," Del said, savoring the fresh coffee. "I've had my encounters."

"Looks like you're packing up," the man said. He put the coffee pot back on its warmer.

"The weather's getting bad. Plus, we had a member of our party get sick."

"Do any good up there?"

"No. But I'll be back. These mountains got a good vibe."

The trading post owner smiled. "That's what the old people said. They claimed the Sasquatch moved through here every year. Used that big valley with the lake as a route to go north into Canada. The Sasquatch would rest there for a while. Let the old and the young catch their breath. Fatten up a little. It was kind of like some people go to the shore."

"I was at the little lake. Did a little fishing myself. The boys and I had a nice fish fry."

The trading post owner frowned. "There's another lake. Bigger. Upstream. It's a hard climb. That was the Sasquatch watering hole. It's not the kind of place you want to go unless you know what you're doing in the wild. You look like you could handle it."

"That'll be my destination next trip."

"I'll draw you a map." The men shook hands. "What's your next stop?"

"Midwest. A place called Thaxton, Ohio. Some friends of mine are chasing a vampire. Maybe two."

The trading post owner smiled. "From Sasquatch to vampires. Del, some people—even in this town—might call you crazy."

"I might be crazy, Friend. I'll tell you this. I've been hunting Sasquatch for years and never saw one. But I've seen vampires. Killed some. We blew up a whole nest of them on the West Coast, just above the border. One, maybe two, escaped. That's who we're after."

"I wouldn't believe just anybody, Del Hatch. If you say there's such a thing as vampires, I believe you. I grew up in this town. Spent my formative years camping, hunting, and fishing. I've never seen a Sasquatch, either. But I knew the old stories and stayed out of everything but the fringes of that mountain range when *they* were supposed to be migrating. Had a buddy of mine go up country and was never seen or heard from again. Not a trace. That was before this town became a tourist trap. That disappearance was bigger news than the dang traffic light is now."

"I'm going to Thaxton because I think my friends need me," Del said. He finished off the rest of his coffee and declined a refill. "I'll be stopping to piss every mile, if I have another."

"Know the feeling, Del. You might want to look at the arrowhead collection. I added a few new ones. We have an old timer who follows the old ways. He knows where the Indians camped, hunted, and cleaned their game. He won't tell anyone where he goes, because he knows there are guys who would destroy the places. He knows where there are burial mounds." The trading post owner chuckled. "There have been those who tried to follow the old scout into the woods, to find his secrets, but he knows they're after him and loses them pretty fast. Fast enough that they end up sore and tired. Sometimes lost themselves."

"I'd like to meet a man like that," Del Hatch said. "Spend an afternoon on a porch in the shade, chew the fat. We might have some things in common."

"Next trip. That's a promise."

CHAPTER THIRTY-FOUR

Eva bent over a table in the library downtown from where the vampire colony had been destroyed and scanned the local newspaper. She was alone in the cavernous room, surrounded by row after row of shelves filled with books. The table sat in front of two closely spaced columns, which protected her backside. She had trashed the dirty western outfit infused with Bo's crusted blood and replaced it with new jeans, a melon-colored blouse, and Nikes. Her hair fell loosely around her shoulders. Eva spoke, read, and wrote in several languages. However, English was her least practiced, and progress was slow. With her finger, she followed down a column of news oddities. Her flesh was plump after feeding at sundown. She had moved from abandoned building to abandoned building, leaving a trail of dead junkies, most of whom had yet to be discovered.

A small article caught her attention, and she tapped her finger over the print and smiled. It was just a squib. Eva felt a presence in front of her. She smelled a female and looked up to see the librarian, with folded arms and glasses perched on the tip of her nose. "You'll have to finish up, miss. We're closing in a few minutes." The woman unfolded her arms to adjust her wristwatch as if calling attention to the time.

Eva smiled and stared at the woman. Her head turned slowly, and her mouth opened. "I'll give you a few extra minutes while I close the main desk. I love your blouse. Was it a Christmas present?"

"No. It's new," Eva said. "I stole it from a woman I killed last night. I'm reading the story now."

"How wonderful." The woman showed no emotion, swayed back and forth a few times, and turned to leave. "I'll let you get back to reading."

After the woman was gone, Eva returned to the story:

```
Once sleepy town besieged by crime


THAXTON, Ohio—This small city is the kind
of place where they roll up the sidewalks
at 9 pm. That was until recently when
three punks had their throats slashed in
gruesome murders at a mall movie theater.
Meanwhile, a van carrying blood and organs
was robbed of donated blood. There are no
suspects in the murders that occurred
after a movie ended and the theater
emptied. Several moviegoers told police
the murdered trio might have been
harassing others before and during the
movie. In the blood heist, officials
suspect the thieves thought the van was
hauling money to local banks and mistak-
enly made off with two coolers of donated
blood. The stolen blood has not been
returned or found. This occurred at a time
when blood supplies were at an all-time
```

low. Some town residents linked the recent
crime wave to cult activity. However, city
officials deny the accusations, claiming
Thaxton has never had any cults.

Eva smiled. *My little rabbit has returned home. He is now a man. No longer the weak virgin boy with sweet blood. A trip to Thaxton is in order. It is time we are reunited.* Eva returned to the main library desk, where the mesmerized woman had just closed her purse. "I need a map of the United States. One that shows highways."

The woman walked down a row of shelves and returned soon with a map. Eva spread it on the desk, and let her finger trace a line across the country. As her digit neared Ohio, Eva concentrated on the city names. She tapped on Thaxton several times. "Thank you. This will do." Eva folded the map carefully.

"You can't check that out," the librarian said. "It's from the reference section. We don't lend them."

Eva grinned. "That is all right. I don't intend to bring it back." She stared at the woman.

"I understand," the librarian said. "Perhaps you could mail it."

"Certainly."

Eva spun on her heels and walked from the library. She stuffed the map into her back pocket. That was the extent of her packing for the trip to Thaxton. She checked directions at the nearest corner street sign and blurred away. Some miles away, Eva slowed at a rest stop along the interstate to pick the bugs from her teeth and eyes and redo her hair. She cruised the eighteen-wheeler parking lot on foot, hoping to find a ride. Sunrise was a few hours away. It would be nice to feed again and find a place to hole up for the daylight hours.

She pulled out the map, opened it, and stood in the lane truckers used to exit the rest area. She appeared to look at the map and seemed perplexed. A big rig approached her. The driver ran through a couple of low gears, building up speed for the exit, the ramp, and the interstate. There was only one way to go on this ramp—east. Eva pretended not to notice the truck's approach and held her face behind the map. The driver pumped the brakes and gunned the engine, producing the noise of hissing air brakes and a growling diesel engine. Eva was unphased. The rig ground to a halt.

The driver set the brake with a loud exhaust of airbrakes. He opened the cab door and hung out. "Say there. Need some assistance?"

Eva lowered the map, exposing her smiling face. The middle-aged driver wore a checkered shirt that barely contained his girth, jeans, and an old, frayed Caterpillar baseball cap. He had a long, graying unkempt beard that extended to the middle of his chest, and he was immediately captivated by the young woman before him. He dropped from the cab and approached slowly.

"I'm lost," Eva said. "I want to go east to Thaxton, Ohio."

"I know Thaxton. It's not a big place. It's kind of like every-where else. Its best days are behind it. The industry is all dried up."

"My dad lives there. I'm going to see him."

"Where's your car, dear?" the trucker wanted to know.

"I don't have one," Eva said as if the answer was obvious. Here she was, standing in the middle of a parking lot with only a map to her name.

The trucker screwed up his face, stroked his beard a few times. "How'd that happen?" He looked around the lot as if he were expecting her car to suddenly materialize and the joke would be on him.

"Happen? I never had a car," Eva said. "I met this guy on the computer. He promised to drive me to Thaxton for two hundred dollars. I paid him upfront. We stopped here for gasoline. I gave him more money for food. It was my treat because I was thankful for the ride. I had to use the bathroom. When I came out, he was gone, along with my...stuff." Eva shook her fists. "He has my purse, my wallet, my identification papers. He could take my identity."

The trucker closed his eyes and shook his head. The long beard swayed back and forth across his chest. "He got you good. Real good. Son of a bitch! Excuse my French."

"That is not French," Eva said.

The trucker's eyes narrowed. "I guess it's not French," he said slowly. "It's just an expression. I don't like to see you in such a spot. It's out of my way, but I'll drive you to Thaxton. See that you get home to your daddy. I'm ready to pull out now, heading east. Can I buy you something to eat before we go?"

"No, thank you," Eva said, with a smile.

"By the way, my name is Bill. I just filled my thermos. How about some coffee?"

"I never drink...coffee."

Eva climbed inside the cab's passenger side. Bill helped her close the seat belt. Bill put the truck in gear and pulled out, said "And away we go!"

"Jackie Gleason," Eva said, looking at Bill. "A funny man."

"You know Jackie Gleason. I thought you would be too young."

"My brother Gerrard and I watched TV when we were... younger."

"Very good," Bill smiled. "One thing you should know. I like to drive at night. Usually stop somewhere around sunrise to get some shuteye. Then I eat, tend to some business, and hit the road again after sundown. You can use the sleeper compartment. I'm not going to get all touchy, feely with you. That sound okay?"

"Perfect." Eva closed her eyes and pretended to sleep.

CHAPTER THIRTY-FIVE

Bo had been identified by a goth security guard at Thaxton Hospital after she slowed down blurry security footage that was thought to be full of glitches from old cameras. It turned out the blurred smudges that streaked up and down hallways at night were not camera malfunctions but Bo Bentwood, her high school class-mate, who had gone missing more than a year earlier from college on the East Coast, moving at super-human speed. The questionable security footage coincided with the disappearance of blood from the hospital laboratory, a fact the board of directors decided to keep secret. Afterall, there were always more blood donors.

The goth was stunned. There was only one conclusion—Bo was a vampire. Rather than examine the film closely, the hospital decided to buy new cameras with use-it-or-lose-it grant money. The twenty-two-year-old goth, Lydia Sangsweet, kept her suspicions secret, sharing her discovery only with Betty Armond, a Thaxton luncheonette owner, in the diner she frequented after her overnight shifts. Betty, in turn, spilled the beans to Kazmer Savoy, her newest steady customer and best tipper.

Kazmer sat on The Roxy theater balcony a few feet away from Bo, who was encased for the daylight hours in his mummy sleeping bag in the dreamless nothingness vampires entered at dawn. Never a nightmare; never so much as a twitch. According to vampire tradition, Kazmer, as an undead Shadow, should divulge what Betty told him. By not telling Bo, he could seal his doom. Kazmer played out scenarios in his mind. What if Bo found out about Betty and Lydia? The women should be eliminated. They should disappear. Their suspicions, their knowledge, buried with their bodies. Kazmer's pick and shovel stowed in the back of the van had gone unused for some time. Lines of rust developed on the pick points and shovel edge. Would Bo kill them, even to protect himself? Consuming stolen human blood and sparing human lives seemed to be working. But would his outing enrage him to the point of murder?

Regardless, Kazmer was convinced Bo would make things worse. Kazmer imagined he would set up a meeting with Betty and Lydia, perhaps in the restaurant after hours. He would ask them to promise never to divulge Bo's secret. It was a matter of life and death. He doubted immediately that it would work. Both women had already told what they knew. By now, more might have been included in their circle of forbidden knowledge. Kazmer would have to convince Bo to leave town.

Kazmer rolled and lit a cigarette in the theater's near darkness. He inhaled deeply, held the smoke in his lungs for a long time, and released it slowly through his nose. He spit a few tobacco flakes from his lips, tapped off some ash, and inspected the smoke's glowing end. How would he persuade Bo to leave Thaxton? Set up in a new place. A larger city with several hospitals. Perhaps a location with what they called a trauma center. There would be so much donated blood that it would be difficult to keep track of it all. Kazmer smiled and inhaled the cigarette again. Instead of the vampire mesmerizing the human, Kazmer would mez the vampire.

A few feet away, Bo unzipped his sleeping bag. The smell of death rose from the floor.

"Good evening, Mr. Bo. I assume you are rested."

"What else would I be, Kaz? Can you imagine what it would be like if I dreamed? Was terrified by my life with Eva? Can you picture me spinning in my sleeping bag, screaming all day?"

Kazmer grunted. He was not off to a good start. "It is time we leave Thaxton and find another place."

"Why do you say that?"

"It's not safe."

"The Roxy is perfect."

"I hear in the restaurant when I take breakfast. There is talk a man was seen on the hospital video. So far, you have not been identified."

Bo reached for the cooler and pulled out the last three blood bags. He kneaded them to mix the contents. "I like Thaxton. After all, it's my hometown and I know my way around. I have a routine."

"Routines can be dangerous," Kazmer said. He had pulled out his tobacco and rolled another cigarette.

"What about your routine of going to the restaurant every day? That can be dangerous. They can probably already recognize you. Identify you."

Kazmer lit the cigarette and inhaled deeply before releasing the smoke. "I listen to gossip. It is a good place to learn what goes on in the city. You hear things that are not in the newspaper. And I must eat."

"Well, I want to keep tabs on my father. I can tell he's having a rough time."

Kazmer was quiet. He puffed on the cigarette. "We will have to be ready to go fast."

Bo extended his fangs and bit into the first bag; he sucked loudly to drain the contents. He held up the second bag to inspect its contents. "I'm going out tonight for more blood. I'll hit the hospital again unless I run into that blood van." Bo punctured the second bag, drained the contents, and flipped the empty container on the growing heap of discarded bags.

"Maybe I will go out, too. It is early and I am hungry," Kazmer said.

Bo looked at him while kneading the blood bag, and Kazmer smoked the rest of his cigarette. Bo returned his attention to the bag and punctured the PVC with his fangs. Several long sucks emptied the container. Bo wiped his bloody chin with his palm.

"You ready to go, Kaz?"

"Ready."

Kazmer stubbed out the remainder of his cigarette and followed Bo to the main floor and the emergency exit they used to enter and leave the theater. Outside, Bo blurred away without saying a word. Their trust in each other had reached a point where they no longer had to explain their actions. Kazmer walked the half block to Betty's.

INSIDE BETTY'S, the luncheonette owner and a young, black-haired girl sat at a table. Clad in a black security uniform, the girl had to be Lydia, Kazmer thought. She had black lipstick and black nail polish. Kazmer walked to the back of the restaurant, where the women sat.

"Sorry, Al. We're closed. Jack went home early. The grill's off. The coffee's gone."

"I came to talk about the video."

Betty stood. "This is our lucky day. We were just talking about you. I'll put on some fresh." She looked at Lydia. "Want coffee, honey?"

"If you have a pound of sugar to go with it," Lydia said.

Betty hurried behind the counter and deftly started a pot of coffee. She returned in a moment out of breath. She introduced Lydia and Al West. They sat at the table. Betty and Lydia started talking at the same time. Kazmer couldn't understand the jumbled conversation. He held up his hands. The women turned silent.

"Have you told anyone what you found?" Kazmer asked. His jaw was tense.

"It's just us three," Lydia said. She pointed her finger at each of them. "We didn't want to tell everybody. What if we're wrong? We could be wrong, but I don't think so."

"Do you have the video here?"

"I have it on a disk at my apartment," Lydia said. "Betty is closed. We can all go there and watch it. I have a big monitor. You'd be surprised at the detail."

Kazmer smiled. He looked at Betty. "What about the coffee?"

"No worries, dear. I'll put it in a carafe."

Betty turned off the lights, and ensured the doors and windows were locked. While Kazmer and Lydia waited at the door, Betty poured the coffee into a carafe. At the door, she handed the carafe to Lydia while she dug out her keys to lock the door.

"Is it far?" Kazmer said after they were outside.

"We can walk," Lydia said. She juggled the carafe from one hand to the other.

Kazmer smiled. He felt the handle of his stiletto knife concealed inside his hoodie in the secret pocket. They walked a block, made a left at the corner, and walked a half block. Lydia lived on the second floor. As they climbed the stairs, Kazmer thought there would be time to kill the women, return to the theater, and bring back the empty blood containers to make it appear Betty and Lydia were the thieves. He'd wipe off his and Bo's fingerprints, then press the women's dead hands to the containers. This might allow Bo and Kazmer time to remain in Thaxton. Bo would not know about the murders. Although it was a betrayal of his master, it was the best plan to keep Bo safe.

Inside the apartment, Lydia seemed to forget the video. She pulled mugs from the kitchen cupboard. She waved her hand at the stacked dishes. "I got all these at the Sally. A complete set and not a chip on them. Can you believe it?"

"What is the Sally? Kazmer said with a frown, examining the ceramic mug.

"Salvation Army," Betty said.

"Of course," Kazmer replied as if he should have known.

Lydia moved around the small apartment like a dervish, describing a sofa bought on Craig's List, table lamps found at a yard sale, an area rug given by her mother, and curtains donated by an aunt. She opened the door to the bathroom. "Towels like new," Lydia chirped. "Came from an estate sale. Never used. The people were hoarders. Got them for almost nothing." She led them through the bathroom, stopping to flap the shower curtain. "Freebie!" The bedroom was on the other side of the bathroom. "Look at this. The entire bedroom set I got for fifty bucks from a doctor at the hospital. Fifty bucks! It's like brand-new. The doc's daughter wanted a new set." Lydia stopped to catch her breath. "And the sheets!"

Betty grinned and nodded approvingly.

"Maybe we should look at the video before it gets too late," Kazmer said.

"Yeah. I have to be at the hospital at midnight. That's when my shift starts."

Kazmer looked at Lydia and smiled. "Graveyard shift."

"That's what they call it," Betty said.

They returned to Lydia's living room and a table with a computer and a large monitor. Lydia sat at the table. Betty passed out coffee and then stood with Kazmer behind the goth girl. Lydia slipped a thumb drive into a USB port. The computer hummed to life. The trio gathered around the monitor. Lydia used a wireless mouse to call up the video. They all leaned in. Betty smacked her lips with anticipation. Lydia hummed as if she were nervous while she moved the mouse about. The hospital hall appeared on the screen along with a time and date stamp. Kazmer fingered his knife and pulled it from the secret pocket. It was not the first time Kazmer struck two victims at once, so fast neither could scream.

Kazmer waited for the moment the women were in the right

positions. His knife would strike one and slash her throat open, followed by a deft move to open the second neck. The murders would be completed in a moment. Kazmer would take the thumb drive and erase everything while he finished the coffee and checked what was in Lydia's refrigerator. The women moved closer to the monitor. It was perfect. He could slice across both throats in one move. Two deaths within a second. Kazmer wiped his hand on the hoodie lining. He clutched the knife handle in its secret pocket with his right hand and opened the hoodie zipper with his left.

"Getting warm?" Betty asked.

"It's the hot coffee," Kazmer said.

"I know. Me, too," Lydia chirped with a smile, looking at Kazmer. Their eyes locked.

Kazmer didn't want the hoodie to snag the knife when he drew it into the open. Any delay might allow one or both women the chance to scream.

Lydia turned back to the monitor. "There he is," she whispered.

Kazmer eyes darted to the monitor.

Bo appeared in the screen's bottom left corner for an instant and turned into a smudge. Kazmer froze. Bo looked at the camera. Frowned. There was no doubt about it. The figure on the monitor was Bo.

Lydia started to talk. "This is the real-time footage. You see this thing that looks like a fingerprint. It moves in a blur from one end of the hall to the other in a second, maybe less. Now I'm going to slow the video down." She moved the mouse around the tabletop, clicking commands.

Betty said "Ohhh," in a soft voice. "You can do all that."

Kazmer wasn't listening. He stared at the precise part in Lydia's hair and her scalp. He watched her long-fingered hand grip the mouse. Saw a vein in her wrist thump while she slid the mouse around the table. Kazmer moved to the side to inspect Lydia's small ear. A mole on her neck. Kazmer believed his slash could bisect the little mole.

Lydia turned suddenly and smiled with a mouthful of white, straight teeth. He looked into her dark eyes. "What do you think, Mr. West? Do we have something?"

Kazmer looked away to focus on Betty's rounded shoulders, then her hand scratching a chin full of fine hair.

"Well, what do you think, Mr. West?" Lydia repeated.

"Do you have a boyfriend?" Kazmer asked. "You're very pretty."

Lydia blushed. "I don't. I was always different, the type that other kids made fun of. That has followed me into adulthood. I'm the odd girl with an odd job."

They locked eyes again. "Know what I mean?" Lydia said, her color returning to its normal paleness, while her eyes filled with tears.

"I know. I was the same," Kazmer said. He cleared his throat.

"Have some more coffee, dear. There's lots of it," Betty said. She flew to the counter to fetch the carafe.

Kazmer pulled his hand from the hoodie and let it hang empty at his side. After a lengthy pause, he said, "I think you have something, Lydia. I can't say what it is. It is definitely a person. How would you know it is a vampire?"

"I knew we did the right thing by letting you in on this," Betty said smiling, nodding her head, opening the carafe, and pouring coffee into their mugs.

Lydia smiled at Kazmer. "I know it's Bo Bentwood who's been stealing blood from the hospital. What do we do next?"

CHAPTER THIRTY-SIX

Eva found a tablet and pen inside the big rig's cluttered sleeping compartment. She composed a succinct note in her elegant handwriting and attached it to the exterior of the heavy curtain that separated the compartment and cab. Inside the compartment, she covered herself with a blanket to protect herself from direct sunlight.

Bill saw the note when he woke and slid open the cab's shades. It was late afternoon. He turned toward the curtain—his neck was stiff—opened his mouth as if to say something, thought better, and decided to heed the note. The last thing he needed was to listen to a grouchy woman all night while he drove. Bill grimaced and stretched his neck. He stroked his beard twenty times, his custom before going out in public, and made sure he had his wallet and keys. Before he climbed to the ground, stretched his frame, locked the truck door, and headed toward a restaurant at the rest stop, Bill wrote his own note to Eva under hers

Please lock door if you leave cab before I get back. I have keys.

He squeezed in all the words at the bottom of the page. Inside the restaurant, Bill sat at the counter and ordered breakfast. Although the sun was setting, it was morning to his metabolism, and breakfast was in order. That's what he told the chunky young waitress who took his order and paused patiently to listen to a man who hadn't had much company all day. He downed one cup of coffee and pushed the empty back to the inside of the counter for a refill.

"I hope this coffee helps me go boom boom before I hit the road again," Bill said, with a sneaky smile. The waitress blushed and walked away.

After he ate, had the waitress fill his thermos with more coffee, and paid the tab, the coffee worked its magic, and Bill retired to the restroom. It was clean and bright, the kind of place he wouldn't mind sitting in for a while. He picked up a discarded newspaper and plopped himself on a toilet inside a stall, where a new roll of toilet paper hung. Sometimes, life was good, even for a lonely truck driver on the interstate. While the coffee finished its last act, Bill scanned the headlines and read a few articles that caught his eye. One in particular, murders and a blood heist in Thaxton, Ohio, he would share with Eva.

Before he wiped, he tore the article out carefully, along the column edges, and placed it in his shirt pocket. Bill felt renewed after he left the stall. His belly was full, and his bowels had been emptied. He tossed the newspaper in the trash, washed his hands, and splashed cold water on his face. He was ready to hit the road again.

When he returned to his rig, it was dark, and the cab was empty. Had she taken off with another person? Left him here wondering what happened? How long should he wait? She said she had no money. Then he saw a few words scribbled above her first note, which lay on the dashboard.

Be back in a few.

Her elegant script filled all the remaining open space on the note.

Bill settled into the driver's seat. He poured himself coffee from his thermos and sipped it slowly. He watched other truckers leave the parking lot. In a few minutes, Eva was at the passenger side. He unlocked the door, and she climbed in.

"Whew," Bill said. "You find some perfume. Smells like the restroom disinfectant."

Eva laughed, clapped her hands.

"Not that it's a bad smell. Just strong."

"It's the soap. I tidied up a bit while I was in the bathroom."

Bill sneezed. Sniffed. Wiped his nose with the back of his hand.

"You can drive with the windows open," Eva said.

"No. the smell is fine. I just have to get used to it. You want to get some food?

"Already ate."

"Coffee?"

Eva smiled.

"You don't drink coffee."

Eva showed her teeth. "I'm ready to leave if you are. And away we go!"

Bill chuckled. "And away we go." He started the diesel engine.

<hr>

They drove for several hours, mostly in silence. Eva feigned sleep and leaned against the door. After a while, Bill touched Eva's arm. She was startled.

"My God, you feel cold!" Bill blurted. "You want me to put the heat on?"

"I'm fine," Eva said. "Leave me alone."

"Sorry. I wanted to ask if the radio would bother you. I usually play it when I drive at night."

Eva turned her head toward him. Stared. "You can play the radio, Bill. Nothing too...wild."

"I don't like this hip hop, hop hip, whatever they call it. How about some classic rock?"

"Sounds good," Eva said. "You can't beat a classic."

Bill fiddled with the radio. Tuned in a station and looked toward Eva. She frowned. Bill tried again. The second time she rolled her eyes. Bill twisted the dial, showing frustration. He stopped again. This time Eva smiled. Bill returned his attention to the road and drove through the remainder of the night. Bill said he would pull off at a rest stop ten miles up the interstate. The sun crested the horizon. Eva crawled into the sleeping compartment. Despite the strong disinfectant smell, Bill noticed another odor, sweet and sickening.

"Is the do not disturb sign still in order for the daylight hours?" Bill said.

"Yes. Please."

"Alrighty then."

They continued on for two more days and followed the same routine. Eva remained in the sleeping compartment all day. Bill slept in his driver's seat, waking with a stiff neck. Bill ate and used the bathroom near sundown. He returned to the cab after dark to find Eva had gone. She returned soon, claiming she ate. He had not given her money for food. She always smelled of disinfectants. On the day before they were to reach Thaxton, Bill pulled in at a rest stop. Eva was already in the compartment. The unpleasant odor she carried had grown stronger.

Rather than sleep through the day in the cab, Bill was glad to get away from Eva. He was happy he would be rid of her soon and couldn't wait to pull into Thaxton. The reststop restaurant was nearly empty. Most people used the restrooms, bought food for the road, and were back on the highway as soon as possible. Bill bought coffee and finding no discarded newspapers, bought one, and found a booth where he could stretch his legs. He moved his cup to the side, where the waitress would see it, and spread out the newspaper on the table.

The first headline that caught his eye.

Does a serial killer stalk the interstate?

In short order, Bill discovered four women had been murdered in recent days in and around interstate rest stops. Curiously, the victims were drained of blood. Police had little information. The investigations continued.

Bill moved to the counter and hauled his coffee cup and the newspaper with him. "What's with these murders?" he asked the waitress as she refilled his coffee.

"I'm scared shitless. That's what's going on." She pointed at the back wall with her arm holding the coffee pot. "I gotta park way the heck out there. We have staggered shifts, so when you punch out you leave alone."

Bill removed his Caterpillar baseball hat and scratched his scalp. "All women?"

"You better believe it."

"What do the police say?" Bill replanted his cap and sipped his coffee.

"Police don't say nothin'. A deputy coroner let it slip about the blood loss. He called it exsanguination." She pronounced the word slowly as if she were in a spelling bee. "Not that nobody'd know what *that* was, but a girl on dayshift did. She had some college before she got knocked up. She knew what exsanguination was. She was right there. Saw the body. It was in the women's bathroom. We have a kind of network among us girls, up and down the rest stops. Help each other out. Warn one another about creeps who spook around the rest stops looking for runaways and such."

"Any runaways among the women murdered?" Bill stirred his coffee slowly and then licked the spoon.

"No. That's the odd thing if you ask me." The waitress moved closer to Bill. "You look like a trucker. I figure I can trust you. *They* say two of the girls were hookers. I ain't telling you anything you don't know about rest stops and lot lizards if you're a trucker. One was a woman on vacation with another woman, driving through, and the fourth was an old broad going home with her hubby to New York State. She wore a ton of jewelry—all untouched. I repeat, untouched."

Bill looked up at the waitress. "Well, it seems like the only thing stolen was..."

"Their blood."

Bill choked on his coffee. He thought of Eva, resting in his rig right now. Why was it so important for her to remain hidden during the day? Identification. Her story seemed flimsy. "Anybody get a look at the killer?"

"No witnesses," the waitress said. "I think the murderer had to be a man. Someone with a lot of strength. They say the old broad with the jewelry put up a fight. She was a big woman who had been quite an athlete when she was young. The newspaper said she was a swimmer."

"Nowadays lots of women work out," Bill said. "If they were killed in bathrooms for women..."

"I see your point. Could be a trans. We get them in here. I never have the time to watch what bathroom they use."

Bill returned to his rig slowly, meandering through the parking lot filled with eighteen-wheelers, surveying the tractors and the custom paint jobs. Someday he would have his own Freightliner. Bright red. His name Bill Hines Hauling in silver lettering. He had always intended the lettering to be in block letters. Now he decided it would be in an elegant cursive similar to Eva's fancy writing. He smiled at the thought.

BILL HINES HAULING.

His own business. He could see his rig in the distance. The closer he got the more determined he was to give Eva the boot. He would make sure she had another ride to Thaxton, even though it wasn't that far anymore. He wouldn't leave her high and dry again, as she claimed she was. He'd even give her spending money for the remainder of the trip. Eva had proved to be a problematic traveling companion. Secretive. Hiding herself during daylight hours so no one would catch a glimpse of her when he passed another vehicle. What about her odd smell and the overpowering smell of bathroom disinfectants? To top it off, there was good and bad food on the interstate. She had no opinion of the secretive meals she consumed at rest stop restaurants apparently paid for with money she didn't have. And who in her right mind didn't drink coffee while driving across the country?

Eva would have to go. Bill unlocked the driver's side door, opened it, and climbed up. After he was inside, he pulled down the shades as a courtesy to block the slanting morning sun from the cab. He sat quietly for a moment, breathing heavily, imagining how to break the news to Eva. Several ideas flashed through his mind. He wanted to remain calm. There was no sense in causing a scene in the parking lot among his fellow truck drivers.

Bill thought he had it. He shook the curtain that separated Eva from him. "Eva, I'm afraid we have to part company."

She was silent on the curtain's other side. Bill opened his mouth to speak. This time he would be louder.

"If that's what you want, Bill," she said, before he launched into his reason.

Bill tried to peek between the curtain panels to determine her reaction to the news, but he knew the compartment interior was dark and the panels overlapped. She was quiet and didn't move. He chewed on his lower lip. "I'm glad you understand. It's just that I'm not accustomed to passengers and I gotta bypass Thaxton."

The curtains parted in a flash. Eva grabbed Bill by the neck with her clawed fingers and hauled him into the bunk. She sank her fangs into his neck and sucked several large swallows of blood. It was just enough to force unconsciousness. She let Bill's head fall and lapped up blood from her chin and his neck with her long tongue. She stroked Bill's beard. Bill moaned.

"I'm not done with you yet, Bill. I'll save the rest of you for tonight before I look for my next ride."

CHAPTER THIRTY-SEVEN

Persimmon tapped her finger, blew off her face the elusive hair strand that defied pinning back. Her gaze left the newspaper and trained on Jane Jennings from across the La De Da Motel room. Jane watched cartoons on the television—Foghorn Leghorn. Her shoulders shook with laughter. Old Harriet, Goldenrod, and Mad Maggie sat with her on the bed for what was a women's morning.

Persimmon stood, approached the three. Stood silently. Old Harriet piped up. "Would it kill them to put El Kabong on for once? I always liked the noise his guitar made when it hit somebody over the head."

"Too violent," Mad Maggie said. "Not for me, though. I like El Kabong. I'd like him better if he carried a machete, but then you wouldn't get that kabong noise."

"Ladies, I have an announcement," Persimmon said, interrupting the laughter.

"Oh. That sounds serious," Mad Maggie said, looking up at Persimmon with a frown.

Persimmon cleared her throat, pushed the hair behind her ear. "Jane."

Jane cringed.

"I think you've learned enough self-defense to be vampire bait. Are you ready?"

"I guess so," Jane said, receiving congratulation hugs from Mad Maggie and Old Harriet. "What do I do?"

Persimmon moved her newspaper from the bed to the table and spread it out with her hand. "One thing nice about slow news days," Persimmon said, tracing her finger down a column, "is that they fill space with stories like this."

Persimmon's finger stopped on a small article and tapped the headline. *Does a serial killer stalk the interstate?* The women huddled around the table to read the short article about the interstate killings. After they finished reading, the women looked at Persimmon.

"It looks like Eva is on her way to Thaxton," Persimmon said. "There might be a serial killer who thinks he's a vampire, but I'd say it's *our* vampire. She might be here already. She doesn't have a connection with Jane, but Bo does. Every person releases pheromones. A scent. The vampire's highly developed sense of smell might be able to tell us all apart. Bo will certainly recognize Jane. That's what I believe. Therefore, we want to get Jane out and about town. We'll walk the streets and hit all the places where blood was stolen, especially the hospital where Bo struck several times. He's bound to go back."

"When do we start," Old Harriet wanted to know.

"After sundown," Persimmon answered.

"Then I'll have time to shower?" Jane said.

"No. I want you to smell like you did when Bo attacked you. As much as possible. I want your dirty laundry, too. We'll split up and cover more territory. We know vampires can detect a virgin and a pregnant woman by scent. Look at Bo and Lisa. We hope enough of Jane's pheromones will linger to attract Bo. If we can kill him, I think Eva will be vulnerable. It's only a theory based on my experience and the Brethren's knowledge."

Persimmon said she would work on their patrol pairings while they rested. They would begin an hour before sundown. Eva should not be much of a factor unless they stumbled across her by accident. She would not know about Jane. Overboard George and John Bargain were informed of the plan before the group retreated to their separate rooms. George had good news. Del Hatch's Sasquatch hunt plans had gone sour. He was on his way to Thaxton.

"Great. I hope he doesn't decide to blow up the La De Da when he gets here," Bargain said.

"Not Del," Overboard George said with a mile. "He'll be ready for a soft bed when he gets here, after sleeping on the ground out in Washington State. I hope he got that BAR and plenty of ammo with him. We might need it for Eva. No way she's gonna outrun a 30.06 slug."

"Don't cough up a lung," Bo told Kazmer. He placed a hand on his shoulder. "You pick up a cold in that restaurant you go to? Or it could be those nasty cigarettes you inhale."

Kazmer sat in a balcony theater chair inside The Roxy. He managed to control his coughing fit. "Not cold. Not cigarettes. I cough when I am up here. I think it is the mold."

"Maybe we should find another place. Have you been scouting one out?"

"I think we should move to a different city. Far from here. It is not safe anymore. There is too much news about murders. Stolen blood. There are stories every day in the newspapers. It could attract the Brethren."

"I don't fear the Brethren."

"You should," Kazmer said, rolling a cigarette, and wiping his running nose.

"I think they got lucky on the coast. They'd never trace us here. This would be the last place they'd look. For all they know, I was killed in the explosion that took down the colony. I think you are too cautious."

"Cautious is good. Do you want me to get the van ready?"

"No, Kaz. We're staying in Thaxton. You can find another place in town if you think mold bothers you here." Bo squeezed Kazmer's shoulder.

"You worry too much, my friend. After dark, we will take a walk to see if your sinuses clear."

THE BRETHREN GATHERED in Persimmon's room in the early evening. Vampire hunters always knew two things: the exact times for sunup and sundown. Today was no different. The matter of a few minutes could spell disaster for a Brethren or a vamp. Persimmon, Old Harriet, and Jane would travel together to spread pheromones. Overboard George and Mad Maggie would be in a separate car along with some of Jane's dirty laundry. Goldenrod and John Bargain would be dropped off downtown and walk the streets with another bundle of dirty clothes.

"I'm so embarrassed to have you guys carry around my wash," June said, blushing. "I hope it doesn't stink too bad."

"If your wash helps bag a vamp tonight, you'll be more than happy," Old Harriet said. "It can't smell any worse than *we* did when we were all living on the street."

They dispersed from the room and into the cars, not wanting to attract any attention. Most La De Da Motel guests stayed a night, two at the most. Therefore, it was unlikely the Brethren, who were already camped at the place for a week, would raise a red flag. Persimmon and Overboard George, in separate vehicles, exited the motel parking lot and drove in opposite directions. All three squads had walkie-talkies. Goldenrod and John Bargain were dropped off downtown. Jane's clothes were tied in a bundle that fit under Bargain's arm. Gold took Bargain's free hand as they walked along the street. They passed Betty's Restaurant, which appeared to be closing. The window lights snapped off as Bargain peered inside. The Roxy Theater loomed ahead.

"This is the place OG thought looked suspicious," Gold said. "Deserted and a good place for a vamp to camp." She felt the .9 mm pistol concealed in the waist of her jeans. Bargain carried a similar weapon. Both had stakes.

"Let's check it out, leave some pheromones to linger," Bargain added.

They walked around the area under the marquee and examined the detached ticket booth barely large enough to accommodate one person. The narrow door on the booth's back was locked. A roll of dust-covered tickets lay on the desk under the front glass. The tile floor under the marquee was dirty. Tiles were cracked and missing here and there. A pile of rotting leaves and wind-blown trash had accumulated against the theater's front doors. It appeared no one had entered from this direction in years. Bargain looked into the dark lobby, cupping his hands around his eyes. He shook his head. Looked at Gold.

"I'd love to see the interior. I love old theaters."

"I'm sure you'd be disappointed, Babe," Gold said, taking his hand again. "The inside is probably worse than out here."

They stepped back to look at the marquee top. A few scattered letters remained. "How are you at Wheel of Fortune?" Bargain said. They stood in the gathering darkness, trying to fill in the blanks between the remaining letters to fathom what film, which movie stars, were the last shown inside.

"Well?" Gold said. "What's the answer?"

"I need a vowel to solve the puzzle."

They tired of the game and walked to the side of the theater and several rusting emergency exit doors. They examined each. One had an oily handprint near the center, where there was a slight gap between the two doors. Bargain fit his fingers inside the gap and pulled. The door didn't budge. Gold called his attention to a fresh-looking scrape mark on the concrete sidewalk.

"Somebody with a lot more strength than I have has been going in and out rather recently. Maybe OG was right. This might be a good place for a vampire."

"We'll let Persimmon know," Gold said. "Maybe we all can come back in the daylight with a crowbar. "I wouldn't want to face a vampire now in the dark—even Bo. We'll need backup."

Gold used her phone to take photos of the handprint and door gap. Another focused on the scrape on the pavement. They rubbed Jane's clothing over the door and a metal light pole at the corner. They returned to the front of the theater, took one last look at the marquee letters, and walked up the street.

As soon as Gold and Bargain left the theater's vicinity, the side exit door opened, dragging on the sidewalk. Bo and Kazmer exited the building and closed the door. Bo sniffed the air. His mouth grew slack. "She is here. I knew it. That girl just stood here outside this door. I can smell her scent. It is the same as at the vacant motel on the West Coast."

"It can't be, Mr. Bo. Impossible."

"I tell you she was here, Kaz. Do you doubt me?"

Kazmer lowered his head. "No, Master. If you smell her, as you say, it must be a trick of the Brethren."

CHAPTER THIRTY-EIGHT

THE SWIMMING POOL WAS OPEN AT THE LA DE DA MOTEL, and the first to try its chilly blue water was Del Hatch. In fact, Del, who had checked in a mere two hours ago, relaxed on one of the chase lounges he had helped the owners haul from a storage shed. Because he was already wearing his bathing suit, Del had insisted on hosing off dust from the weatherproof chairs and lounge cushions. When there was work to be done, Del was always at the right place at the right time, so it seemed. It had been a long drive more than halfway across the country from Washington State, and Del was about to doze off behind his sunglasses.

The sun felt good after the miserable Washington weather and his failed Sasquatch hunt. The hint of a smile creased Del's face. He thought of the slim Brethren from the UK, former special forces, expert in everything that could spell mayhem to enemies. She was the closest thing there was to a real 007. He wondered what Guacamole and her British accent could be doing at this very moment. Guacamole had taken a moniker, as all Brethren did, so members could not give up their fellow members' real names to vampires, under torture or mind control. Although Del never knew

Guacamole's real name, he imagined the warm scent of her skin, the time they spent together at the old funeral home and later at the Brethren ranch home strongholds. Such was the arrangement. He might never see her or hear from her again. Del hoped she had a similar memory of him.

Del's eyelids fluttered under his shades. He was about to sink into sleep when there was a sudden ruckus near the pool, giggling, running feet. His eyes snapped open. Peals of laughter and the "Cannonball!" holler he remembered from old Navy days echoed off the semi-circle of cottages that surrounded the pool. Overboard George splashed into the pool's deep end near Del, covering him with a curling wave of frigid water. Del sat up and pulled off his glasses with the wet lenses. His teeth set to chatter before he could issue an oath. Persimmon followed with a graceful dive. Mad Maggie and Jane navigated the pool steps, hand in hand, the cold water sucking breath from their lungs. Del's eyes focused on his grinning friend, elbows resting on the pool's coping.

"Serves you right for sitting so close to the water," Old Harriet called from a chair in the shade. "You won't see me drowned by no cannonball."

A wet reunion followed. Jane was introduced. The party moved into Persimmon's room. There was a lot for Del to catch up on. Details about vampires were never discussed over telephones. Bo was in the city, possibly holed up in the vacant movie theater downtown. Eva, the ancient vampiress, was headed to Thaxton on the interstate, with a trail of grisly murders in her wake. She might already be in Thaxton in an apparent attempt to join Bo. More Brethren were en route to backup their numbers. They were not about to take Eva and her supernatural powers lightly.

Persimmon drew up plans quickly while toweling off inside her room. They would watch the theater and canvas Thaxton's two graveyards connected to old parishes inside the city and three cemeteries on the outskirts. Disturbed ground, recent burials, and mausoleums with broken locks were suspect. All were likely places

Eva would rest during daylight hours. Her strong claws were able to dig into the hard ground deep enough to keep off the sun's rays. Vampires had a penchant for resting among the dead. Therefore, cemeteries and graveyards would be the Brethren's first targets.

———

Despite rain the next day, the Brethren broke up in twos and began their searches. Del Hatch and Old Harriet found the Bentwood plot by accident, attracted by two newer-looking graves.

"Bo's mother," Del whispered with solemnity, standing next to her grave. Rain dripped off their ponchos. "I wonder if Bo knows."

"If Bo's in town, like we think, he knows," Old Harriet said. "It's hard to keep a secret from the undead. Keep your eyes peeled. He might be able to move around on a day like this. Heavy clouds. No sunlight. We might bump into him."

"My eyes are always peeled. Even with Sasquatch sex pheromone sprayed in them." Del and Old Harriet laughed.

"You keep that BAR ready to go?"

"It's ready. I cleaned it last night before I went to bed," Del said with a wink. "That gun's action works like spreading butter."

"It sure shot old Fagan full of holes," Old Harriet quipped.

"And you and Mad Maggie finished him off with your machetes. He looked like sushi."

Old Harriet ran a hand through her hair. "I lost half my hair when that old fanger exploded into flames in front of me. Persimmon said Fagan was only about a hundred years old. Imagine how Eva's going to go up after we stake that bitch. It'll be like an H-bomb."

"That's an event we don't want to miss," Del said. They moved across the cemetery, recrossing the terrain, moving down a few rows with each pass, ensuring all the ground was covered. They stopped to give Old Harriet a rest and sat under a mausoleum's portico to get out of the rain.

"One thing about vampires when you kill them. They don't ask for mercy," Old Harriet said. "They just stare at you. Even when they see you ready to deliver the lethal blow. It's a look of hate."

"That must be the instant they realize they're taking the express route to hell," Del said. "That's where I think they go."

"Me, too. Who else would want 'em?"

"You want to rest while I cover that section on the hillside? It won't take me long."

"I'm fine," Old Harriet said. "In the old days, I carried some heavy bags from the food bank to my tent. Didn't have no car. Had to walk *and* fight off crazy people who wanted to help themselves to my stuff. Too damn lazy to walk across town themselves, but happy to steal my food."

Del Hatch smiled. "You're a force of nature, Old Harriet. When we get this Eva burned to a crisp, I might take you on a Sasquatch hunt. You might give me and the boys some good luck for a change."

"I wouldn't mind seeing a real Sasquatch. Can't be any worse than a vampire. And I saw plenty of them. Just so you know, though, when it comes to camp life with the boys, *I ain't easy.*"

"I believe that, Old Harriet," Del said, smiling. "The Squatch does stink. I smelled them a few times at night. Never seen any, though. They're elusive. Always a step ahead of me."

"Ever take a sniff of the undead? They're potent, too. Real rotters they smell like. Ever smell a human that's been dead for a while?"

"I have, Old Harriet. More than once."

"Me, too, Del. On the street. Sometimes you'd find an OD in a box or tent after they sat in the heat. Usually smelled them before you saw them. Enough to gag a maggot."

The rain turned into a mist, and they continued walking, breaking up the cemetery into grids, using roads to define the sections. The rain stopped while they started the final grid. After a few minutes, patches of blue sky appeared, and sunlight slanted through the sky.

Del received a call from Persimmon while he and Old Harriet stripped off their ponchos next to Del's SUV. "OG says we spotted a Shadow coming out of the theater," Del repeated. "You know what isn't far behind." Del winked at Old Harriet.

"A young man who's allergic to the sun's direct rays," Old Harriet said.

"I have some more news," Persimmon said over the phone. "Guess who just blew into town and just registered at the La De Da?"

"Well?"

"Guacamole."

CHAPTER THIRTY-NINE

Bo came to consciousness slowly, as he did sometimes.
The vampire disease raged in his throat. He needed blood, and his bagged supply had been consumed.. Bo unzipped his mummy sleeping bag slowly. The cadaver stench escaped his cocoon and permeated The Roxy balcony. Kazmer coughed once when the smell reached his nose. He sat in a theater chair listening to his transistor radio. Kazmer's long, crooked nose twitched a few times as he became accustomed to the odor.

"I need blood, Kaz. I'm making a hospital run as soon as it's dark." Bo emerged from the sleeping bag, plopped down on a seat near Kazmer.

Kazmer turned to Bo and removed his tobacco pouch from his hoodie pocket. "Not a good idea."

"It's like going to the Acme. I'll be in and out in less than a minute. Have food for the rest of the week." Bo smiled. His once beautiful teeth were stained from drinking blood.

"They might be waiting, Mr. Bo."

"Nonsense. The hospital hasn't reported blood loss from the

lab. It hasn't been in the newspaper, like it was for the mobile drive I hit."

"Hospitals keep records on blood donations. They *know* blood was stole from the laboratory. They don't report it because they don't like bad—what is the word?—publicity." Kazmer raised a knowing eyebrow toward Bo. Then he turned his attention to rolling a cigarette.

"How would you know, Kaz?" Bo looked at the man as if he were a misinformed child.

"I know. It is my job as Shadow to learn as much as possible. While you sleep, I am out in the world. I hear things. I learn the hospital knows about the missing blood. Everyone is concerned. Still, they say nothing. They add security. They change cameras. They get good cameras that don't make mistakes."

"Let them try to stop me. I'll lay a bruising on them, Kaz. After tonight, the door to the lab will be propped open. There'll be a clear track for my...entrance and exit. You know, like in cartoons. Exit stage left."

"I hope you are correct." Kazmer said after a moment. His face showed worry. To avoid Bo's gaze Kazmer inspected his cigarette one last time and lit it. "Do you want me to bring the van? I can park down the street from the hospital. Have the motor running for a fast getaway."

"I can blur faster than you can drive the van. Besides, you never go over the speed limit." Bo stood wit his hands on his hips. The matter was settled. Bo would go alone. He blurred from the balcony to the exit door in an instant. He was outside on the sidewalk, with the door relocked, in another.

Kazmer raised the hand that held his cigarette to make a point and add a warning, but Bo was already gone. From his seat on the balcony, he heard the first-floor theater exit door scrape open and closed. Kazmer shook his head, took a long drag on the cigarette, and released the smoke slowly from his lungs.

Bo was accustomed to blurring now. It was as easy as moving in real-time. There were no more slamming into things, making awkward turns, stopping too short, or whizzing by a target. He vaulted over fences and walls, jumped to and from rooftops with hardly a sound, and navigated long straightaways at breakneck speed while avoiding traffic and pedestrians. He negotiated Thaxton's streets and alleys noiselessly, stirring up dust and dry leaves in his wake.

At an intersection, he sensed the approach of a box truck from the right, hurdled over the cab and under the traffic light. A pedestrian on the corner might have been amazed by the light's sudden motion above, swinging on a night when the air was calm.

Bo streaked toward the hospital. He passed an ambulance racing in the same direction. The siren caused his sensitive ears pain, but in a second he was beyond its high-pitched range. The vampire disease supplied the energy for Bo's dash through the night. It wasn't necessary to breathe. His leg muscles didn't cramp or tire. He didn't sweat or overheat.

Bo arrived at the hospital. He stopped at the corner behind a recently clipped large evergreen shrub. Trimmings lay on the ground scattered around the bush. Bo smelled sap. He was no worse for wear than if he had stood in his hiding place for hours. He watched two security guards packing sidearms at the emergency room entrance. He recognized one as Lydia Sangsweet, an old high school classmate. In a moment, others dressed in scrubs joined the security officers outside. Bo's eyes darted back and forth from person to person. He raised the hood on his jacket.

After a few seconds, the ambulance roared to the entrance, cut the siren, and halted. As if choreographed, paramedics shot from the ambulance, the scrub-clad workers surrounded the vehicle's back door. Lydia and her partner moved inside the entrance and held the wide, sliding door open. A gurney slid from the ambulance; its wheeled bottom telescoped open to support the patient. Bo watched the commotion with interest, his head cocked like a puppy's. The attendants surrounded the gurney and directed it toward the entrance. Within seconds, the patient had been unloaded from the ambulance, and the gurney that held him streaked through the waiting room toward the ER examining rooms. Even faster was Bo Bentwood, who catapulted himself from his hiding place through the closing ER door. One foot hit the floor inside the door, and he jumped over the gurney and its attendants. Bo zigzagged up the hall, avoiding more hospital personnel and litters that crammed the hall. No one noticed a thing.

Bo didn't care about the congested hall. He turned a corner and raced toward the laboratory. Blood was on his mind. He imagined he smelled and tasted it. The back of his throat was on fire. Bo stopped for an instant outside the lab. Finding the door locked, he twisted the handle, broke the lock, and pushed it open. The lab was mostly dark. Inside, he blurred through the now familiar room to the freezer guided by the green and red LED lights on computer screens. Analyzing equipment hummed softly. The place smelled of disinfectants. Bo rifled through the blood supply. Pouches plucked from the freezer were transferred inside his hoodie. Bo had become a connoisseur. He preferred certain blood types. There was the elusive AB negative, held by just one percent of the human population, and AB positive, almost as rare, but Bo liked A negative the best, more readily available at eight percent of the population. However, good old O positive, held by thirty-five percent of humans, was what he seemed to drink most often and was good in a pinch.

The vampire disease raged. Bo's tongue swirled around his mouth in anticipation. It would be nice to warm the chilled blood, but the vampire disease demanded feeding. He didn't know whether he could wait to return to The Roxy and have Kazmer warm the pouches next to his body. Poor Kazmer. He would sit on the theater balcony with several pouches pressed against his skin, against his chest, and under his arms, shivering, grimacing while the chilled blood warmed to body temperature.

Little did Bo realize security personnel—it was Lydia's idea—

watched closed circuit video at night, waiting for an anomaly to appear on the new security cameras. When Bo's blur appeared, security officers pulled a newly installed steel gate across the hall outside the laboratory door and locked it. Bo focused on the blood he sorted and not noise in the hall. After all, if someone walked in on him Bo could mesmerize that person who ultimately would not remember their encounter.

Bo turned to the hall door, smiling at his haul. One arm secured his bloody booty inside the hoodie. He swung open the door and faced the closed barred gate and a half dozen security guards with guns drawn. A few beefy men in scrubs backed up the guards. Bo hissed and slammed the lab door. "Come out," one of the guards hollered. "There's no way out."

Bo scanned the lab's interior. No windows. Another door proved to be a closet. The vampire disease raged inside him, now more than ever with blood so nearby. He grabbed a cooled pouch, punctured the plastic with his fangs, and sucked greedily. There was no time to massage the blood inside the bag to mix it thoroughly. He downed the blood and tore open another. Guzzled it, and let it pour down his throat. A third bag followed. The cold blood soothed his throat. Bo swirled his long, vampire tongue around his lips to catch the blood that escaped his mouth. Bo stopped. Smacked his lips. The thirst was satisfied for a moment. He returned to the freezer. Replaced the consumed pouches with more frozen blood. He picked up the empty pouches and pressed them to the bottom of a trash can.

Outside in the hall, Bo heard the metal bars scraping across the floor. The security guards planned to attack. They could never overcome him. Their bullets, if they were fired inside the hospital, would have no effect.

His biggest problem was being identified. At least Lydia might remember him. He could not let that happen. He would blur through the guards as soon as they opened the door. He would be gone. They wouldn't know what direction to chase him. The guards mumbled outside the lab door as if making plans on the fly. Bo heard the bars slide back across the floor. It sounded like the bars were back in place and the guards were between Bo and the barrier. He would have to fight through the guards and then tear through the steel. There could be casualties. He wouldn't stand for that. Bo looked around the room again. A vent in the ceiling caught his attention. He extended his claws. Jumped. Tore off the vent cover. Jumped again. Tore through the ceiling next to the vent. Crawled on top of the ductwork, shimmied along its length, at times squeezing under pipes and conduits filled with wires.

The security guards burst into the room with guns leveled. Bo was gone. A single bag of frozen blood, which had slipped from Bo's hoodie, remained on the floor. He had already passed over several rooms, made a turn, and crawled toward the emergency room waiting area. He moved slower now, trying to remain as quiet as possible. He sensed people below him under the ceiling. By the time the security force retrieved a ladder and sent Lydia above the ceiling—she was the smallest and lightest—there was no trace of Bo.

The sound of his wiggling over the ductwork seemed to come from all directions at once. Lydia was afraid to follow a vampire above the ceiling, even if it was a vampire who had been a cute kid in high school. Security guards urged Lydia on from the ladder behind her. They told her to follow the duct where Bo's body had wiped it clean. Lydia climbed down the ladder. She said the dust bothered her and she was claustrophobic. Who else wanted to try, she repeated several times. There were no takers. Reluctantly, Lydia returned up the ladder and above the ceiling. She climbed on the vent and crawled after Bo.

Bo continued along the ductwork that branched out in several directions. He didn't want to stop but kept following a straight line he thought was directly over the hall. Finally, Bo passed over an intersecting wall below him. He thought he must be in the ER waiting room. He heard various chatter below, noise from a television in the distance. Ahead there was a loose metal strap supporting the ductwork and the piping sagged toward the ceiling. Bo hoped the sagging duct would hold his weight.

He had drunk three pouches of blood and carried more inside his hoodie. He was not willing to leave his booty behind. Bo decided to continue. He couldn't go back. He heard the guard who followed him on the ductwork and felt the vibration. Bo shimmied toward the sag. As he reached the lowest point he crashed through the ceiling and landed in a chair next to an elderly woman.

"My God!" she cried. Others screamed around the waiting room. The security force charged down the hall toward the commotion.

"Sorry, ma'am. Maintenance." Bo stood. He adjusted the blood bags inside the hoodie, pulled the hood forward to hide more of his face, and walked into the night through the sliding door that opened in front of him. Then he was gone.

CHAPTER FORTY

Guacamole and Del Hatch's reunion in front of the newly arrived Brethren and the group already tracking Bo was hilarious. The encounter near the pool even attracted some of La De Da's other lodgers, who slinked inside the group, possibly expecting a wedding ceremony. Del smiled and chuckled. Guacamole showed her beautiful smile against her dark skin. After a moment, they embraced.

"Is that a stick of dynamite in your pocket, big guy, or are you happy to see me," Guacamole said in her British accent. She wore what appeared to be army fatigues, although tighter and more stylish, with pants bloused inside her highly polished black boots. She was exactly as she appeared—a force to be reckoned with.

"A little bit of both. Man, you smell good enough to eat."

"If he heats up anymore, that dynamite might go off," Old Harriet said from her lounge chair in the shade. "Better push him in the water to cool off."

The group laughed, including the strangers who infiltrated the Brethren and had no idea they were surrounded by skilled vampire hunters. Those lodgers were disappointed there would be no wedding, and possibly a slice of cake, especially after Persimmon called the group to order and told them to meet in her room in five minutes.

In five minutes, the group assembled. Some had to stand. Old Harriet sat on the extra bed, her back against the headboard. Mad Maggie pulled out paper ready to take notes, but Persimmon waved a finger back and forth and tapped her head. John Bargain raised his cell phone with a gimble to record, but Persimmon shot him a glance and he dropped his arm. Goldenrod, who stood next to Bargain, rolled her eyes. The meeting details had to be memorized. Other than the tomes that recorded fighting vampires, and new idiosyncrasies discovered about the undead, the Brethren kept virtually no documents that could be traced, either by vampires or police.

Although some of the Brethren had been present on the West Coast for the attack on the vampire colony, there were some new faces. They were introduced. Jane Jennings explained her role in attracting Bo. It was not the first time a victim's scent was used to lure one or more vampires to staking. If vampires had one weakness, it was the intoxication they felt for humans that attracted them. Then, of course, there was the vampire disease's unrelenting demand for blood, a thirst that made the back of their throats feel like they swallowed sand.

The new Brethren were split up in twos to share rooms. Another room held the group's arsenal—crossbows, bolts, long and short stakes, an assortment of pistols and rifles, ammunition, and razor-sharp machetes and knives. The arsenal was delivered to a room central among those the Brethren rented, and a do-not-disturb sign was hung on the doorknob. Inside the room, four Brethren guarded the weapons.

Despite the foolhardiness of two vampires, even one a thousand years old, attacking a Brethren encampment, the vampire fighters took every precaution. Guards were posted, and Brethren took turns sleeping. It was a design developed in the Middle Ages when there were horses to defend, too. A design that had proved effective in protecting Brethren and killing vampires through the centuries.

Persimmon cleared her throat. The room fell silent. She looked around at the faces. She smiled at some. Winked at some. Then she began.

"By now you should all know we're after two vamps, the ancient Eva and a newbie, Bo Bentwood. Eva's been around a long time. Our forefathers hunted her during the Middle Ages throughout Europe and England. Bo was turned by Eva on the West Coast at the colony we destroyed a few months ago. I don't have to tell you it will probably take multiple bolts and stake thrusts to kill Eva. She's smart. She resisted the virgin blood we spread in the colony tunnel, while it drove the other vamps crazy and to their demise.

"Bo might not be your typical newbie fanger. He *might* have inherited some of Eva's prowess simply by drinking her blood when she turned him. For whatever reason, Bo seems loathe to kill humans, to drink their blood. Instead, he has taken to robbing blood banks and hospital laboratories where human blood is stored. Our gal behind the scenes, Goldenrod, discovered that during her snooping. We believe Bo has killed, but only a few, and he might have done it reluctantly."

"It's hardly believable, I know," Persimmon said, to the murmurs from the Brethren. "But I have some recent news Old Harriet received.

"Before I start," Old Harriet said," I want to tell *again* those of you who were on the coast that the cake you got me was the best I ever ate."

"You didn't have to wear it," a Brethren interjected from the back of the room.

"That was an accident," Old Harriet said, searching for the male voice in the crowd while the laughter died down. "I'm talking about the second cake—the one we ate. But now to the news. I called Lisa to check on her baby—the one Eva almost killed. We got talking. She said after Bo was shot and Eva brought him back to the colony, Bo begged to die. He didn't want to be a vampire. By that time, he had lost a lot of blood and was out of it. Eva made the decision to turn Bo, even though Lisa and Jimmy wanted her to let Bo die." Old Harriet paused for a moment. She looked around at the group. "Lisa and Jimmy knew that. So, my point is, maybe Bo still doesn't want to be a vampire."

There was more grumbling among the Brethren.

"Think about it," Persimmon said, bringing the room back to order. "That would explain the blood drive thefts." She shrugged. "It doesn't change our approach to Bo."

"No mercy," Overboard George called out.

"And we knew him when he was human," Mad Maggie added. "He's not Bo anymore."

"It does limit the places we have to look for him," Persimmon said. "He has hit Thaxton Hospital several times, and local blood drives that were advertised."

"We ought to have our own blood drive," Jane Jennings said. "I'll donate blood."

Persimmon twisted her mouth and looked at the ceiling for a moment. "It'll only take a little blood, Jane. Just enough to attract Bo." Persimmon said.

Red Beet raised his hand. "Will there be Shadows?"

"I doubt Eva has taken any yet," Persimmon said, "but Bo has Eva's old Shadow, Kazmer, in tow."

"I sat two stools over from him at the lunch counter at Betty's Restaurant while I was scoping out The Roxy the other day," Goldenrod said. She pinched her nose. "He's a real stinker."

"Gag a maggot," Old Harriet chimed in. "I know what they're like. Allergic to a bath."

Persimmon nodded. Raised a finger. "The gruesome twosome tend to rent a motel room and shower before they go out in public. It seems like they might need another cleanup from what Gold smelled. Keep your eyes open. They might show up here at the La De Da after dark."

"How can they stand themselves?" Jane said.

Old Harriet piped up again, squinting a knowing eye. "My mother used to say, 'A fox doesn't smell its own hole.' Meaning they might not notice it."

Persimmon outlined her plan to attract Bo to the Brethren. Jane would spend the day in the sun. Get sweated. No showering. Tomorrow she will leave a trail for the vampire to follow.

"EVER SMELL ANYTHING SO RIPE?" Jane said the next morning. "I hope this works."

"Not since I lived on the street," Mad Maggie said. "This'll work."

Persimmon drove Jane to the Roxy. She instructed Jane to rub her hands over and her arms and legs against street light poles, mailboxes, street signs, and anything that wouldn't give her a splinter. They averaged two or three stops a block all the way back to the La De Da, including the arsenal doorknob and frame.

"Can I get a shower now," Jane wanted to know. "I have most of my skin rubbed off."

As evening approached, a contingent of Brethren waited inside the arsenal, weapons ready. Persimmon told Jane she should get a shower and return to the arsenal. She handed Jane a long stake with sharpened point. Just in case.

Jane walked toward her room, dragging the stake's blunt end on the concrete walkway. There was still another hour until sundown and plenty of time to shower and change clothes, rejoin the Brethren in the arsenal for what she hoped would be the last night of Bo Bentwood's short, unnatural life. A few muscle cars lined the parking lot in front of the motel. A car show was scheduled for the weekend, which brought motorheads from all over into Thaxton.

She had seen a billboard on the highway and posters around town. Someone had plastered one on The Roxy's ticket booth window.

Jane, although no car enthusiast, stopped twice to admire custom paint jobs and splashes of bright chrome erupting through car hoods. She froze when her eyes spotted a white van ahead, pulled in backward, among the parked show cars. She fingered her long stake. Pulled her room key from her hip pocket, making sure it was pointed correctly to slip into the door lock.

Jane took a deep breath and ran toward her room and into the arms of Kazmer Savoy, who stepped from beside the white van into her path. Kazmer deftly covered Jane's nose and mouth with a cloth soaked in chloroform, a lesson he learned from the interstate trucker who had briefly kidnapped Lisa, lifted Jane off her feet with one arm and caught the falling stake with his free hand before it could clatter on the concrete.

Kazmer placed Jane inside the back of the van, threw in the long stake, climbed inside the driver's seat, and as was his custom, started the engine and pulled out slowly, creeping toward the La De Da parking lot exit.

KAZMER DROVE below the speed limit. Kept the rear-view mirror trained on the unconscious Jane instead of the road behind him. He made sure she breathed regularly and had not yet regained consciousness. She would be more trouble than any woman he had encountered—worse than even Lisa, who stabbed him and escaped from him.

Bo was infatuated with this woman. That was the problem. He should take her outside the city to a secluded spot. Slip his stiletto knife through her ribs and puncture her heart. He knew how to guide the blade with his deft fingers. He had murdered many times with the knife he always carried. She would be unconscious and never feel her death. That knife would end the problem. His pick and shovel were in the back. He would bury her where she never would be found. Her scent would disappear from Thaxton. Bo would forget about her.

However, he had already lied to Bo, his master. He hadn't told Bo someone had identified the vampire. It was unthinkable for a Shadow to betray a vampire master. It spelled death for the Shadow when the master discovered the lie.

Kazmer rounded a curve in the road. Jane rolled from one side of the van to the other. She was still unconscious.

Kazmer had a second idea. He could pull over and let her lie along the roadside. Someone would find her. Surely, she would flee from Thaxton and cease to be a problem.

A third option—returning her to Bo—was the worst. She might escape again. She would have to be fed and cleaned. The woman would become Kazmer's problem. If Bo turned her, Kazmer would have two new vampires to watch over and train in the vampire way. As he drove through the setting sun, he fingered the stiletto knife inside his hoodie. Then he felt something else in his pocket, which he pulled out. It was the sling Bo had made him when the two child vampires injured Kazmer back at the vampire colony.

He held the sling in his fingers. He squeezed the cloth in his meaty hand. Looked at the dirty rag while watching the road. Receiving that sling was the only act of kindness Kazmer had ever known. There was a wide spot on the road ahead. Kazmer swung the van around and headed back to The Roxy. He would take the girl to Bo.

CHAPTER FORTY-ONE

The Brethren paired up in their assignments for the night, while a contingent remained in Persimmon's room. Old Harriet was tired after being on post most of the day across the street from The Roxy. She had the night off and made her way back to her room, passed the armory and Del Hatch's room, where she could hear Guacamole laughing from inside.

That Guacamole even laughs like the British.

Ahead something shining caught her eye just off the sidewalk next to a muscle car's oversized tire. Couldn't be money, she thought. Perhaps a fancy cigarette lighter. She quit smoking years ago. Still, you never knew when a shiny cigarette lighter might impress. She scanned the nearby area in fear some motorhead might be searching for the lost treasure. With no one in the vicinity she skipped the last few steps, bent over to see what shined in the near dark.

It was a room key—the same number, 1 3—she shared with Jane now that more Brethren had moved in. Old Harriet pressed her index finger to her lip and thought. Jane went for a shower. How would she get into the room without a key? Old Harriet had her own key. Did Jane go to the office for another key? La De Da was a swell place, but how many keys would they have for one room? Old Harriet continued to her room. Knocked on the door. There was no answer. The room was dark. Old Harriet opened the lock with Jane's key. Nudged open the door.

"Jane? It's Old Harriet. I found your key outside. I'm checking to see if you are all right." Old Harriet turned on the room's ceiling light. Found the bathroom unused. Old Harriet pressed her index finger to her lips again. Walked outside and locked the door. Thought a moment. Ran the short distance to Persimmon's room.

Old Harriet burst into the room. A half dozen crossbows trained on her immediately. Old Harriet raised her hands.

"It's Jane. I think she's gone." Old Harriet held the room key between her fingers. Let the key fob dangle. It twisted back and forth reflecting light off its smooth surface. "I found her key in the gutter. She never made it to the room. I just checked. No light on. Nothing's been disturbed."

The Brethren started an immediate search of their fellow members' rooms. Perhaps she stopped to trade notes with someone after the meeting, but no one had seen Jane after she left Persimmon's room. Except for the Brethren guarding the armory, the rest of the group convened back in Persimmon's room for a head count and a solution to Jane's disappearance. The Brethren were silent for a long time. Most looked toward the floor while they contemplated. Fidgeted with coffee cups, soda cans, or water bottles.

Scenarios soon swirled. There was no reason to believe Jane abandoned the Brethren when they were close to killing Bo. She wanted to finish Bo herself. She would not be so foolish to go after Bo herself and risk running into Eva. Why would she leave the new clothes the group bought her? Had someone with drugs lured her away? She had not been clean for very long and might try to find a fix.

Finally, Old Harriet piped up from her perch on Persimmon's bed. "If you want my opinion, I think that big goon, Kazimotto, or whatever his name is, took her. Jumped Jane in the parking lot. She probably fainted when she saw him. He's a nightmare in the daylight." Old Harriet looked toward the ceiling and cried, "Heaven help the poor girl. In the company of goons and vampires."

Silence followed again. Persimmon looked at Guacamole.

Guacamole arched one dark eyebrow. "Road trip?"

Persimmon smiled. Looked at Overboard George.

"Anybody know what's playing at The Roxy?" George asked.

"*Night of the Living Dead*," Mad Maggie said.

"I suspect they been showing that for a while," George added.

Old Harriet and a few Brethren would remain in Persimmon's room. The armory guards would stay in place. Old Harriet balked. "I'm going with the road trip. Ain't missed a vampire killing in almost a year. I sure want to be there for Bo's goodbye party."

"You up to it, Old Harriet?" Persimmon asked. "You've already had a long day in the sun."

"Try and keep up with me."

"I don't like attacking at night," Persimmon said, "especially in a big place none of us are familiar with, but Jane might have little time. From the intel we gathered on Bo, I don't think he'll kill Jane, but we must consider that Eva might be there and Kazmer is armed."

"I say we save Bo for Jane, and I finish Kazimotto, or whatever his name is," Old Harriet said, lifting her machete in its scabbard over her head.

"You are one ferocious little lady," Del Hatch said with a wink.

"And don't you forget it," Old Harriet said.

THE SUN HAD SLIPPED below the horizon on a warm late spring evening by the time the Brethren reached The Roxy. Three vehicles. Ten vampire fighters. All armed to the teeth—crossbows, long and short stakes, pistols, machetes, and long jungle knives with serrated blades. Mad Maggie and Old Harriet carried only machetes. Old Harriet wished she had one of the stakes made from her old chair on wheels, but they had already claimed the hearts of vampires. Del Hatch toted his BAR slung over his back, extra clips of 30.06 armor-piercing bullets, a crossbow, extra bolts, and his personal jungle knife strapped to his leg. The Brethren approached the old theater from opposite directions. When the three groups were within eyesight of one another Overboard George led the group down the alley to the side entrance. He counted down the row of emergency door exits until he reached the door Bo and Kazmer used to enter and exit the theater, the one that had fresh scrape marks on the concrete sidewalk.

Before the Brethren left the La De Da Motel, Persimmon gave the final instructions. The theater, at least from the exterior, appeared similar to one Old Harriet was familiar with as a child. After they were inside the door, the fighters would split into three groups. Overboard George would sweep up the theater's left side, cross the stage, and return through the theater on the right side toward the lobby. Persimmon and Old Harriet would go directly to the lobby. Guacamole and Del Hatch would go directly to the balcony. Any group that found vamps or anything interesting would call out. There seemed little chance of keeping the raid a surprise, especially with the difficulty they expected forcing the emergency exit door open.

Everyone arrived at the emergency doors. John Bargain pulled out his cell phone and gimble. Persimmon shook her head no. "For posterity," Bargain mouthed equally silent. He sidled next to Persimmon and whispered. "Who among the Brethren has seen an ancient vampire erupt in flames? Die the permanent death?" He smiled at Persimmon. The other fighters waited for her response.

"All right, but if you upload any of this to your channel, to the internet, I will personally castrate you."

"I understand," Bargain said. "This is for Brethren only."

Overboard George and Del inserted their fingers in the seam where the two emergency doors met. They each took a deep breath. The rest of the vampire fighters waited expectantly. The doors swung open easily and silently.

"You think they're waiting for us?" Old Harriet whispered. "You think Jane did a Bo, told the vampires our plans while she was mesmerized?"

"I don't know," Persimmon said. "It's too late to retreat, or the vamps will get away. This is where we stop them, either one or both of them." Persimmon looked at her fellow Brethren. "Ready?"

The Brethren nodded.

"We stay with the original plan. Go!"

CHAPTER FORTY-TWO

Kazmer stood next to the water-filled orchestra pit inside The Roxy. He held two take-out meals from Betty's Restaurant in a paper bag gripped in one closed fist. He twisted his mouth and cranked his head toward his shoulder. He grunted.

Water dripped from the hole in the roof into the pit. He was amazed that such a drip could fill the pit, enough to float a baby-grand piano. He noticed the piano had moved during the last day from the pit's far side near the stage to the near side close to the audience. Kazmer could take a step onto the instrument's hinged top if he so desired, but he knew his weight would capsize the instrument and dump him into the unsavory black pool.

Kazmer held an unlit cigarette between his lips. It was a smoke one of the old geezers from Betty's Restaurant gave him earlier in the day, a popular brand of filtered cigarette. He never liked the mild tasting American smokes, preferring the strong loose tobacco he rolled himself, a tobacco that reminded him of the old country. There was something about rolling a cigarette, the hope of making it perfect, the anticipation of the first inhale that he found as calming as that initial rush of nicotine.

Two things perplexed him before he returned through the theater to the balcony, climbed the wide staircase to the balcony, and dug into his food—how the orchestra pit filled from a small drip overhead and why did the piano move across the water when there was nothing to propel it. Kazmer stared into the black water, thought it looked like the water that sometimes flooded the mines where he worked in the old country. He grunted again and turned toward the back of the theater.

It was just before sundown. Kazmer's eyes had become accustomed to the darkness in the theater's extensive interior with its peeling paint and mold-covered surfaces. Its funky aroma. Bo would wake up soon. He still had blood from his last hospital heist. Therefore, Bo might stay in, and they would continue Kazmer's English lessons. He held today's edition of the Thaxton newspaper under his arm with news about the last blood heist. Despite the hospital's attempts to keep the missing blood a secret and solve the problem internally, too many staff, patients, and visitors had seen Bo's escapades. Had seen him ripping through the ceiling, landing in the hospital waiting room, and disappearing suddenly in a blur.

Now, they must leave Thaxton for another city. It was only a matter of time before they were discovered. Before Bo was identified. The girl bound on the balcony would be a problem unless Bo mesmerized her into compliance. *Compliance* was a word Kazmer had learned earlier in the week and decided to use and think about as much as possible.

Kazmer climbed the stairs to the balcony. He scared two rats as they frolicked on the landing. *That's all we need. Now there will be more rodents.* He looked down at the paper bag that contained his evening meal and food for the girl. Grease spots already showed through the paper sack.

Jane cried silently when Kazmer appeared inside the balcony door. He approached her and checked the rope knots that bound her wrists and ankles. He untied her wrist restraints behind her back and retied them with her hands in front. He pulled her food and a bottle of water from the paper bag and put them beside her.

Kazmer warned, "Don't make any trouble or I will knock you out again." He pulled the bottle of chloroform and a rag from his pocket. "You must *comply* to the master's desires. You are his now. Life can be good, like I have it, or it can be bad. It will be your choice."

"Fuck you, Beetlejuice. My name is Jane, and I don't belong to any vampire."

Kazmer pursed his lips. "Eat and stay quiet or I will knock you out again. Then you will never know what he does to you. You scream and I will knock you out. You cause trouble like you did at the factory, and I will knock you out. Remember what I say. You must comply."

Kazmer moved to the balcony's first row of seats, raised a cloud of dust when he dropped into one and opened his meal. Kazmer ate slowly, covering almost everything with packets of ketchup. He heard Jane's meal container snap open. Her water bottle opened. Kazmer smiled. She complied, he thought. Kazmer finished his food and downed a plastic bottle of Diet Coke. Then he lit the American cigarette he had saved. The taste was smooth. He still preferred his own loose tobacco and immediately rolled his own cigarette after he stubbed out the filtered smoke. Kazmer kept a wary eye on Jane, turning his head toward her every time he heard her move.

The zipper on Bo's mummy sleeping bag opened. The smell of the grave followed almost immediately. Kazmer wondered how long it would take Bo to recognize Jane's scent. How surprised he would be! Kazmer smiled after he inhaled deeply on his cigarette.

Bo erupted from his sleeping bag. Blurred to Kazmer at the balcony's rail. "She's here, Kaz. I smell her." Bo looked around. His mouth dropped open. Kazmer saw shock and surprise on Bo's pale face.

Kazmer chuckled. Cigarette smoke encircled his head, making

him squint. "I caught her, Mr. Bo. Just for your pleasure. Jane is in the back." Kazmer waved the hand holding the cigarette toward Jane.

"Jane?"

"Her name is Jane. She told me, Mr. Bo." Kazmer smiled broadly.

"Not Jane. *Her!*" Bo looked confused. He sniffed the air and scanned the theater stage.

Kazmer looked at Bo. Studied his eyes, an act Shadows rarely did with their vampire masters. "I don't understand." He quickly lowered his gaze.

Jane coughed when Bo's odor reached her.

The piano in the water-filled orchestra pit bobbed. The movement, even in the near dark, caught Bo and Kazmer's attention. They leaned over the rail to watch the activity below. Bo sniffed the air again. Black water lapped over the piano's dusty top. The instrument floated to the pit's rim, and bumped the edge several times like a docking boat. Then it remained still in the water.

"What the fuck just happened Kaz?"

"Jane is in the back," Kazmer said. They stared at each other again.

"No."

"She is," Kazmer said. He pointed his cigarette to the rear

"No, Kaz. It's *her*."

"Isn't it *she?*" Kazmer waited for an answer. There was silence in the old theater.

The piano lid burst open. It flew off its hinge. Sailed across the theater. Shattered as it smashed into the wall. Eva stood from the piano's interior, a smirk on her face. Her first step plucked several off-key wires. Broke one. They sounded discordant. She planted a boot on the auditorium floor and leaped through the air to the balcony. Landed a step from Bo. Kazmer kneeled immediately.

Eva straightened her back and pointed her chin toward Bo. She had fed recently. Her skin was taut and youthful looking. She wore a new tight-fitting cowgirl outfit, although it smelled dank from the orchestra pit water. She cupped a palm along Bo's cheek.

"You are no longer my little rabbit." She smiled. "No pounding heartbeat. No sweat. No fear. Your flesh is as cold and hard as mine. You are one of us. A vampire. We will have wonderful times, Bo. Spend centuries together."

She placed a hand on Bo's shoulder and pulled him toward her, but Bo resisted and took a step back.

"What troubles you, Bo? Was my entrance such a surprise? Was I too dramatic?"

He stepped back again and kicked the long stake Persimmon had given Jane before she disappeared. Kazmer had carried it to the balcony and thought of hurtling it into the stage curtains for fun but soon forgot it. Eva blurred behind Bo, retrieved the stake, and returned to her original position. She hefted the weapon.

"This is Brethren craftmanship," Eva said. She examined the point. "Kazmer?" She pulled Kazmer to his feet.

Kazmer lowered his head. "The Brethren are in the city, Mistress. They are at the La De Da Motel."

"I know!" Eva screamed. She broke the long shaft in half like it was a pencil. Threw the two halves on seats nearby. "I know everything." Her eyes bulged. Her face was contorted. Black veins stood out under her face and neck's pale skin. "Do you think I couldn't follow you? Do you think I can't sense the presence of the Brethren? Kazmer! Who is this cunt *you* have tied up in the back?"

Kazmer stuttered. "She is Bo's pet. We caught her today."

"*We?*"

"I caught her today, Mistress. She was almost Bo's first time."

"Now he's in love. How tender." Eva blurred to the back of the theater. She stood over. Jane. Bo followed in an instant. Kazmer clambered up the steps and remained respectfully behind. Eva lifted Jane like a rag doll. The captive sobbed and struggled to free herself. Her feet dangled off the floor. Eva sniffed. Smiled. "You are the one whose scent they spread all over town so Bo would follow you back to the—what was it?"

"La De Da," Kazmer whispered with his head bowed.

Eva dropped Jane, who tumbled to the floor, and rolled down the steps and against the balcony rail. "Bo, you didn't feed on her." She threw her head back and laughed. "Vampires don't feel love. I might drain her now." Eva reached for Jane again, but Bo jumped between them.

Eva extended her claws. Rolled her shoulders. Narrowed her eyes to two slits. "Protective? I have fed, but I can always drink more."

"When I was your pet, nobody could touch me," Bo shouted. "She is my pet now and nobody touches her."

Eva smiled. She raised a clawed hand to her cheek and raked claw marks across her face that healed immediately. She licked a drop of blood from her finger. "Kazmer! Are you no longer my Shadow?" She looked toward Kazmer.

"I live to serve you, Mistress." Kazmer flattened himself on the floor before her.

"Then why did you leave me to rot underground on the West Coast? Where is your loyalty, Kazmer? Bo?" Eva spread out her arms. "You live in the lap of luxury in this theater. Do you care about me? Do you wonder if I survived? Did you dig through that mountainside in search of my body? Noooo! You leave me like...roadkill."

"It was my error, Mistress," Kazmer said, sobbing, averting his eyes from the incensed vampiress. "I thought it would be better for Bo if I stayed with him. He was the first to crawl from the ground. You know how it is. A new vampire needs training."

"Do you suppose you, a human, would train a vampire? How dare you!"

Kazmer continued between sobs, "Even though I have limited knowledge of such things, I did not want Bo to fall into a trap I might see."

"So, you bring this little chickadee here? A Brethren! I will strip off your flesh, Kazmer. You will wail in agony for days. When you are healed, I will do it again. Maybe then you will learn." Eva raised a clawed hand ready to strike.

"I told Kaz I wanted the girl," Bo said calmly. "I still want her. She is mine until I decide otherwise."

Eva blurred to Bo. Looked into his eyes. "Are you truthful?"

"I am," Bo said.

"You are already strong. I can no longer read your mind." Eva stepped back. "I believe you, my little rabbit, until you give me reason to distrust you. You never could lie to me. I suspect you still can't." She paused for a moment and looked into Bo's eyes. "How I miss your pounding little heart."

Eva looked at Kazmer, who still trembled. "Rise, Kazmer. Your new master has saved you. Receive my blessing." Kazmer stood slowly, unsteadily. He breathed heavily. He approached Eva and bowed. She kissed him lightly on the top of his head. Keeping his eyes lowered, Kazmer retreated to a nearby theater seat. He immediately started to roll a new cigarette.

Eva looked around the theater. "Such a grand place. Who has not eaten? The human girl had chicken. Potatoes.

"French fries, you cunt."

"Bo, your pet needs to be trained., I will be happy to do it," Eva said with a snarl.

"I will handle her," Bo said.

"Very well. And dear Kazmer. You ate a cheeseburger and... french fries. Bo? Have you fed? I think not."

"Not yet," Bo said. He pulled a hospital cooler from under a seat, opened it, and offered Eva a bag of blood. She massaged the bag for a moment. Then she sniffed it. Opening the bag with a claw, she drained its contents, spilling blood on her checkered shirt. She slurped up blood that ran over her chin with her long vampire tongue.

Eva belched, and a foul odor filled the air. "Is this what you live on?" The vampiress looked incredulous.

"I've taken a few human lives, by accident, but I decided to kill no more," Bo said. He looked at her for a reaction. There was none at first.

"Never? Never!"

"Never," Bo said softly. "This is what you made me. A monster."

Eva was silent for a moment. Her chin trembled. She clapped her hands once, sending echoes off the walls that sounded like a gunshot. Eva's head rolled back; she laughed as if she had never laughed before. Peals of laughter echoed off the balcony walls. She walked as if intoxicated. She slapped the backs of the seats, raising clouds of dust. She fell into one of the seats. More dust rose. Eventually, she fell silent and eyed Bo with disgust.

"How long do you think the vampire disease inside you will allow you to drink this?" She tossed the empty blood bag over the balcony rail.

"I'll drink it as long as I can. Until something better comes along. Maybe synthetic blood. Who knows?" Bo approached Eva along the curving aisle of seats. "But I will never kill again. I didn't ask to be a vampire. I didn't want to live forever. I begged you to let me die. But no. You had to save your *little rabbit*. Lisa and Jimmy asked you to let me die. I was riddled with bullets. No one could have saved me—even if you blurred me to the hospital. You were the only one who could save me with an unnatural life bent on murder."

"I was not ready to let you go, Bo," Eva said. "Kazmer loved you, too. Didn't you, Kazmer?"

"Yes," Kazmer answered sheepishly from his seat. "I did not want to lose Bo. He showed me kindness."

"So, what has been done can't be undone," Eva said with finality. "Throw yourself off a skyscraper. It will hurt when you hit but you will heal. Blow your brains out with a gun but you will heal. Try to step into the sunlight or fall on a stake. The vampire disease will not let you end your life and *its* existence inside you."

"I've already tried it," Bo said.

"Killing is a natural instinct to a vampire," Eva said. She stood, strode to Bo, and touched his arm lightly. "The human lives you take are not important. Did you care about the cattle that were ground up for the cheeseburgers you loved as a human? It's the same. You will see."

"It's not the same," Bo protested. "Humans have lives, souls."

"Human life is inconsequential," Eva said. She turned to Kazmer. "How many humans have you killed?"

"Many."

"Do all those lives affect you? Can you fall into your human sleep without a troubled mind?"

"I sleep. Some who I killed would have killed me."

Eva stood with her hands on her hips. "How many were innocents?"

Kazmer twisted his mouth. "Many."

"And do you grieve for them?"

"To be honest, no," Kazmer said.

"I do grieve," Bo said. "I grieve for my brother and my mother and my father who has lost his entire family. I grieve for the innocent souls I took since I am a vampire."

Eva showed the coldest expression Bo had ever seen. She looked at Kazmer. "I would have trained you better. I see we have no future together, Bo, the way you are now. You are a danger to yourself and a danger to those around you. The authorities will see you on cameras. You will be identified. You will be tracked down and destroyed. Although you are already strong, the Brethren are stronger with their many members and their knowledge of the vampire ways." Eva raised her head. Pointed her chin at Bo. "I will go on alone until I find another Shadow. Kazmer, you may remain with Bo or follow me."

"Mistress, with your permission, I will remain to help Bo. He will need my help."

"Bo will make you a powerful vampire, Kazmer, if he lives long enough to turn you. I will leave now. When you return to the vampire way, Bo, you can join me. You will know how to find me. Goodbye."

Eva prepared to blur away but stopped suddenly. She raised her finger. The claw extended. She stooped down behind the balcony railing. Bo and Kazmer followed her. All three heard jovial voices—men and women—outside in the alley.

"The Brethren?" Bo whispered.

"Too loud." Kazmer shot Bo a quick glance. He reached behind and grabbed the two halves of the long stake the vampiress had snapped in two.

The people outside groaned, cursed, and huffed. Eventually, the emergency door below in the auditorium inched open, emitting an ear-splitting screech as the metal door bottom scraped on the concrete sidewalk outside.

Eva's head snapped toward Bo. "Make sure that bitch doesn't give us away. It might be the Brethren and the noise is a trick."

Kazmer pulled his bottle of chloroform and rag from his pocket. "I will put her out for a while. I will not hurt her, Mr. Bo." Kazmer crawled away. After a brief scuffle, Jane was silent at the back of the balcony. He returned to Bo and Eva. Kazmer looked at Bo nervously. There was only one way out of the theater for him—the door that had just been pried open.

Bo patted Kazmer's arm. "We'll get out of this together."

Kazmer returned a smile.

Eva watched the auditorium with interest.

"What the fuck, people. Can we make a little more noise, please?" a curly-haired heavyset man in shorts and a T-shirt called, cupping his hands around his mouth, as he stepped through the emergency exit door. "If there are spirits here, you shits just scared them away."

"Fuck you, Wilson," a tall, thin man said while he hauled a trunk through the door.

"This is serious stuff, people. I want some serious attitudes. It's going to be a long, long night before we crawl out of here at daybreak."

Eva and Kazmer stared at Bo, expecting answers.

Bo rolled his eyes. "It looks like The Roxy's been invaded by paranormal researchers."

CHAPTER FORTY-THREE

The paranormal investigators made trip after trip carrying in microphone stands, boxes, coils of wire, monitors, a folding table, backpacks with more stuff while the heavyset Wilson stood surveying the theater with the aid of a powerful flashlight. He panned the light over the stage curtains, the ornate faux boxes on either side of the stage, too small to accommodate actual people, the orchestra pit with its now damaged floating baby grand piano, the balcony, the projector room with its several square cutouts behind the balcony, the rococo molding and designs with their peeling paint and missing pieces.

"This was quite the place back in the day," Wilson mused. "Makes you wonder whether anyone ever died here. I hope so...."

"Of fright during a monster movie?" said a tall, lanky woman with close-cropped green hair, who passed him carrying a cooler.

"Maybe took the big one," Wilson finished, "and didn't know how to get out. Or," Wilson raised a finger, "someone spent so many happy hours here that they returned to spend eternity after death."

"That's gruesome," a slim man said. "Hey, boss, where are we setting up central? I hope not on the balcony. I don't want to carry all this stuff upstairs."

"No. No," Wilson said. "The clear area by the orchestra pit. Just don't set up too close to the water. I don't want anybody to get fried tonight."

"There's chunks of plaster all over the floor," the slim man said. "The table and chairs won't sit right."

"Well, Billy, find a broom and push it out of the way. Look behind the stage. There's got to be a broom somewhere in this place. When we're done, Cheryl can set up the table and start to wire the monitors. When you're done, we can put the genny over by the door. Point the exhaust outside. We don't want to be overcome and join whoever's already here."

A short muscular man in a white T-shirt leaned through the door. "Hey, I'm going to move the van."

"Make it quick, Mark," Wilson said. "We have a lot of work to do before the ghosts come out. I hope someone remembered to bring in the food."

"I carried it right by you," the green-haired woman said. "You didn't see me?"

"I love you, Cheryl," Wilson called. "Too preoccupied on this place to notice. It's a shame the city's tearing it down. It should be a historic place. That's what happens when absentee landlords let a place go to ruin."

"At least we'll record her final days, from what it looks like now to the actual demo," Cheryl said. "It will make a nice keepsake that will make us a little income. Everybody will want a copy."

"It's about time we see a paycheck for all the work we do," Billy said.

On the balcony, crouched behind the rail, the vampiress whispered, "I agree. The food is here. I will show you tonight how a vampire kills, Bo. After you smell blood in the air, the blood of several people, their terror, and the disease inside you will make you kill. You will enjoy the hunt, no matter how short it is. You will relish the hot splash of blood running down your throat. The panic in your victim during the final moment of life will intoxicate you as much as the blood itself. My little rabbit, you will become a real vampire tonight."

"Never," Bo hissed.

The vampiress looked at Bo. She snarled, "I want to watch this—how do you say it—play out before we feed. It should prove to be amusing, I think. What do you say, Kazmer, my faithful friend?"

"I think we should leave now. I don't like so many people near our only exit. What if we are discovered? What if they realize there are vampires here?"

"No one will be left alive to tell a story," Eva said. "*That* is how we survive."

"The authorities..." Kazmer started.

"Will be clueless, as always, especially in these modern times," Eva said with finality.

Kazmer lowered his eyes.

"Remember, Bo. The disease inside you relishes the death of your victims. The disease will reward you for the fear you inflict." Eva smiled. "This will be wonderful."

Billy found a long-handled push broom behind the stage and swept the floor clean near the orchestra pit, pushing plaster into the water. He tossed the broom on the stage when he was finished. He and Cheryl set up the table in front of the first row of theater seats. They cleaned the seats as best as possible, raising dust that made them sneeze.

"I hope these seats aren't infested with lice or anything," Cheryl said. "Maybe I'll sit on the floor tonight."

"Nothing could survive—especially bugs—all these years the place has been closed," Billy said. "Even a bug has to eat."

Mark carried over three monitors to capture video from cameras they'd set up around the theater. Cheryl fetched coils of cable to run between the cameras to the monitors.

MEANWHILE, Wilson walked up the theater's incline to the lobby. He inspected the concession stand, clean of any food, not even a candy bar wrapper. A dead rat, mummified, lay inside the empty popcorn maker. Just like a roach motel, it got in but couldn't get out. Not a single kernel remained, although there was a quantity of rat droppings. The rodent, with its face pressed against the glass, seemed to smile with its yellow protruding teeth and mummified mouth, as if its final meal had been satisfying. Stains covered the theater's front interior, apparently from a leak outside on the marquee.

Wilson peered through the front doors around the old posters and signs plastered on the glass. He crossed the lobby to a door with the script LADIES in faded paint. He opened the door. The restroom was dark. Wilson flicked on his flashlight. He scared himself when the flashlight caught his image in a dust-covered mirror. He looked around as if to make sure none of his team had followed him in and saw him jump. There were toilet stalls with a few missing doors. Pedestal sinks without faucets. A long, ornate sofa with slashed cushions. Two more mummified rats. Wilson smiled. All worth filming for the group's vlog—especially close-ups of the rats.

Wilson returned across the lobby to the men's bathroom. He opened the door and found a long downward carpeted staircase. Pitch dark. He propped open the door at the top with a piece of plaster he found nearby, which shed some wan illumination from a streetlight outside that shined through the front doors and into the shaft. He turned on the flashlight and proceeded downward.

It was necessary to navigate the stairs with his feet at an angle because the steps were narrow and the risers short. Three lengths of handrail had been cobbled together along the stairwell's length, but the middle section was missing and lay at the bottom. The wooden steps under the carpet creaked with every step. He turned to shine the flashlight over his shoulder because the creaking sounded like it was behind him rather than under his feet. Was it merely an echo? Wilson was losing his nerve and thought of returning to the lobby but decided to continue.

He was halfway down, pressing his hand against the wall where the railing was missing when the door above slammed shut. He jumped. Cursed. Lost his balance. Tripped down several steps until he caught the next section of the rail and yanked it off the wall. Wilson stopped to catch his breath. He trained his flashlight up the stairwell to the door. A long spring from the door to the jamb vibrated after an initial twang. He sighed. That spring still worked after all this time and its tension closed the door with a bang despite the wedge under it. Except for his flashlight's beam, Wilson was surrounded by darkness. After he caught his breath and his heart stopped hammering, he continued down the steps with one hand on the loose railing, the other panning the flashlight around.

Wilson reached the bottom of the steps and another door. Something—a rat most likely—scurried unseen in the darkness. The door pulled open, as the one at the top had. He immediately noted the spring on the door's interior and let the door close noiselessly behind him. The faint odor of old disinfectant remained trapped inside the closed restroom for years. Black and white tiles, some cracked or missing, covered the floor and walls. A row of mostly smashed sinks and built-in tall ceramic urinals occupied one wall. A row of stained, dried-up toilets in doorless stalls stood opposite.

Wilson held his flashlight under his arm while he bellied up to one of the old urinals, with its many hairline cracks, to relieve himself, letting the stream carve up an ancient dust-covered web that still retained a few dried insects suspended in a spider's silk. He sighed again. Fixed his jeans. Noted his heartbeat was normal again, finally, with two fingers pressed against the side of his neck. It was the first time he had been calm since he descended into this hell. He smiled. This bathroom would provide more video documentation.

Wilson trained his flashlight on the door. Followed its beam to the door and pushed. The door moved a few inches and bumped into something. Stopped. *That fucking railing. Should have moved it when I had the chance.* He was trapped. He knew the team would never hear him under the theater. *Fucking Phantom of the Opera creepy. I'll never live this down.* His friends were like that. Wilson took a step back and put his flashlight on the floor so its beam pointed toward the ceiling. That gave him a little light to see where he was going. He didn't want to miss the door and slam his body into the wall.

Wilson prepared to throw his considerable weight against the dust-covered door. *One, two, three!* He charged and hit the door with his beefy shoulder. The door banged off the wall, ricocheted back, and struck him in the face. Wilson cursed. He reeled back and caught himself as he was about to fall. He felt his nose and returned to the flashlight. There was no blood on his fingers. He rubbed his nose again and wiggled the cartilage back and forth. It was sore but did not appear to be broken. Wilson pushed the door again. It opened easily, halfway, with a twang from the old spring. He let the door snap closed.

Wilson retrieved his flashlight from the floor. Pointed it toward the door and pushed. It glided open. The door spring twanged again. He raised the flashlight. Found a cowgirl on the first step grinning at him. Her eyes were ablaze. Her fangs were extended. Wilson dropped the flashlight. It went out. The vampiress tore open Wilson's throat and drank with gusto.

Behind the balcony rail, Bo and Kazmer watched the paranormal investigators piecing together their equipment. "I'm not starting the genny until we're all connected," Mark said. "I don't want to siphon gas from the van before dawn like last time. Don't want to get shocked, either."

Go for it," Cheryl answered. "You're our sparky."

Billy approached the central table. He carried a television camera on a tripod and a long coil of wire. "This looks like another three-man investigation. Where the fuck's Wilson?"

"Good question," Cheryl said from her cross-legged seat on the floor. "The food's with us. He might actually be doing something... somewhere. By the way, it's a three-*person* investigation. Let's keep the terminology correct."

"I stand corrected," Billy said. "I'm going to set up this camera on the balcony."

"Did you hear that?" Kazmer whispered, keeping an eye on the activity below. "We should leave now."

Eva blurred to their side. The front of her shirt was covered with fresh blood.

"Hey, I thought I saw a shadow on the balcony," Mark said, looking up from a monitor he was connecting with cable. "Out of the corner of my eye. In the middle, first row."

"You fucking with me because I just said I'm going up there to place a camera?" Billy said. He panned his flashlight over the balcony.

"Swear," Mark answered, raising his right hand. "I'll go upstairs with you."

"Never mind. Do your sparky work," Billy said. "I'm going to look for Wilson while I'm at it and haul his ass back here to do some work. He thinks he's in charge just because he had the idea for this investigation work while we were all buzzed at the bar."

"This sounds like fun," Eva said. "Let's hide and surprise them. Where the projector is. Bring the girl."

Eva, Bo, and Kazmer crawled up the steps in the darkness and disappeared into the projection room. Bo carried Jane over his shoulder.

"This is amazing," Eva said after they were inside. "This was the projector. It looks like it could still show a movie. All we need is a movie."

"And electricity," Kazmer added. "What do we do with Jane? She'll be waking soon. I don't want to knock her out again so soon."

Eva looked around. "Lock her in the closet over there."

Bo was obedient. He carried Lisa to the closet. Placed her inside, closed the door, and locked it."

"There's a bathroom over here," Kazmer said. "The three of us can fit in." He patted his hoodie pocket. "I need a cigarette."

"You'll have to wait. We don't want them to smell the smoke," Bo said.

"Yes, we do." Eva clapped her hands. "Let them follow the smoke. Don't you see? That will be the surprise. We'll jump out."

"Then what?" Bo wanted to know.

"We'll see what happens."

Kazmer grunted.

THEY SQUEEZED into the tiny bathroom inside the projection room. A toilet and sink. Kazmer sat on the toilet and rolled a cigarette. Bo held the lighter for him to see. Eva was pressed into the corner and suppressed giggles with her hand cupped over her mouth.

Meanwhile, Billy set up his camera on the balcony to encompass most of the theater below. It could be adjusted later. He dropped the cable over the balcony to Cheryl, who waited below. She uncoiled it down an aisle to the table and monitors. A second camera set on the stage showed the performance area and behind the curtain. The third camera pointed from the orchestra pit back toward the lobby. Recorders to communicate with the dead would be left on the steps to the balcony and carried around the theater to various locations. Eventually, Billy returned to the monitor table, panning his flashlight as he walked.

"Wilson?" Mark asked.

"No sign of him," Billy said, "although the concession stand was empty, so maybe he made a visit there."

The group chuckled.

"Let's all do a walkthrough before I start the genny," Mark said. "We'll turn the cameras on, make any final adjustments we need, and get going with this investigation, with or without Wilson."

The paranormal researchers walked toward the back of the theater. Inside the lobby, Cheryl sniffed several times, and said, "I smell cigarette smoke. It's putrid."

"I smell it, too," Mark said. "It could be a smoker trying to communicate. Make initial contact through what it remembers best. Doesn't it make sense that a spirit would communicate through cigarette smoke because smoking was not allowed inside?" He stepped away from the rest. "Is there anyone here? Anyone who wants to talk with us? We're not here to hurt you."

"How do you hurt the dead?" Eva giggled from inside the cramped projection room bathroom.

Downstairs, Mark's voice boomed. "We want to talk with you."

"My name's Cheryl. I'll be happy to talk with you. Hear your story. Why have you remained here in the theater? Where will you go when this place is torn down?"

"Waiting for the second movie to start," Eva quipped. "This is —how do you say it—too much."

Kazmer grunted. Bo moaned.

"Over here," Billy said, up three steps on the balcony staircase. "I think the smoke's coming from the balcony. I didn't smell it before when I was up there." The three joined together and walked up, stopping after each step.

"I hope there's nothing on fire up here," Cheryl said.

"How could there be?" Billy said. "There's no power in the joint.

"Maybe somebody's living up there," Cheryl said. "You know. Squatters. Does it smell like an electric fire?"

"How the fuck would I know? It smells like fire. Nasty."

"You're the sparky, Mark. You should know," Billy said. "Where's Wilson when you need him."

"Like he could charm a real fucking ghost," Cheryl said. "He's probably the one who lit the fire. He might be a firebug in addition to his long list of perversions."

They proceeded up the wide staircase side by side, one step at a time before stopping to listen.

"We'd like to talk to you," Cheryl started again. "We want to be friends. You can talk to us." The group traded nervous looks. "I think the smell is stronger as we go up."

"Definitely stronger. It could be electrical," Billy said

"It's not electrical!" Mark hissed. "If you had taken the time to look, the wires to this building are cut at the pole outside. The meter is capped. There is no electricity running through this fucking theater. The only way this place will carry any electricity is if it's struck by lightning."

"Did anyone check the weather lately?" Cheryl said. "I don't care what you say, Sparky, to me, it smells electrical," Cheryl shook her head and sighed. She began again. "Is anyone here? We are your friends. We want to talk. Get to know you. We'd like to know your name. Is there more than one person here?"

"How did you die?" Billy called. "Did you die here, or did you come here a lot during your life? What were your favorite movies? Are you a movie star from the past?"

"I don't believe this," Mark said. "I think I'm going to go home."

Eva could take it no longer. She couldn't control her laughter. She pounded her fist on the wall three times.

The paranormal researchers ducked on the steps just below the balcony landing. They held hands and grinned. "Breakthrough!" Billy said. "We have breakthrough."

Billy nudged Cheryl in the ribs. She cleared her throat. "Hello? My name is Cheryl. Can you show me you are real by making a noise again? Can you make three noises again? That would make me and my friends happy."

Eva knocked on the wall again. Bo rolled his eyes. Kazmer looked worried.

"Excellent!" Mark chimed in. "Are you making the smell we detected downstairs? If you make one knock for yes and two knocks for no it will help us understand."

Eva knocked twice.

"Oh!"

"Wow!"

"Did you hear that? That means..." Billy stopped for a moment to think. "Is there another person up here who can make the smell?"

"Knock once for yes. Twice for no," Mark said.

Eva knocked on the wall once. The paranormal investigators were beside themselves. Cheryl jumped up and down. High-fived with the others. Eva reached across Bo and opened the bathroom door a couple of inches to let out more smoke. She instructed Kazmer with pantomime to blow smoke through the opening into the projection room. Kazmer was near the end of this cigarette but complied. Eva threw back her head and laughed silently. Then she closed the bathroom door. She clasped her hands and waited. The paranormal investigators called again with their questions. Eva snickered. Ignored them.

The stronger smell of smoke reached the investigators. "Are you blowing more smoke?" Billy called.

"Yeah. Up your ass," Bo whispered, smiling. "This is incredible. How can people be this stupid?"

Eva beat on the wall. Kazmer's shoulders shook with silent laughter. He wiped tears from his eyes.

The paranormal investigators climbed the final few steps to the balcony landing. "Where are you? Are you on the balcony?" Billy called.

Eva answered immediately with two raps.

"Can we see you? Are you in the old projection room?" Billy called.

Eva rapped once. The paranormal investigators looked from one to another in disbelief. They approached the projection room with caution. They held hands again.

Billy said, "Go ahead, Sparky, lead the way."

Mark stepped forward and pulled open the door. He looked back at his friends. Grinned. "You know, we should have this on video. Who's going to believe us?"

"I'll run down for a camera," Cheryl said.

"No time. Let's go in," Mark said. "We don't want to miss the moment." After they were inside the projection room, Mark closed the door, as if that act would prevent ghosts from escaping. They spread out in front of the door.

"Are you inside the projector?" Cheryl said. "No answer. Are you still here?"

"Give them time," Billy said.

"I heard a moan," Cheryl said. "It was definitely a moan."

Billy snapped his fingers to get their attention. He cupped one hand over his mouth. Pointed another finger at the closet. Cheryl approached the door and opened the hook latch. Let her hand rest on the doorknob for a moment. She cleared her throat. Took a deep breath. Looked back at Billy. He motioned for her to pull open the door fast.

Cheryl took another breath. Opened her mouth as if to say something, then closed it. She pulled open the door violently.

"What the fuck!"

Jane moaned and fell into Cheryl's arms. Cheryl screamed and let Jane drop to the floor with a thud. The three paranormal investigators shook with fright and screamed. They threw their arms over their heads and fled from the projection room.

Eva was bent over with laughter, but she recovered soon. A sneer crossed her face. She blurred from the balcony, propelled herself over the rail, and met the paranormal researchers in their mad dash at the bottom of the steps. One look at Eva's face paralyzed them with fear.

"Sparky," Eva crooned.

The vampiress's claws and fangs extended. Her face was contorted by the vampire disease. Black veins appeared below her pale skin. One swipe of her clawed hand opened Mark's windpipe. He dropped to the floor, choking on his own blood. Eva laughed and Cheryl and Billy ran in opposite directions.

The vampiress caught Billy first. Dragged him by the ponytail and sank her teeth into his neck. She took a few long sucks and dropped the body. She caught Cheryl near the entrance. Grabbed her throat and threw her across the theater, where she crashed into the wall. Eva immediately blurred back to Bo and Kazmer, who had returned to the balcony. Jane sat in a seat, slowly regaining consciousness.

CHAPTER FORTY-FOUR

On the balcony, Eva clapped her clawed hands and laughed. "I don't know when I had so much fun. A century ago, or more perhaps. They came to hunt for ghosts and found vampires." She turned to Bo. "There is blood left in all the victims, except the one in the basement. I suggest you feed before the blood turns useless."

"Never," Bo said. "I will not drink blood from corpses. You didn't have to kill them. We could have scared them out of here. That might have been fun."

"Kazmer, you have some influence with Bo," the vampiress said. "Help me convince him."

"I have tried, Mistress," Kazmer said with lowered head. "This path we take is a dangerous one. Bodies can be buried. Crimes of theft get noticed."

Eva confronted Bo. "It might be different if I had been there when you emerged from the chrysalis, my little rabbit. Even though Kazmer has killed many, *I* might have made a difference in the way you think. The silly way you behave."

"Nothing or no one can change me. Not you or the vampire disease that burns my throat raw."

"The vampire disease is to be embraced," Eva said, almost wistfully. "Look at Kazmer. He cannot wait for the day he is turned. He and his brother served vampires, including me, for years for the... opportunity to be one of us. To live through the centuries."

"That is true, Mistress. I will give you my neck this instant. I dream of the three of us hunting together."

"You see, Bo. The vampire disease will never be cured. There is no cure. You must accept it. Bend to its desires, and it will repay you, keep you young, strong, disease-free, impervious to the weather, with senses that are many times greater than those of humans. The powers the disease gives will protect you and *it* through years to come. If humans by chance injure you, the disease will heal you. Their bullets and knives and stakes will leave no scars. You will be whole again." The vampiress stopped for a moment. Her body shuddered. "And the taste, Bo. The taste of human blood, fresh and warm, sipped or gulped. Whatever way you like it. How do they say it? You don't know what you are missing."

"Do you think I enjoy living in this rat-infested dump, with its leaking roof, falling plaster, and mold?

Eva looked around. Peeked over the balcony's edge into the theater. "I think it's rather—what is the word?—quaint."

Kazmer grunted from the several rows behind them, where he checked on Jane's condition as she revived slowly from the chloroform.

"I'd rather be back home in my room, in my own bed, and seeing my father every day instead of on this dirty floor," Bo said. "Living at home might not be normal for a guy my age, but it's better than this." Bo threw out his arms and let them drop to his side.

"Maybe your father or Kazmer can buy cow's blood at the butcher. Tell them in the store you have a rare blood disorder."

Bo's head snapped up.

Eva laughed. "It would never work, dear Bo. Animal blood will do for emergencies. I know. *I've done it.* Most vampires have. The vampire disease evolved like any parasite, over countless millennia. It now feeds on human blood to extend *its* and your existence. It will always come first."

"I haven't always been a good person, as a human or a vampire, because I did kill in the heat of the moment, on the first night I came out of the ground," Bo added, looking into Eva's eyes. "I've taken a vow never to take another human life."

"That could be a costly mistake. You will be on your own. The Brethren will surely learn about your activities, hunt you down, and stake you. I hope the rest of the world does not discover you. It will ruin everything for our kind." She walked a few steps away from Bo. "Goodbye, Bo. It is too dangerous to be near you."

Eva paused, preparing to blur. She stopped and cocked her head. "There are people in the theater," she hissed.

"More paranormal researchers?" Kazmer asked. He stopped midway while rolling a cigarette.

Eva looked back at Bo and Kazmer. "The Brethren!"

Kazmer scanned the theater below and pushed his tobacco pouch inside his hoodie pocket. "They're chaining the emergency doors closed," he whispered.

"Idiots! That won't stop me," Eva hissed. "They are here, Bo, because you were foolish enough to take the girl. We three could have left this city undetected. The Brethren have always been clever."

"There are ten or twelve of them," Bo said.

"Yes," the vampiress said, drawing out the word. She sniffed the air. "Excellent. I detect the big black man and the small woman we had in the cages at After Dark. The ones who escaped. They must have joined the Brethren. How wonderful." She smiled broadly as if making plans.

The vampires crouched behind the balcony rail and listened for a moment.

"They have spread out," Kazmer said, peeking over the top. "Some are on stage. Some crossed the theater. Some are on their way to the lobby." He looked hurriedly between Bo and Eva. "When they are all in the back, I am going to drop over the edge and run for the door. The van is a half block away." Kazmer held the two halves of the long stake. "I'm ready to fight my way out."

"I will kill the couple who escaped me at After Dark and blur into the night," Eva said, with a smile on her face. She pointed at the hole in the roof. "Bo, we will probably never meet again."

"I'd take you with me, Kaz, but I'll have Jane," Bo said. He returned to Jane, who was still groggy.

"Leave the bitch," Eva demanded.

"No. The Brethren will think she was a Shadow in their ranks and kill her. That would be like *me* killing her."

The noise on the balcony attracted the Brethren's attention. Five Brethren fanned out across the theater, their crossbows trained on the balcony. The rest headed toward the lobby and the stairs to the balcony. Outside, the paranormal researchers' generator started. The theater, including the balcony, was flooded with light from powerful lamps the group had set up on stage. Del Hatch slipped through the door, wrapped a heavy chain around the push bars, and padlocked the chain. He wore his powder blue jumpsuit with bloused pant legs and one of his Sasquatch baseball caps. The BAR was slung over his back. Del picked up his crossbow and took up a position with the Brethren in front of the balcony. John Bargain started his video. Goldenrod stood behind him with her crossbow ready to fire.

The rest of the vampire fighters climbed the steps to the balcony carefully, shoulder to shoulder. They swept their crossbows back and forth to cover the open spaces, some aimed high, some low, expecting a vampire assault at any time from any direction. Old Harriet and Mad Maggie were crowded in the middle with their machetes raised. Their jaws were set. They both remembered Bo and the vampiress. Neither would hesitate to hack apart the two vampires. Then they'd watch for the lethal bolt or stake strikes to incinerate the fiends.

Old Harriet thought back to when she lived on the street near After Dark. She remembered friends she lost to the Whistlers, Eva, and her brother the ancient vampire Gerrard. With every step, the face of a lost friend passed through her mind. A tear formed in her eye. Would this really be the end? Mad Maggie recalled being caged inside the After Dark basement with Overboard George while he endured the ravages of withdrawal symptoms and she feigned the sickness while the vampires waited for their blood to clear. Maggie remembered the fight to escape After Dark, their return to the dank basement with a rag-tag group of junkies with improvised potato guns, and the fury and surprise on Gerrard's face when a lethal stake hit his heart.

Eva moved across the balcony. Crouched. It appeared she intended to blur through the hole in the roof. Del Hatch fired his crossbow. The bolt caught Eva in the shoulder. She roared. Dust from the old chandelier lights rained down.

"Look at the trouble you fools have caused," Eva hissed. She was enraged. Black veins stood out on her face. Her fangs and claws were extended. "Bo, you take Kazmer."

"No!"

"She's not going anywhere." The vampiress extended a claw and swiped it through Jane's neck. Her head fell back. The wound spouted a fountain of blood.

"Noooo!" Bo screamed.

Eva laughed and pulled the arrow from her shoulder. The hole was already healed. More bolts ricocheted off the railing and sank into the ceiling. One hit Bo on the thigh. Two impaled Jane's body. Bo dropped Jane into a balcony seat. The impact caused her head to loll backward over the seat and detach, hit the floor, and roll across the aisle. It settled upright as if watching the trio with a surprised look on her face.

"Ta ta," Eva exclaimed with a flip of her hand and a smirk.

Bo grabbed the pointed half of the stake from Kazmer's hand and lunged at the vampiress. The point pierced her plaid cowgirl shirt, snapped a button in half, and penetrated her cold, hard flesh. Eva looked at Bo in amazement. The stake stopped suddenly, as the vampire disease rallied the thoracic organs to wrap around the shaft, ensnare the stake to save Eva and itself. Bo pulled the vampiress to him, encircled her back with his free arm, and thrust the remainder of the stake upward with all his vampire's strength. Its fire-hardened point split the shriveled, dead heart. Eva took a step back. Her mouth opened. Black blood poured between her lips and from her nostrils.

She appeared to mouth, "*Bo.*"

The Brethren unleashed a salvo of bolts from the theater floor and the back of the balcony. The vampiress and Bo were hit multiple times. She staggered back a few steps. Kazmer took a bolt in the shoulder, another in the neck. Bo grabbed Kazmer and blurred to the emergency door they used to enter and leave the theater. Bargain caught everything on camera. Del Hatch and Goldenrod fired their crossbows and reloaded.

Eva collapsed and erupted in a great conflagration. Flames, smoke, and noxious gas filled the balcony. The Brethren retreated down the steps. Old Harriet and Mad Maggie brought up the rear.

"Maybe the place will burn down," Old Harriet said, with a giggle. "Then they won't have to tear it down."

"I told OG we needed to bring torches," Mad Maggie said.

"You don't see something like this every day," Del Hatch said.

Bo reached the emergency door. He looked down at Kazmer. The bolt in his shoulder was not fatal. The one in the neck passed through, tearing it open. "Kaz," Bo whispered. His friend was dead. Bo let him slide to the floor.

The balcony was engulfed in flames. The old carpet and seat

fabric were ablaze almost immediately. Flames roiled over the ceiling and down from the balcony, catching some of the lower seats on fire. Bo tested the emergency doors. As he prepared to push them out of their hinges, the combined Brethren released another salvo. Bo looked like a pin cushion. Black blood covered his back. Bo turned and faced his nemesis. In the seconds it took the Brethren to reload, while Bo started to heal, he saw Overboard George, Mad Maggie, and Old Harriet. He smiled at them and drew an X with his bloodied finger where his heart was.

EPILOGUE

Del Hatch grinned ear to ear. Guacamole in her pink bikini sat on his lap poolside at the La De Da Motel. The Brethren had taken over the swimming pool for the afternoon, before they pulled out of Thaxton, going their separate ways.

John Bargain and Goldenrod sat in their motel room editing his video from The Roxy. Bargain would return to his life as a vlogger of the macabre.

The East Coasters packed their bags for their trip home, where Persimmon would lead them to a new base on the East Coast.

Del Hatch would return East, always ready to hunt Sasquatch.

Some Brethren would not fight together again. Some might not survive their next encounters with vampires, but they all would remain friends.

AFTERWORD

After three novels, I got to like Bo Bentwood and Kazmer Savoy, even though they were not nice people. Bo was not a nice human or vampire, although he did have somewhat of a conscious. Kazmer was a pathological killer who had no concern for human life. However, eventually he developed a soft spot for Bo. Afterall, I spent many hours with the duo while I wrote this trilogy—some 300,000 words. I didn't have a definite ending until I reached the last few chapters of *The Reluctant Vampire*. I toyed with the idea of having Bo and Kazmer ride into the sunset (sunrise) or middle of the night. Would they blur, with Kazmer carried piggyback on Bo's back? Would they drive off below the speed limit in the infamous white van that ended up with as much mileage as the characters? Would survival necessitate a fourth novel? I didn't think so. Don't they say something about too much of a good thing...

I also liked Del Hatch. He started as a minor character, soon to be written off or drained of blood but blossomed into something more. I hope to let him star in his own novel or a short story. One with at least one Sasquatch, of course. That's why I inserted in the third novel chapter about Del on a Bigfoot safari in Washington

State while the Brethren tracked vampires. I wanted to keep him fresh in the reader's mind. We will see what happens to Del. The idea is on the back burner.

John Bargain, the mad vlogger, was another character I liked and one who survived three encounters with vampires in two novels, so he might come back in some form. He started as a vlogger taking a whiz behind a bush at the mall and meeting Eva. At the time he was allotted a few paragraphs before he slipped off the page into character infinity. He survived that encounter in the second novel and then he showed up when the Brethren attacked the vampire colony. Then he managed to kill two fangers. That's what happens when you keep asking "what if..." or "what else could go wrong in this scenario?" He managed to finish the trilogy mostly unscathed. And who couldn't like Persimmon, Goldenrod, and Guacamole? All strong female characters and leaders. They were merciless when it came to vampires and tender with the men they liked. I have a soft spot for all three. They might do well on a Sasquatch hunt. The back burner is now on low.

ABOUT THE AUTHOR

Dean Alan Conrad is a former newspaper reporter and columnist. He is a graduate of the Pennsylvania State University with a degree in English. He lives in Pennsylvania and always has been interested in everything spooky.